Song of the Siren

A FIVE DIRECTIONS PRESS BOOK

A Novel

C. P. Lesley

SONGS OF STEPPE & FOREST 1

ISBN-13: 978-1947044180

Published in the United States of America.

A Five Directions Press book

Cover images: Elżbieta Krasińska, *Portrait of Katarzyna Branicka, Countess Potocka, 1825–1907* (oil on canvas, 1841), public domain, no. 128942, National Museum of Warsaw; Jan Nepomucen Głowacki, *View of Wawel Castle* (1847), public domain via Wikimedia Commons. *Map:* Adapted from "Poland and Lithuania in 1526," CC BY 3.0 Mathiasrex, based on work by Hallibutt, via Wikimedia Commons.

Book and cover design by Five Directions Press

Five Directions Press logo designed by Colleen Kelley

Five Directions Press

O, thou art fairer than the evening air
Clad in the beauty of a thousand stars.

—Christopher Marlowe

BOOKS BY C. P. LESLEY

The Not Exactly Scarlet Pimpernel

Songs of Steppe & Forest
Song of the Siren

Legends of the Five Directions
The Golden Lynx (1: West)
The Winged Horse (2: East)
The Swan Princess (3: North)
The Vermilion Bird (4: South)
The Shattered Drum (5: Center)

Tarkei Chronicles
Desert Flower
Kingdom of the Shades

CONTENTS

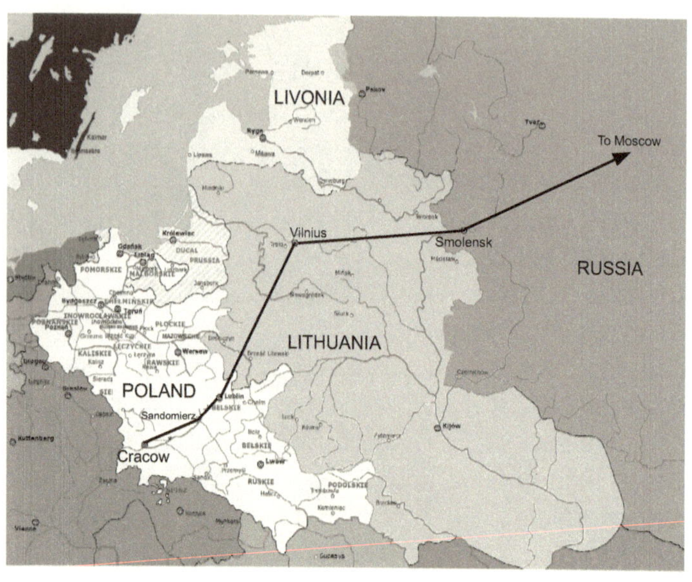

Poland-Lithuania and Russia, 1525–1558

The lines mark the path of Felix and Juliana's journey.

Cast of Characters

(in alphabetical order by first name)

FICTIONAL CHARACTERS

NOTE THAT IN THE 1540S "LITHUANIAN" REFERS TO A SUBJECT of the Grand Duchy of Lithuania, whatever his or her ethnicity. Many of those subjects were in fact Ruthenian—that is, residents of areas now part of Belarus, Ukraine, or western Russia. "Russian" likewise refers to subjects of the grand prince of Russia, regardless of ethnic origin, and "Polish" to subjects of the king of Poland, who was also the grand duke of Lithuania although the governments of the two realms remained separate until 1569.

Adam Tarlo: Polish nobleman; one of the envoys who accompanies Juliana and Felix to Moscow; schoolmate of Felix and nephew of Samuel Tarlo.

Alexei Bulatovich: Christianized Tatar sultan in Russian service, formerly known as Tulpar; Maria's husband and father of her children, Alexander and Dosya. (In Tatar usage, sultan means "son of a khan," not "supreme ruler," as among the Ottomans; the Russian equivalent is tsarevich.)

Bogdan Ostrogski: Lithuanian nobleman whose uncles have defeated the Muscovite army in battle and are prominent defenders of Orthodox Christianity within the Grand Duchy of Lithuania; one of the envoys who accompanies Juliana and Felix to Moscow.

Emilia Sobieska: Juliana's replacement in the affections of King Sigismund Augustus; a seventeen-year-old beauty.

Felix Ossolinski: Scion of a prominent Polish noble family whose accident at sixteen diverted him from the typical aristocratic military career to scholarship and diplomacy; hero of *Song of the Siren.*

Fyodor Mikhailovich Koshkin: Juliana's estranged husband; a high-ranking Russian nobleman.

Ilya Shuisky: Russian prince, nephew of Iosif Shuisky.

Iosif Shuisky: Russian prince, head of the Shuisky clan; dominant figure in the Russian government from the death of his older brother, Vasily, in October 1538 until 1541; determined to regain his position in 1542 and to counteract Konstantin Belsky's moves against him.

Juliana Krasilska: Fyodor Koshkin's wife and Alexei's former concubine, known to them as Roxelana; originally a Christian slave from the area that is now northwest Afghanistan; heroine of *Song of the Siren.*

Konstantin Belsky: Russian (formerly Lithuanian) prince, dominant figure in the Belsky clan and antagonistic to Iosif Shuisky, whose power in the government Belsky seeks to limit or circumvent.

Leon Laski: Polish nobleman; one of the envoys who accompanies Juliana and Felix to Moscow.

Lev Mikhailovich Glinsky: Martin's cousin; part of the Russian branch of the family.

Lyuba Fyodorovna Koshkina: Maria's eleven-year-old sister.

Maria Fyodorovna Koshkina: Eldest daughter of Fyodor Koshkin; wife of Alexei Bulatovich and mother of Alexander and Dosya. Her marriage to Alexei gives her the title of tsarevna (khan's daughter or daughter-in-law).

Martin Glinsky: Lithuanian nobleman whose cousin Elena married Vasily III of Russia; one of the envoys who accompanies Juliana and Felix to Moscow.

Samuel Tarlo: Polish nobleman and friend of Felix.

Simon Belsky: Lithuanian nobleman related to Konstantin Belsky; one of the envoys who accompanies Juliana and Felix to Moscow.

HISTORICAL CHARACTERS

As often happens with medieval and early modern people, we have limited information about Lithuanians, Poles, Russians, and Tatars, even royalty, who lived in the sixteenth century. To the extent possible, I have ensured that details about real people included in Songs of Steppe & Forest match the historical record, but often these details don't extend much beyond dates of marriages, deaths, and sometimes births. Therefore, these characters' appearance, personalities, words, and motivations are just as much my invention as those of their fictional counterparts.

Bona Sforza: Queen of Poland and Grand Duchess of Lithuania (r. 1518–1548); wife of Sigismund I "the Old" and mother of Sigismund Augustus.

Dmitry Belsky: Russian prince, older brother of Ivan Belsky (here called Konstantin), who generally stayed out of the feud between his brother and the Shuisky clan; prominent in diplomatic circles in the 1540s.

Ivan IV "the Terrible": Grand Prince of Russia (1530–1584, r. 1533–1584); crowned tsar 1547.

Sigismund I "the Old": King of Poland and Grand Duke of Lithuania (r. 1506–1548); co-ruler with his son, Sigismund Augustus, after 1529/1530.

Sigismund II Augustus: Grand Duke of Lithuania (1529–1572) and King of Poland (1530–1572), co-ruling with his father until the latter's death in 1548.

Chapter One

Wawel Castle, Poland, December 1541

"LADY JULIANA WILL LIVE," A MALE VOICE SAID. "NOT AS SHE did before, of course. I doubt the young king will have much use for her now, despite her charms. It's too bad about the scarring. She was a beautiful woman." The dispassionate tone contradicted any hint of concern implied by his words.

Was? She *was* a beautiful woman? I lay flat on my back, too weak and dispirited to demand that he explain what he meant. I tried to force my eyelids open, but I hadn't the strength even for that. Trapped in a nightmare world, I huddled, shivering, waiting for the ogre to appear at the door. I pushed and twisted, but my arms weighed heavy as granite on the bed and my feet stuck to the mattress.

The doctor's callous verdict echoed in my head. Too bad about the scarring? She *was* a beautiful woman?

Tragedy bared its teeth, sucked me into its vortex. Without my face I was nothing. I had no purpose, no means of survival, no self. I existed to mirror the desires of men, to fulfill their passions while expressing none of my own. My beauty was the only currency I possessed. If I couldn't use it to draw men to me, I would starve. What point, then, in living?

Tears slid from the corners of my eyes, wetting the linen beneath my head. I lacked the power to wipe them away. "Oh, look," another voice said. My maidservant, Hanna. "She's crying. Do you think she heard you, Doctor?" A soft cloth touched my cheeks.

"Perhaps." The doctor still sounded indifferent, as if discussing my case at some society of physicians. If I had the energy, I would slap him. "I see no sign that she's awake, but I've had other patients report things I said under similar conditions. Smallpox causes extreme exhaustion. She may be able to hear but not respond. Just in case, you should talk to her, reassure her, like this."

Garlic-inflected breath passed my nose, and I guessed he had bent closer to examine me. "You will recover, Lady Juliana," he said, and this time I heard actual kindness in his voice. "The worst is over."

But I knew he was wrong. The worst lurked somewhere down the road of a bleak future, waiting to pounce when I was least prepared to resist.

"I look hideous." I slammed the silver-backed brush against the dressing table. "Take the glass away, if you love me." Two weeks had passed since the doctor's pronouncement, and I shuddered every time my reflection forced me to face the damage caused by my illness. In place of the flawless skin that men once yearned to caress, I saw a countenance peppered with indentations and red-tinged scars, one for each pustule that had dried and fallen off. Twenty-seven years old, and smallpox had ruined my life.

I'd thought that nothing could exceed the torment of Advent—lost in a blur of fever, rash, back pain, and fatigue. I had since come to realize that my suffering then could not possibly compare with the catastrophe that followed. At the height of my illness the pustules had covered my entire face and neck, hands and feet, as well as assorted other places hidden by my clothes. Their passage to the land of memory left me looking as if someone had taken a small skewer and stabbed it all over my forehead and cheeks.

"It's not so bad, Lady Juliana," Hanna said as she laid the hand mirror on the dresser and picked up a comb. "I got some pink powder from the apothecary. We'll cover up the marks, and no one will notice a thing."

"Of course they'll notice," I snapped. "I used to have perfect skin. Now I'm grotesque!"

Hanna meant to be kind—I understood that—but her efforts only made me more aware of my ugliness. Still, I covered my face with both hands and mumbled an apology. She had cared for me throughout that miserable month when I lay like a stone, wishing death would put me out of my misery, and the not much less miserable two weeks when I hid in my chambers, writhing whenever I thought about how others would react when they saw me. I didn't know which prospect horrified me more: the hand extended in courtesy while a rigid countenance strove to mask pity and condescension, or the turned shoulder conveying outright revulsion. So I kept to my rooms, claiming weakness, postponing the moment when I must face the world.

Today that moment had arrived, in the form of a royal summons. And not the summons I might—under other circumstances—have welcomed, from King Sigismund Augustus. My former lover had withdrawn at the first mention of smallpox. I didn't dare imagine his reaction when he saw my ruined face. I said a silent prayer that he'd taken himself off to Vilnius once more. In the present situation that seemed unlikely, but one could hope.

No, this summons came from his mother, Queen Bona, who had chosen to celebrate the seventy-fifth birthday of her husband, King Sigismund the Old, in full Italianate style. That his birthday also heralded the entry of the new year 1542 and took place amid the ongoing observation of the Twelve Days of Christmas merely increased the pressure on his loyal nobles, including me, to attend.

To be sure, attaining the age of seventy-five was a rare occurrence, one worthy of as much pomp and acclaim as a grateful court could provide. Most people I knew counted themselves fortunate to see fifty-five. And I had nothing but respect and affection for King Sigismund, an enlightened ruler and a genial and cultured man who had treated his son's attraction to me as one more reason to accept me into his royal household. I wished him well—and Queen Bona, too. More passionate in nature than her husband, she had a reputation for taking her son's women—whether current mistresses or potential wives—in extreme dislike. But for some reason she tolerated me. Now that her son had moved on, my comfortable residence at Wawel Castle depended on her good will.

Indeed, her attention flattered and reassured me. Nothing dooms a courtier, especially one not of noble birth, faster than royal disregard. She had even, out of consideration for my recent ailment, exempted me from the royal banquet that formed the centerpiece of the celebration. I need only attend the reception preceding the meal. But if she had ordered my presence at the banquet, I would have endured the hours of toasts and heavy food without complaint. It didn't matter whether I enjoyed the festivities or not. If summoned by the queen, I had no choice but to obey.

While these thoughts roiled my brain, Hanna pulled the comb through my hair. A steady stream of meaningless reassurances poured from her lips. I let them roll past me, neither listening nor responding. Every stroke brought its own instant of agony, tugging against the incompletely healed sores on my scalp, ending too soon because the lustrous tresses the physician had so callously ordered shorn during my illness stopped at my ear lobes. Hanna strove for gentleness, but I winced as the scabs tore and I felt the ooze of blood against my tender skin.

In my crimson velvet gown, high-waisted and long-sleeved, no one could mistake me for a boy. My headdress would conceal the chopped and patchy hair. And I could expect one day to see my nut-brown mane, unlike my ravaged face, restored to its old glory. Yet still I grieved, as if this small loss were the only part of the disaster I could allow myself to feel.

For in truth, the costs of my illness extended far beyond my looks. I had come so close, with Sigismund Augustus, to achieving my ultimate goal: a life where I could support myself without the aid of a man. The young king had promised land and riches, and he certainly had those things to give. But one need not pension or marry off an ugly former mistress. And since I could no longer find another protector to replace him, I would die in poverty.

Unless I returned to my detestable husband. But even dying in poverty was a better choice than that. Fyodor had run off six months after our wedding, leaving me to suffer arrest and ignominy, then had the nerve to show up almost a year later acting as if nothing had happened. I swore then that I would never go back to him, and I'd earn my living in the stews of Cracow before I broke that vow.

The thought set me glancing sideways at the mirror. Again I recoiled in horror. Why hadn't I sent a message hours ago, when I first received the summons, saying I had suffered a relapse and couldn't rise from my bed? Instead I had tried to please, as always.

I groaned. "I can't do this, Hanna. People will think me the veriest witch."

Hanna stopped mid-stroke, astonishment visible in the angle of her comb. "But you must, Lady Juliana. I told you, we'll put on the pink powder. You'll look fine. Besides, you can't stay here. Not when Queen Bona has summoned you."

Speaking of witches ...

Queen Bona Sforza, late of Milan and Bari, grew herbs in her garden that, according to rumor, she used to dispatch her enemies. She had once given such an herb to me—for the detestable husband. I hadn't used it on him, although I admitted to having been sorely tempted, but the memory of the shock on his face when I showed him the vial compensated at least in part for the suffering he'd inflicted on me.

"Yes, of course," I said. "I didn't mean it." Hanna needed to have such things explained to her, or she would take them into the kitchens and alleys, spreading allegations I could ill afford. "Put on my headdress. We can't keep the queen waiting."

"There, Lady," she said when she finished. "You look pretty as a painting."

Of the *Danse macabre* perhaps. Bracing myself, I stood, picked up the mirror once more, and examined my court dress. The high collar with its small ruff concealed the craters on my chest. The puffed sleeves drew attention away from my thickly powdered face, and the black velvet snood with its gold rim concealed my snipped and straggly hair. Slow of understanding or not, Hanna worked wonders with pots of cosmetics. From the other side of the room a person might mistake me for my old self.

"Excellent, Hanna," I said. "Truly excellent. Return after supper to help me undress."

She curtseyed and withdrew. After one final shudder at the mirror I placed it on the dressing table, straightened my shoulders, and left the room.

Can't keep the queen waiting.

As I'd half-expected, one could hardly move within the formal reception rooms without treading on someone's toes. Except for the tiled stoves in the corners and the central dais that held the thrones atop a scarlet carpet ringed with oriental designs, every square inch of space held a lord or a lady in elaborate clothes. Lutes and hautboys sounded from the far side of the room, mingled with men's voices singing a ballad in Italian. But so many courtiers filled the space between us that I couldn't catch so much as a glimpse of the musicians.

The tension in my stomach eased. In such a crowd, who would worry about one former mistress with a marred face? To counteract the dimming sun of the January afternoon, candelabra hung from the ceiling and dotted small tables about the room, threatening to set ablaze the full sleeves and trailing skirts but softening harsh angles and lines. Hanna had been right: her pink powder might do the trick after all.

Stopping every few feet to greet those I recognized, accepting their inquiries and good wishes with the best grace I could manage, I slowly drew closer to the thrones. Since Queen Bona had demanded my presence, courtesy required me first to make my obeisance to her and her husband, a detail that offered a ready escape from the more probing questions with which the ladies I had supplanted in the younger King Sigismund's affections would no doubt choose to remind me that I no longer held that special place.

While awaiting my turn for the royal presentation, I intercepted a muttered conversation. A leftward flick of my eyes revealed two men I didn't remember meeting before. The one I could see in profile was young and good-looking, with dark brown hair and eyes and a bearing I recognized as military. The other had his back to me: I got an impression of sandy hair beneath a blue velvet cap and broad shoulders emphasized by princely robes but not much more.

"They say that two weeks ago a man tried to assassinate the queen, right here in her own garden, where the witch grows her poisons," the dark-haired man said, speaking so low that only years of practice in eavesdropping made it possible for me to discern his words.

Assassinate the queen? While I was ill? I had to bite my lip to keep from crying out. Who would do such a thing and why? I edged closer, hoping for details.

I knew the queen was not universally loved. Many members of the gentry considered her extravagant. They accused her of stiffening her husband's spine against them, of indulging her son, of opposing the planned marriage between Sigismund Augustus and Elisabeth of Austria that was supposed to secure the Polish-Habsburg alliance, and—perhaps the worst sin in their minds—buying up landed estates that they viewed as their own. But *assassinate* her? How could that serve their cause, whatever that cause might be?

"Yes," the sandy-haired man said. "The guards caught him in the garden with a musket. He shot at her, but thanks to divine providence, the devil's weapon misfired, injuring the attacker rather than the queen."

"And where is the villain now?" The avid curiosity in the young man's voice echoed my own. Yet I also heard something else that I couldn't quite put my finger on. Trepidation? Disappointment?

"He lies in the king's dungeons," Sandy-Hair said. "Awaiting summary execution at the king's pleasure, I assume. But first he must name his co-conspirators."

"And he hasn't done so?" Dark-Hair asked. Definitely, I heard something odd in his tone. An eagerness, almost, as if he had a personal stake in the answer. I didn't dare look their way again.

"Not to my knowledge," said Sandy-Hair. I heard none of the suppressed emotion in his voice. "But he will, soon enough. The rack is a powerful persuader."

"Although not one that invariably procures the truth," Dark-Hair noted.

I had no opportunity to hear more, as the line before me cleared. It was my turn to congratulate the king while showing his wife that I had obeyed her command. As I walked forward, I surveyed the queen.

She appeared unharmed. No evidence of concern or fear showed on her face or in her stance. Yet I noticed that she monitored the crowd with more watchful intensity than normal. She trusted the world no more readily than I did. It was one of the traits that drew me to her—and perhaps explained her kindness to me. We were, in that sense, kindred spirits. I wouldn't mention the attack. How would I explain my knowledge? Nevertheless, I admired her aplomb.

Only then did I realize that the dais contained three thrones, not the usual two: one each for Sigismund, Bona, and Sigismund Augustus. I sighed. Of course, the young king and co-ruler would celebrate his father's birthday. Only a visit to Cloud Cuckoo Land could explain my thinking otherwise, even for a moment. I plastered a smile on my face and did my best to appear unmoved by anything but gratitude as I sank into the deep curtsey required when greeting royals, murmuring my thanks to the queen for her invitation and felicitations to the older monarch on his birthday.

The elder Sigismund accepted my good wishes with his usual cheerful calm. He too showed no signs of unusual strain, despite the recent attack on his wife. "We trust you find yourself fully recovered, Lady Juliana. We rejoice to enjoy once again your quick wit and graceful presence." A tall man of solid frame, now stooped with age but not fat, he still bore traces of the strong and noble countenance that rumor had attributed to him even at forty, when he at last ascended to his brothers' throne.

Nicely done, I thought, not believing him. "Thank you, Majesty," I said. "Your kindness honors me."

Queen Bona extended a hand, and I brushed my lips across the back, as was the custom here, before releasing it and rising at her command. "I echo my husband's words," she said. "For a while, we feared to lose you altogether. A severe case, the doctor said." She managed to make it sound as if she meant every word, for which I thanked her, both in my own head and aloud.

"I too am glad to see Your Majesties in good health," I said. A statement not much more honest than her own, for Bona had not worn as well as her husband, perhaps because of her six pregnancies, which had yielded the one precious son and a handful of daughters. Even so, I didn't need the circled portrait on the wall to see that she had once been lovely in that elegant Italian way. She could still spark a light in her ancient husband's eyes; her upright posture would have done credit to a dancer; and her dress, as always, reflected the latest fashions from Rome or Venice while respecting the changing needs of middle age. I could take lessons from her. She responded to my good wishes with an appreciative nod.

Reassured by their welcome, I glanced at the third throne. King Sigismund Augustus, at twenty-one less than a third his father's age, resembled his sire enough that watching them side by side I had no trouble imagining how the older king must have looked in his youth. Tall and slender, with good legs and broad shoulders, Sigismund Augustus had a handsome face and a sensuous mouth, the touch of which I remembered too well.

But today the expression in his eyes chilled me, as they say, to the bone. I had seen them hot with lust, warm with laughter, soft with concern. I had never encountered the utter revulsion I saw on his face as he surveyed me from head to toe, then turned his gaze away.

Shocked beyond words, I stared at him. I hadn't loved him, but I'd enjoyed being the center of his attention. And I would have sworn he loved me—up to the very day when his lackey delivered a letter conveying his lord's condolences and best wishes for my recovery, together with a box containing the pearl choker Hanna had clasped around my neck an hour ago, which now throttled me in truth. I hadn't seen Sigismund Augustus since. Hadn't even been able to read the letter for a month, as I was already sick when it arrived. I had accepted, then, that he wouldn't return to me. But I had never anticipated such public and complete rejection.

There was worse to come. I followed the direction of his gaze, and my spirits, already crushed by his contempt for me, sank into the earth like demons returning to their infernal home.

So much for Hanna's pink powder.

The most beautiful girl I had ever seen stood at the edge of the dais. She couldn't be more than seventeen, a decade younger than I. Blue-eyed, with hair the shade of primroses, she boasted a roses-and-milk complexion as perfect as mine had once been but fairer than my sun-kissed cheeks, in that style for which poets—and, it seemed, kings—yearned. Her dress of cobalt blue reminded me of the one I wore in the days when Sigismund Augustus first selected me as his paramour, but of course updated for the latest style. Everything about her glowed with youth.

When Sigismund Augustus beckoned to her, she came to his side at once. He placed an arm about her waist, studying her with the same caressing gaze that he used to bestow on me. "Lady Emilia Sobieska," he said over his shoulder. Then, as if my humiliation were not complete, he spoke to her. "You have heard of Juliana Krasilska, my love. This is she."

No "Lady" for me, I noticed. He had called her "my love." And the sound of my last name—conferred on me by him and derived from *krasa*, a word meaning loveliness or grace, here spoken in tones that transformed it into an insult—put the final period on my shame. Blinking back tears, I glanced at Queen Bona, who regarded me with what looked like sympathy, although I feared that I also detected a hint of triumph. Only the old king paid no attention, accepting the good wishes of the next bowing courtier.

Sigismund Augustus was a king, not the only king but a present and future king, and Queen Bona—sympathetic or triumphant or both—ruled as wife and mother. Calling on every emotional resource I possessed, I dipped my head, murmured a polite and proper response to the introduction, curtseyed once more, and withdrew into the crowd. My stomach hurt, I felt a flush in my cheeks that

I doubted even Hanna's powder could hide, and my limbs trembled under the onslaught of a hideous concoction of rage, terror, and grief that would do a sorceress proud. But I succeeded in hiding myself among the throng of courtiers without stumbling.

When I'd attained a suitable distance, I turned and found a vantage point amid the throng. Queen Bona gazed into the distance, her face a study in contemplation. Her son ogled the young Emilia as if he'd forgotten not only my present but my past existence. And Emilia herself stared straight at me, as if she'd followed every step of my shame-filled retreat.

No question what *she* was feeling. Every line of her showed the complacent contentment of a cat in a creamery. Queen Bona might consider my ouster a victory, or she might not, but I had no doubts that Emilia rejoiced at my discomfiture.

Chapter Two

Wawel Castle, January 1542

BUT IF THAT HIDEOUS MOMENT MARKED THE NADIR OF MY day, my agony didn't end there. As if freed by Sigismund Augustus's disdain, the aristocrats of the Polish court closed ranks against me. I strove to smile as great ladies greeted me with kisses that came nowhere close to my cheeks, asked in voices dripping with false sympathy how I tolerated the ravages of the smallpox and the loss of the young king's affection, bemoaned the loss of my beauty, and deluged me with equally false compliments on how well I was holding up amid my slew of misfortunes. As I moved among them, I looked for the two men I had seen before, but I failed to find them—either because they had already left or because the press of the crowd kept us apart.

Meanwhile, the emotional assault continued. I endured the cold stare of Sebastian Branicki, who had once gone to great effort to supplant his king in my bed—a campaign I hadn't rewarded, having no illusions about who made a better protector. Others who had importuned me without ceasing greeted me, if they bothered to greet me at all, in ways that underlined the message that my days as the sought-after beauty had ended. Even Jan Radziwill, the one-time sponsor of my detestable husband and for the last four and a half years an irrepressible (if also unrewarded) suitor for my heart—or at least my body—congratulated me on my recovery without so much as a hint of his former interest. I allowed irony to drip from my voice as I thanked each of them for his concern and for a moment rejoiced to see the offenders flush, but it was a hollow victory, and I left one after another without delay.

In truth, I found myself shaken. My time first in Vilnius, then in Cracow, had provided a refuge I didn't fully appreciate until I watched it dissolve before my eyes. After a life in slavery, followed by a disastrous love affair and a marriage broken before its first anniversary—all of them undertaken in lands that hid their women behind walls—I'd responded to the warmth and civility of the Polish court as a flower opens to the dawning sun. I loved it, and bolstered by Sigismund's attention, I believed it loved me. Only now did I understand that the court loved its kings and its queen. In the end I was the outsider I'd always been—tolerated so long as my pretty face appealed to men in power but kicked aside like a mangy cur when I lost my looks. Even here in this world where I'd briefly felt at home, I had, as my masters often told me, no value in myself.

So what happened next took me completely by surprise.

Discouraged, needing a place to recover from the assault of the no longer welcoming crowd, I glanced around the room and discovered a chess game off in an alcove to one side. I hadn't met the players before. One man had a collar-length brown beard already touched with white, his massive shoulders widened further by the puffed and slitted sleeves of the current style, his black cap dotted with pins and a gold medallion that matched the one hanging from a chain about his neck. His companion I guessed to be my age or close to it, with chestnut hair and gray eyes, a short and rather dapper beard, and a solemn, clever face. I wondered if he ever smiled.

Their dress spoke of old money and landed wealth. I assumed that, like most of the people in the reception area, they belonged to Polish or Lithuanian gentry families. Their casual handling of the chess pieces, their disinterest in the social games of the court, likewise suggested that they belonged there by right of birth. I deduced they were neither merchants nor hangers-on like me. And given the reaction I had encountered so far from others of their ilk, I could expect them to ignore me unless I forced myself on their notice, in which case they would make their distaste clear.

I didn't plan to do anything so foolish. I'd endured enough freezing courtesy for one day. Another half-hour, and I could return to my chambers to lick my wounds. But to withdraw too soon would insult the queen, and with every moment that passed I understood that offending Bona would pitchfork me into the very predicament I sought to avoid. I had, after all, no other means of support.

Trying to hide my distress, I glided toward the table and sank onto the covered bench next to it. Neither man so much as turned his head.

I released a breath I hadn't realized I was holding. To give further verisimilitude to my presence on the bench and to deter conversation, I pretended an interest in the board.

Within minutes I no longer needed to fake fascination. My second master took quite an interest in my education, if only to make me a more entertaining houri. He taught me music and poetry, drawing and dance, the arts of the bedroom—and chess. I saw at once that the younger man would win, so when he snapped his head around and asked in a rather supercilious tone, "Well, Madam, what do *you* think?" I didn't hesitate. I had no reason to care if he thought me ugly, but some perverse instinct urged me to demand his respect.

"Mate in five," I said.

His eyes widened, his eyebrows rose—and, my goodness, he *did* know how to smile. Quite a charming smile, in fact, although I didn't give him the satisfaction of responding in kind. Instead I stared straight at him, daring him to comment.

"The lady plays chess," he said. "But how in five? I see seven." He pushed himself upright with both hands on the table and bowed to his opponent. "Apologies, Samuel, but I must see how she would solve it. If she can."

That did it. I forgot my many woes, took the seat he'd left open, and made my first move. Samuel, if that was his name, countered exactly as I had expected. I moved another piece, and the man whose seat I occupied said, "By the rood, I missed that one! Five it is."

I produced a smile of my own then, taking care that he not see it, and finished the game. When I rose to my feet, the younger man doffed his dark cap and bowed. I noticed, without at first grasping the significance, that he balanced himself by holding onto the chair back. "Felix Ossolinski, at your service, Madam. And may I have the honor of learning the name of such a charming and accomplished player?"

I held out my hand, and he bent over it. Even after four years in Poland, I had yet to accustom myself to having my hand kissed, but this time, for some reason, the brush of a man's lips against my skin didn't make me want to jerk away. "Juliana," I said. "They call me Krasilska."

Again I strove to ignore the sour taste the name left in my mouth. Self-pity was a useless as well as an unappealing trait, one I must overcome without delay.

"And so you are," Felix said with a gallantry I could only admire. Although I doubted his sincerity, his response soothed my heart. Of the many people I had greeted today, Lord Ossolinski was the first to address me as the entire court used to do.

But when I looked at him more closely, I saw genuine approval in his eyes. He didn't turn his face away. His mouth did not tighten or his shoulders tense. Did he not see the pockmarks? He hadn't met me before, it was true, but candlelight and pink powder had deceived none of the room's haughty ladies and indifferent lords, no matter how well they knew me—not even that little snip Emilia Sobieska, who had nothing but my reputation to go on. Despite his initial assumption that I couldn't follow a simple game of chess, I sensed in that moment that Felix might play a special role in my life.

"Good lord, man, don't you recognize Lady Juliana?" Samuel bowed in his turn. He reached for my hand, only to withdraw without kissing it because Felix still clasped it. "Samuel Tarlo, my dear, at your service. I'm delighted to make your acquaintance. Forgive Ossolinski his stupidity. He has just returned from Florence."

Incredibly, Samuel also appeared sincere. What kind of men were these? Unlike any I'd encountered before, if neither my flawed appearance nor my spurning by an entire court could touch them!

But his words drew me as well. Experiencing something close to awe, I looked at Felix. "Florence?" I asked. Since arriving in Cracow, I had met many Italians. Everything I heard from them made me want to visit their country. As sunny and lovely and cultured as Crimea—not like these grim northern climes with their long, cold winters—but with a more enlightened view of women's place in society. And here was someone who had just returned from that magic land. I forgot my ruined face long enough to say, "Then *buon pomeriggio, Signore.*"

"You speak Italian?"

I saw real surprise in his eyes. What had he expected—a once-beautiful idiot? "Not so well as other languages, but yes. I have practiced with Queen Bona and the musicians since I arrived in Cracow."

"And which other languages, may I ask?"

I had his full attention now. "Persian, Tatar, Russian, and of course Polish."

Samuel held out his arm, crooked at the elbow. "Release her, Felix, so that I may escort her to the next room and find some refreshments for her."

But Felix didn't release me. Instead he tucked my hand around his own left forearm and reached for a cane I hadn't seen until then. "Fie on you, Samuel. Leave the lady to me. I want to find out where she learned to play chess and to speak so many languages. As well as what other skills she possesses."

He must be mad. No one at court asked or spoke about another's past or even shared his or her private thoughts. Except when needling or flattering, the courtiers kept their conversations impersonal. Exchanges about art and music, the latest sensation from Venice or Milan, the skills demanded of gentlemen or ladies—anything so long as it remained superficial, flirtatious, and unreal.

But then, I'd had enough of that for one day. If Felix wanted an honest conversation, he could have it.

Although explaining where I learned to play chess and what other skills I possessed would be quite a tale. As I allowed Felix to lead me toward the promised refreshments, I culled my thoughts for a version that I could safely share with a gentleman I'd just met.

At the same time, I wondered about the cane. It didn't escape my attention that Felix lurched as he walked. In a strange way, I found that comforting. It seemed that he too might perceive himself as broken.

Felix seated me at a small table and signaled to a servant to bring wine and cake. Out of habit I sent him a flirtatious glance of thanks, but although I saw a flash of interest in his eyes, I also sensed a subtle withdrawal.

Of course, my marred face. He had concealed his visceral reaction to my ugliness with greater skill than the others, but I should have known better than to mistrust my instincts. I wouldn't make that mistake again. I retreated into the realm of the impersonal.

"Tell me about Florence," I said in the most casual, self-confident tone I could muster. "Is it as marvelous as people say? What took you there?"

The tone didn't entirely convince me, but Felix responded in kind. He even relaxed a bit, as if my calm acceptance of his unspoken refusal reassured him that he could safely converse with me. "Every bit as marvelous. And I went as King Sigismund's representative—to shop for art for the castle walls." He waved an expansive hand, indicating the numerous paintings arranged against the silk wall coverings. I had lived at Wawel long enough to know that he didn't mean those specifically but works like them.

We talked of Florence for a while, and my desire to visit strengthened with each tale. After a while he asked me, "And what of you? Where did you learn Russian, let alone Tatar and Persian?"

Should I answer? But after what I'd endured today, his obvious interest soothed my wounded pride. I decided to share the rough outlines of my past. Not to trust him, of course, because trusting anyone was risky and trusting a stranger quite absurd. But if I told him nothing important, what harm in satisfying his curiosity to this small degree? At least he looked at me when he spoke. The other aristocrats' willingness to fawn over me so long as they considered me a possible pathway to their king, only to thrust me aside like an unwanted scullery maid when I lost that exalted position, still stung.

"I was born in Chorasan," I said. He nodded—letting me know he'd heard of it, I assumed. "In the far north, close to Bokhara. Persian is my native tongue, and I learned Chagatai Turkic in childhood. It's close to Tatar. So when I moved to Crimea seven years ago—"

He interrupted me. "But why did you go there? It's a long way from Bokhara."

I couldn't bear to speak of Tulpar, who went by the name Alexei these days. After giving me the full force of his attention for a month, he had returned to his prior position as a military commander, leaving me in luxury but bereft. I might forgive him someday, but not soon.

"I fell in love," I said, unable to keep the brusqueness from my voice. With luck, it would discourage questions. "But he preferred to live on the steppe, so after a time we parted ways. He did later take me to Russia, though, where I met my husband. I learned Russian first in Crimea. The place is filled to bursting with Russian slaves. Some of them served me there."

I had startled Felix with the revelation of a husband. I didn't like to think of Fyodor Koshkin either, but that memory hurt less than Alexei. Fyodor had abandoned me too, to save his skin, but I'd only pretended to care for him. And I hated every minute I spent in Russia.

"Husbands can be inconvenient possessions," Felix said, his tone lighter than I would have expected. "I trust you rid yourself of yours."

"Alas, no," I admitted. "That is, he hasn't divorced me, although I told him I wouldn't return to him. But he lives in Moscow. He can't touch me here. And I didn't enjoy marriage so much that I wish to repeat the experience. I can survive without a divorce."

Felix touched his right leg. "I understand. No woman would have me, a cripple. So it seems we can both avoid the yoke of matrimony."

I wouldn't have asked, but he hadn't hesitated to satisfy his curiosity about me, and he'd raised the subject of his injury himself. "What causes your limp?"

He shrugged, but I saw a sadness in his eyes that he must have seen in mine when I skipped over my past. "A fall from my horse. Twelve years ago. Youthful exuberance that the horse didn't share when faced with a hedge higher than its shoulders. I was sixteen, a student at the university in Padua, and I broke my right leg. There was no physician to hand, and the bone setter did a poor job. The bones didn't knit properly. I had to leave Italy and finish my education here in Cracow, so that I could live with my parents. I can walk, but with difficulty, and ride at best short distances. A poor excuse for a man."

My own reaction startled me. Pleasing the opposite sex had become, since the age of six, my stock in trade, my guarantee of survival. I put a great deal of thought, as a rule, into getting each nuance just right. Spontaneity was dangerous. I might miss a glance or a gesture that concealed an emotion that might then explode in my face, leading to a beating or worse. Yet I reached across the table and wrapped Felix's hand in mine, looking straight into his eyes—not even flirting but perfectly sincere. I didn't give a thought to my pockmarks.

"No woman worth marrying would care about such a thing," I said.

I swear, I caught a flash of tears in his eyes. I quickly changed the subject to give him time to recover.

The next day, at Felix's invitation, I joined him in the royal library. King Sigismund and his son had amassed an enviable collection of books, which they constantly supplemented with new works from Italy—in addition to the ones Queen Bona had brought with her on her marriage. Many of them came from the new printing presses, themselves a remarkable achievement. Felix said that courtiers could borrow the books, so long as they returned them in good condition, and he'd promised to show me the ones he liked best. Which is how I found myself perched on a ladder at shoulder height, reaching for a quarto of poems in Italian by Michelangelo, when I caught sight of a smaller book in green leather with the familiar lines of Arabic script along the spine.

"Oh!" I stretched out one hand, clinging to the ladder with the other and standing almost on tiptoe, to pull the book toward me. "Where did this come from?"

"Careful, Lady Juliana," Felix said from below. His injured leg made negotiating a ladder, however sturdy, difficult if not impossible, so I'd offered to fetch the Michelangelo while he steadied the ladder. "If you take a tumble, I'll try to catch you, but I may do nothing more than break your fall by collapsing under you."

He laughed as he said it, and the image of us lying in an ungainly heap on the floor *was* funny, so I laughed too. I grabbed the Michelangelo and the small book I'd found and scrambled down the ladder. I handed Felix his book and slipped off the leather tie holding the other closed.

"What is it?" he asked. "Why are you so happy?"

I showed him the cover: green leather flecked with gold surrounding a miniature depicting a group of birds—a peacock, a falcon, waterfowl of various sorts, even a rooster—against a blue hill split by a dark gray stream. A tree in leaf, strangely bent to match the contours of the painting, curved over the hill, and other greenery grew directly from the rocky soil. At top right and bottom left, two small boxes marked with Persian script identified the book.

"It's *The Conference of Birds*. One of my favorites." I heard the pleasure in my own voice. His face reflected mostly bemusement, but he brushed the painted image with a delicate finger. I turned the page and found another painting of a wood in spring, with a single small bird swinging on a branch, its mouth open in song. Beneath it spread flowers in indigo, yellow, and white. Another turn of the page revealed a young woman mounted on a horse, a bow in her hand and a shining band around her hair.

"It's gorgeous," Felix said. "Why a conference of birds?" He touched the rich black script next to the image. This was not a printed book: some unknown artist had copied both script and the numerous images by hand. "You can read this? What is it, Arabic?"

"Persian," I said, still quivering with joy. "I haven't seen one for years. It's a famous story: the birds gather to discuss who should be their leader, and they go on a long journey through a series of valleys looking for the perfect ruler, only to learn at the end that the perfect ruler is themselves. The whole story is poetry, and some of it is beautiful. Listen." I turned another page, looking for the passage I wanted while thinking about how to translate it from Persian to Polish. At last I found it.

Never was jewel after or before
Like that Suleiman for a signet wore:
Whereby one ruby, weighing scarce a grain
Did sea and land and all therein constrain,
Yes, even the winds of heaven.

"Gorgeous," Felix said again, but this time he looked at me, not the book. I experienced a glow of pleasure at his interest. Then a flash of fear that startled me. I sensed my eyes widening and hastily looked away.

Where did that come from? We're in a public place. He means me no harm.

Perhaps he saw my reaction, because he changed the subject. "How did it get here, I wonder? From the Turks, I suppose."

"Or the Crimeans." I turned to the frontispiece and stared in awe at the lettering. "Oh, it's from Istanbul," I said. "A gift from Hurrem Sultan herself." The wife of Suleiman the Magnificent, who had succeeded despite the complex politics of the harem and centuries of tradition in persuading the sultan of the entire Ottoman Empire to marry her. She had long been a beacon of hope to those like myself, condemned to live in slavery for decades.

But Felix nodded, apparently taking the news that I found so extraordinary for granted. "The one they call

Roxelana. Yes, she's a Pole, from what I've heard. Queen Bona writes to her regularly."

Then he glanced at me. "What did I say to make you sad?"

Roxelana. My slave name. I hadn't realized I looked sad.

I released a single sobbing breath and said, "It was my name—Roxelana. Until I converted to Catholicism four years ago and took the name Juliana." I hated to think of that time, yet in a sense I had brought his questions on myself. I owed him an explanation. "Some good things happened while I bore that name, but many more bad ones. I'd rather not talk about it. Suffice it to say that I much prefer being Juliana."

Felix studied me, not moving or speaking, for a moment before reaching out and stroking my cheek. "I'm sorry," he said. "I hope you will tell me one day. But not today. I understand."

Without waiting for me to reply—which was good, because I had no idea what to say—he opened his own book. "Perhaps you'll like this one," he said, his voice as even as if nothing had happened. He read four lines in Italian: "How happy is the garland that adorns her golden hair, so blissful and well-formed out of flowers, each of them jostling the others so that it may be the first to kiss her head." He looked at me, his eyes alight with laughter and something else, and I touched his hand briefly. "It sounds best in Italian, of course," he added.

"Everything does," I said. "It's that kind of language. It's beautiful. Thank you."

"Yes, beautiful." He was still gazing at me as if he didn't even see the pockmarks on my face, and again I wondered what kind of man cared so little for appearances.

I redirected his attention to the books, suppressing the glow that touched my heart. I had, after all, not yet known him for one whole day.

Thus Felix and I became friends—a new experience for me. Most of my life I had struggled with men's lust and women's dislike, neither of which lay within my power to avert or alleviate. I dreaded the memories that skulked in the shadows of solitude, so I lived in constant company, chafed by actions and reactions outside my control.

As the days turned into weeks, Felix and I spent more and more time together. He teased me and questioned me, shared his knowledge of the world—not vaster than mine but different in nature—without judging or withholding. He assumed I could follow him, no matter that I wore skirts and he did not. Compared to the Muscovite nobility, the aristocrats of the dynastically aligned states Poland and Lithuania prided themselves on their familiarity with Latin, their firsthand experience with Italian culture, their love of music and art and intelligent conversation, their grasp of etiquette. These elements of life in the western lands kept me determined to stay here despite the dreadful setback dealt by the smallpox. But even Queen Bona's court maintained a distinction between men who rode and fought and studied and women who flattered and charmed, expressing themselves through their mastery of lute and drawing pencil—areas in which I excelled—rather than scholarly argument.

Except for Felix. At first I saw him as yet another master intent on molding me into the woman of his dreams, but I soon realized that other motives drove him. He enjoyed our exchanges—sometimes arguments, but more often explorations—for their own sake. As we spent hour after hour in endless discussions of everything from human nature to the value of religion and the place of man (and woman) in the universe, I slowly accepted that I had somehow won his respect.

And I enjoyed his company. He was lighthearted, quick of mind and tongue, and funny—traits I had seldom encountered, especially in men. In his presence I learned to relax, to joke, to tease without malice. He was the quintessential optimist, whereas the harsh life I'd led left me an incurable pessimist, but we both loved poetry and painting, languages and the vagaries of those who spoke them, history and politics, madrigals and ballads—and chess.

It was a heady brew, and I soon found myself yearning for the sight of him, the sound of his voice—not only in a romantic way but for the thrill of discovering what unsuspected facet of life he would reveal next, which odd insight of mine would crease his face into that appealing smile or provoke his laughter or applause. I drew designs for my henna paintings, eager to show them to him. I dug Persian poetry from the depths of my memory to share with him. I pestered the court musicians to teach me Italian music for the lute. In his company I came alive.

And if I forgot and out of habit tried to coax and seduce, that instant of withdrawal never failed to remind me that I was no longer the siren whom all men desired. Although Felix clearly enjoyed spending time with me and didn't refrain from the occasional flirtatious comment or glance.

But even as I reveled in my novel adventure into friendship, I heard a clock ticking in my head. For I still had no means to support myself other than Queen Bona's generosity, and my hours spent with Felix, delightful as they were, would not lead me to my goal of financial independence. I could accept that he felt no passion for me—indeed, his focus on my mind and my heart rather than my body contributed a great deal to my growing sense of safety with him. But it meant that I couldn't in good conscience ask him for money. And because I had lost my beauty, no other man yearned for me. Smallpox had stripped my one sure means of survival from me.

Yet however dire my situation, I found myself in a quandary. After weeks of being treated with respect, I dreaded the prospect of returning to life as a man's plaything, assuming I found a man who could imagine me in that role. I also doubted that my friendship with Felix could survive such a choice on my part. Losing him was not a risk I wished to take.

But I saw no alternative, until the day Queen Bona summoned me once more into her presence.

Chapter Three

I APPROACHED THE QUEEN WITH A CERTAIN TREPIDATION. At close to fifty, Queen Bona had the advantage of two decades' more experience than I in maneuvering her way through a complicated and often hostile court. She had married the king by proxy in December 1517, when I was but three, before my father came up with the scheme to sell me to a wealthy local warlord to keep his sons in food. And based on the reports I'd heard, Bona had swept into Cracow and Vilnius like a ship at full sail, leaving opponents floundering in her wake and alternately coaxing and bullying her placid middle-aged husband into making policy and taking action as she saw fit.

Nor had the years mellowed her, so far as I could tell. She adamantly opposed the marriage of her son, Sigismund Augustus, to Princess Elisabeth of Austria, as a result of which the marriage had still to take place, despite having been contracted around the future bride's first birthday, now fifteen years in the past. It was Bona, rumor had it, who had pushed her husband to appoint Sigismund Augustus as co-ruler when the boy was just nine years old. She meddled in politics throughout central and eastern Europe, even maintaining a correspondence with the wife of Sultan Suleiman—the evidence of which I had seen in the library. And she'd attracted the ire of an unnamed assassin—still lingering in the castle's dungeons, I assumed, since I'd heard nothing else about either the attempt or the would-be murderer's fate. I'd begun to wonder if the two men I'd overheard had invented the whole story.

I couldn't guess what the queen wanted with me—or why she permitted me to stay at Wawel, for that matter. I wouldn't have predicted that she might take pity on her son's discarded mistress. I could only pray that she hadn't called me into her presence to tell me to pack my bags. Surely royalty didn't deliver such unwelcome news in person. Wasn't that a task for stewards and chamberlains? Yet there she sat, magnificently attired as always, on her plain wooden throne, her hand extended, looking down her long nose from under painted brows.

I curtseyed low, took the extended hand in mine, and brushed my lips across her seal ring. "You requested my presence, Your Majesty?"

"Rise," the queen said. When I again stood facing her, she added, "You still appear somewhat drawn, although less so than on the day of the king's birthday celebration. We trust you are quite recovered from your illness?"

"Yes, Your Majesty." I touched the pockmarks on my cheek, releasing a pink powdery dust from Hanna's latest application of her sovereign remedy, such as it was. "As much as I can hope to be." Bona nodded her understanding.

I waited. One does not ask royalty what royalty wants.

"We like you," she said after a while.

I hoped the shock didn't show on my face. It was the last thing I'd expected her to say. "Thank you, Majesty."

"Yes," she went on, as if I hadn't spoken. "You have common sense, and you handle yourself with grace. You have not complained or begged, despite this tragedy that has befallen you or even our son's decision to replace you with that pretty but mindless chit. The nobles mutter against you because you yielded to him in the first place, but who can refuse a king? They mutter against us too, for other reasons. And you have gained the respect of Lord Ossolinski, which is quite an accomplishment. You could do worse than encourage him, you know."

"I do know," I said, although the thought of manipulating Felix as I had manipulated so many others made my insides curl in shame, banishing the flash of pleasure I'd experienced at hearing the queen's dismissal of the woman who had triumphed over me. "But Felix doesn't desire me."

"Are you sure?" Bona raised her painted-on eyebrows at me. "It doesn't look that way to us."

My cheeks flushed with pleasure, although again I had to suppress that flash of fear. Could she be right? He did flirt with me, but then what explained the moments of withdrawal? "If he does, it won't serve," I said. "I have yet to secure a divorce from my Russian husband."

Queen Bona gave me a long, assessing stare from under those painted brows. "Well, now you'll have an opportunity to ask him for one."

I blinked, then shook my head quickly to clear it. "Ask him?" I prayed my voice didn't squeak, but I had to admit that sounded like a squeak to me.

The queen's eyes crinkled at the corners. It seemed my dismay amused her. "We are sending Lord Ossolinski to Moscow. The peace treaty that ended the last war between the Russians and our own Grand Duchy of Lithuania expires this year. We have enough trouble on our hands with the Habsburgs and the Tatars, so let us renew our pact with Moscow."

As I listened to her, my dismay expanded to encompass emptiness and dread, the implications of which I couldn't stop to consider at that moment. I had known Felix for two weeks, at the most. It made no sense to act as if the powers above planned to strip my sole comfort from me.

Although it felt just like that.

"You will accompany the embassy," the queen finished.

"Me?" Too stunned to remember the proper court protocol, I stammered questions that probably sounded like protests, although they were more like tendrils of hope. "Why? How is that possible for a woman?"

She leaned back and crossed her arms over her chest. "My dear, do you think we haven't watched you since you arrived at our court? You are a mistress of guile. You calculate every word that drops from your lips. You read each person's place on the social ladder the way others absorb a philosophical treatise."

I stared at the floor, my cheeks hot. It embarrassed me that she saw so clearly that which I'd thought hidden from everyone's eyes but mine.

"Make no mistake," the queen said. "In a diplomat these are admirable, even essential traits. Moreover, your friend Lord Ossolinski tells us you speak five languages, including fluent Russian and near-native Tatar. He asked for you to serve as his personal translator, and we have decided to grant his request. Your task for us will be to eavesdrop on the Russians. Learn whatever you can of their secrets. As for how, you will go dressed as a man."

"As a man?" My shock ran so deep that I could hardly speak the words. "Suppose someone finds out?"

"They won't. You're an excellent actress, and Lord Ossolinski will help you prepare. My husband and I will protect you as well, if necessary. Besides, it won't be for long—a month or two at the outside. Once you reach the Russian border on your way home, you can complete the journey as a woman if you like."

"I suppose." The words stuck in my throat, although I'd grown up in a world where women could, under certain circumstances, dress as men. So the queen's demand really shouldn't trouble me as much as it did. My fears came more from a sense, ever since my illness, that I walked on quicksand. It would be just my luck to have my disguise fail in the wrong company, leaving me vulnerable to rape or worse.

"Where will I get these clothes?" I asked.

"I've ordered the court tailor to prepare them." Bona seemed to take my acquiescence for granted. But then, why wouldn't she? Subjects did what they were told, if they wanted to live in comfort and freedom. "You must leave quite soon if you're to catch up with the ambassadors in Vilnius. There's no time to waste."

I stared, stupefied as a moonstruck cow at the news that she had already made arrangements for my departure, until she laughed and waved the pomander that everyone wore to protect against the plague. "Lord Ossolinski will explain the details. Aid him as he requires, but understand two things. First, we appoint you to act as *our* eyes and ears. We hear disturbing news from Moscow. The boyar clans are fighting again, and we need more detail about what's going on, so we can decide how the outcome of their squabbles will affect us. Second, provide useful information, and we will reward you with property of your own. Then you may marry or not, live with a man or by yourself—even maintain your passionless friendship with Lord Felix, if that's what you both prefer—without concern for your material welfare. Shirk this responsibility, and you have worn out your welcome at our court." Her painted brows rose again as she widened her eyes. "Do we make ourselves clear?"

She offered the very thing I wanted most. How could I refuse? I curtseyed once more. "You honor me, Your Majesty," I said. "I will do as you ask."

She accepted my submission with a careless nod. "Go with God, Lady Juliana, and return in triumph." Recognizing dismissal when I heard it, I withdrew.

I had reached the far side of the double doors before the enormity of her demand sank in. She was sending me back to Moscow, a place I detested, where the husband I'd abandoned could lay claim to my person at any moment. She had ordered me to go dressed as a man, a masquerade guaranteed to create problems with the others on the Polish mission if I succeeded and to threaten my safety, even my life, if I failed. And she wanted me to act as her personal spy, her eyes and ears, to uncover information the enemy preferred to keep hidden. I must travel masked, concealed from my husband, my fellow envoys, and the nobles in Moscow. One slip would destroy me.

Perhaps I should accept that I no longer belong at this court and flee westward.

But the thought had no sooner formed than the impossibility of it struck me. I would be a woman alone, without means of support or protection. No one would take in a stranger—the innkeepers would regard me as a whore and refuse to let me cross their thresholds, assuming I could find money to pay them. I would have to walk and sleep in the fields—in Poland, in January—and my chances of reaching the next town, even in a civilized country like this one, without suffering assault were next to nil.

No, the queen had left me no option but to do as she wished. Whatever I said in a careless moment about working the Cracow streets rather than return to my detestable husband, I had no desire whatsoever to find myself in a situation even worse than the one inflicted on me as a child.

And if I succeeded, I would never again need to beg or placate to keep food on the table. For the first time in my twenty-seven years, I would know freedom.

The stakes were high, but the reward was higher. So I must go forward, and I must succeed.

But how on earth was I going to fulfill my commission, with or without Felix's help?

I set off in search of Felix right away, but he proved elusive. I had plenty of time to brood over my predicament before I ran him down in the music room, where I found him engaged in a discussion of the relative merits of the lute and the virginals.

"There you are," I said, unable to keep the accusatory note out of my voice. "How could you?"

He blinked, expressing an emotion not unlike the sheeplike astonishment with which I had greeted the queen's announcement. "By the rood, Juliana, what's put you in a temper?"

I couldn't discuss his misdeeds before a roomful of musicians in the queen's pay. "Perhaps you could spare me a moment of your time," I suggested, still mad as a drenched cat yet aware that Felix was neither the true cause of my plight nor the real target of my anger.

Indeed, I couldn't have sworn at that moment that anger was the right word. After all, I didn't *want* him to leave me behind while he traipsed off to Russia. *He* hadn't threatened to throw me into the streets if I refused his request. He hadn't even made a request of me, only of Queen Bona. And if he *had* asked me, I might have said yes rather than lose my sole friend, even if it meant returning to the one place among the many I had visited that lacked, in my view, any redeeming value.

But I couldn't yell at the queen, and there he stood looking like an innocent, not like someone who had carelessly tossed me into the middle of a lake while I clutched at phantoms to keep from drowning. I took several deep breaths to stop myself from blurting out my outrage and tried to take comfort from his wary bow and rather befuddled expression as he lurched across the room and held out his left arm so that I could place my fingertips on it while he escorted me to a more private location.

By the time we entered the library and found seats in a secluded corner, I had calmed down enough to apologize. I filled him in on the gist of my conversation with the queen.

He blushed and took both of my hands in his. "I did tell Bona that I thought you would make a wonderful addition to our party. I didn't expect her to twist your arm with such ruthless efficiency—although I should have, I suppose. But we could use your skills, Juliana. It's not just a question of finding out who among the Russians may come out on top, although that's part of it. We've received information that they are stirring up unrest among those members of the gentry who already oppose King Sigismund's reforms. Up to and including plots against the lives of the king and queen."

The attempt to assassinate Queen Bona, which I had heard those two men discussing at the birthday celebration! Had the conspirator talked, then?

I opened my mouth to ask, but Felix went on before I could interrupt. "We know they've sent agents here and to Vilnius. They may also have recruited one of the envoys who visited Moscow last year. We need to find out who those agents are and who oversees them in Moscow. Whose interests the agents serve."

"Stop." I pulled one hand free of his and held it up. "You're moving too fast. I can't follow you. How can warring clans in Moscow benefit from promoting unrest here?"

"It sounds crazy, I know." Felix scrunched up his nose as if the explanation eluded him. "But our king has done much to protect Poland and Lithuania against our enemies. He's subdued the Prussians and signed an eternal peace with the Ottomans, who control the Crimean Tatars—to the extent anyone does. He's expanded our territory and secured our borders. When the younger Sigismund at last marries Elisabeth of Austria, which he will do next year, even the Habsburgs will leave us alone for a while. Sigismund the Old has offered to renew the peace with Muscovy, and you'd think the Russians would want that, especially if they're fighting among themselves. But some may hope that by stirring up trouble, they can weaken and distract him. If so, we must find out and put a stop to it."

I frowned, considering the implications of what I'd heard. "But why send us to Moscow? Why not work on counteracting the unrest here?"

"Oh, there are people doing that too. Our job is to find the spymaster, if we can, and identify those who work for him."

"The spymaster," I repeated, trying to take the information in. "And his agents. In Moscow." It sounded impossible. Did Felix understand how many people Moscow contained? Its government was compact enough, but even so, identifying a spymaster within a month or two would task our abilities to the utmost.

"Whoever they are, they will seek to establish contact with the other side," Felix said. "We want to watch for members of our party with family or other ties to powerful Russians, as well as Muscovites who often visit Poland and Lithuania. The spymaster may prove difficult to discover, but if we keep our eyes open, we should be able to find the agents."

"Can we trust no one on our own side?" I thought of my masquerade, and how much more difficult it would become if I had to suspect everyone of hidden deceit.

"The ambassadors haven't traveled to Moscow before, and they have little to gain from betraying Poland and Lithuania. Some of the others I can probably certify as safe once we gather in Vilnius. And you can trust me, obviously. King Sigismund has sufficient proof of my support." He stopped talking long enough to smile, and I returned the smile.

At the same time, I wondered about the proof. Did Felix make a habit of engaging in—what? Detection? Spying? "You've done this before?" I asked.

"I have," he said. "In Florence, among other places. We can discuss that later. For now, let's concentrate on our present task. Five men went to Moscow last year, plus myself and the usual servants and escort. Most of the servants and soldiers got nowhere near the Russian diplomats. So it's the five who concern us. The king and queen have decided to send them all on this journey. It's not the solution I'd have chosen, but it does get them away from court and avoid punishing the innocent, and I do what I'm told like everyone else. Our job is to watch them, identify the culprit, and prevent him from causing further harm. If we can also find out who among the Russians seeks to cause trouble for the royal family, so much the better. Obviously, we tell no one the true nature of our mission."

I shivered. It wasn't the solution I'd have chosen either, although I liked the idea of protecting Queen Bona—and Poland—from attack. And part of that involved sharing with Felix what I knew. Trust didn't come easily to me, but since we would be traveling together, I would have to trust him to some degree, would I not?

"I heard two men talking at the king's birthday celebration," I told him. "I don't know their names. Both sounded like native speakers of Polish. A young man with dark brown hair and eyes, and another man I saw only from the back. He had sandy hair, and he was about medium height and broad of frame, but I wouldn't recognize him if I saw him again. They were discussing the attack on Queen Bona. I had the impression that the dark-haired man—not so much the other—had an interest in the case. He kept asking whether the assassin had confessed. He sounded—I couldn't guess what. Eager, perhaps, or anxious. But my point is that unless the two of them go to Moscow with us, there will be people we have no way to suspect. And if they do travel with us, there will be others who don't, will there not?"

"There will." Felix drew curves with his index finger against the blotter on the desk, like the doodles children put in their schoolbooks. "I can warn the king, but with so little to go on ... You haven't seen either man since?"

I shook my head. "Just that one day. And I didn't get a full view of them then. I've looked for them, but to no avail."

"Did they see you? Did they know you were listening?"

I frowned, remembering. "I doubt it. I was standing in line, waiting to make my bow to the king and queen." My cheeks flushed hot as I recalled the humiliation that followed. Felix hadn't witnessed that, thank God. Odd to think I had met him such a short time later. "I stood in front of them, off to the right. And they were preoccupied with their conversation. Looking at each other, talking quietly. After the presentation I walked around for a bit." More humiliation. "I didn't see them then, although I did look. But there were so many people I might have missed them in the crowd. Then I was tired, so I retreated to the alcove where you and Samuel Tarlo were playing. After I left you, I returned to my room."

"That's right," Felix said. "You weren't at the banquet."

"No. Queen Bona excused me because of my illness. That was my first day at court since November." I wondered anew about the two men—who they were, whether they posed a risk to me. But they'd done nothing in the weeks since the party, and I hadn't seen them about the court. They seemed an unlikely source of danger. "It would be easy for the men I overheard to find out my name if they asked, but what would they do with that information? I haven't spoken of what I learned until now."

Felix still looked thoughtful, even troubled. "Perhaps it's good that we're leaving so soon. I'm sorry the queen forced your hand, but not that you agreed to accompany me. I'll watch out for you. We need you. How many people can translate from Persian to Polish and Russian to Tatar?" He treated me to his delightful smile. "Besides, I'd miss you, Juliana. I know it's too soon, but I haven't met a woman since I left Padua who could hold her own in a conversation, never mind beat me at chess with such alarming regularity."

"I'd miss you as well, Felix." I was glad I'd told him what I knew, but the journey ahead still troubled me. Our task grew more complicated with each hour that passed. Bad enough when I thought we needed only to spy on the Muscovites. Now we would be watching those in our own party as well—and for evidence of treason, at that. And unless I'd misunderstood, I would be the only translator Felix trusted. Each revelation raised the stakes for the mission, increasing the risks associated with discovery and undermining our chances of success.

Only then did his first sentence sink in. "When *do* we leave?" I asked.

"In a few days." He clasped my hands once more. "You're a quick study, and with so many languages no one will doubt your qualifications as a translator. That's good, because we have barely enough time to teach you how to dress and act like a man. Fortunately your hair hasn't grown enough to pose a problem, and I can lend you my clothes."

"Felix, you could fit two of me in your clothes!" I said. My anxiety vanished in laughter at the thought. He was neither exceptionally tall nor fat, but I have always been slender and slight of frame, although the crown of my head reached somewhere around his nose.

He laughed too. "Your own clothes, then. The king can afford a few suits for a translator. If that's the only problem, consider it done."

"It's the least of my problems." I sighed as the desire to laugh left me once more. He was distinguished by his intelligence. How could he not see what an absurd plan he and Bona had cooked up? "The queen already said she ordered the tailors to stitch for me. But how can I travel among a whole group of male envoys without one of them, probably at the most inopportune moment, realizing that I'm a woman? And there's another thing ..." I hesitated. I didn't want to share the story of my marriage. Had deliberately deflected his questions, in fact. But now I must. "In Russia I'm still legally married. My husband could force me to return to him at any time."

Felix raised my clasped hands to his lips. "My dear Juliana, I won't let your husband anywhere near you. Nor the other men. You will stay with me, and I'll look after you."

I believed he meant what he said, yet I still felt troubled. I couldn't draw back, and wouldn't if I could, so that wasn't the issue. I sought reassurance—that I could succeed, that I could maintain the mask long enough to complete the mission, but also of something deeper, something I struggled to articulate. I wanted him to swear that I would keep his friendship and respect, no matter what happened during our journey. I needed to know that if something went wrong, he wouldn't desert me as so many others had. I wanted to trust him. But I had never received that kind of support from a man, and I had no idea how to phrase the request to elicit the words I yearned to hear.

So much for my ability to calculate, I thought with a bitterness that shamed me.

"Wouldn't you love a chance to live, just for a month or two, as a man? Not to be judged by your face?" He spoke in a coaxing tone and, when I didn't respond, released one hand to brush my powdered cheek. "I know how this aftereffect of your illness troubles you, although it need not."

The thought did appeal, but that wasn't what persuaded me to abandon my doubts. I'd already accepted that the queen had left me no real choice, and if I succeeded, the promised reward would fulfill my deepest goal. And even without that, I wouldn't have wanted to stay safe but lonely in Cracow while Felix went off on adventures by himself. "I suppose," I said. "I've already agreed to go to Moscow with you. God grant that I also return."

Felix leaned forward and brushed his lips across my forehead. "Thank you, Juliana. I promise to keep you safe."

I hoped he told the truth, but safety seemed faraway.

"Bigger, Juliana. Take up space when you walk. No apologies, even implicit. You're young, yes, but a lord. Be expansive." Felix waved his arm to demonstrate, and I copied him—once, twice, half a dozen times until he was satisfied.

Three days had passed since Queen Bona's summons. Clad in shirt, doublet, and hose—and wasn't *that* a strange experience? I might as well be wearing harem trousers!—I had spent every free moment in Felix's chambers practicing how to turn myself into his cousin Julian.

This morning we had received instructions to depart on the morrow. With so little study under my belt, I feared that Julian was destined to remain a sadly effeminate boy. But I had to admit to enjoying my lessons, despite the constant hammering into my head that I needed to speak more firmly, move more aggressively, gesture more widely, bow with a greater flourish, and generally impose myself on my environment as a man would instead of gliding through the hallway attracting attention by the grace of my steps and the occasional seductive glance over a bared shoulder.

Since my illness, of course, I welcomed that last reminder, a response to a habit I strove to overcome. My rejection by King Sigismund Augustus still stung. Not to mention the disdain shown me by Sebastian Branicki, that infernal fool Jan Radziwill, and others of their ilk.

In response to a gesture (broad, of course!) from Felix, I flung myself onto a chair and threw one leg over the arm. My hand claimed the chair back, and I stared straight into his eyes. He laughed and applauded. "Much better. Now stand and cross the room. No mincing."

"I do not mince," I announced with dignity.

Felix grinned. "Yes, you do. Those tiny steps, that graceful sway—what else would you call it?"

"Walking. Or, if you insist, gliding." I raised my chin and assumed my loftiest expression, but his grin did not falter.

"Then no gliding," he said, unabashed. "Men don't glide. And no simpering!"

"I definitely do not simper." I stood, hands on my hips, trying to look aggressive—or at least lordly. "That wretched Emilia Sobieska simpers. I wouldn't stoop to her sort of 'oh, don't think twice about little me' nonsense. If I want a man's attentions, I show him that I do. And if I don't, I can stare him down with the best of them."

Felix's grin turned into outright laughter. So much for aggressive or lordly. I permitted myself an exasperated sigh.

"Well, whatever you call that sideways glance that makes me want to kiss you," he said, "refrain. I can't spend the trip hauling lascivious envoys off my young cousin Julian, never mind lascivious Russians. I doubt you'd enjoy it much either."

I made a face at him, although secretly flattered that he thought I still wielded that kind of seductive power, and crossed the room as he'd asked. My feet in their thigh-high leather boots strode over the tiles, and I realized all of a sudden that in the long, tight hose I could move my legs without having to kick skirts away. I could breathe unconstrained by a stomacher. I imagined the men I'd known—Alexei and his brother and the other Tatar khans with their proud heads and broad shoulders, the way they seemed to fill the space around themselves, their constant jockeying to determine who was up and who down; and the running, shrieking boys who dodged their mothers' hands and raced around the camp endangering life and limb. With each step I took their image into me and made it mine.

When I reached Felix, I swept the cap from my head, extended one leg, and bowed. Then I looked up, laughing as hard as he, because the whole thing was absurd and I had no idea how these unfamiliar gestures could give rise to a persona that I could sustain throughout our journey.

"You'll do, Julian," Felix said, still grinning. "So long as the Russians don't decide to dance after dinner."

"I dance very well, I'll have you know." I demonstrated a slow, twirling movement that I especially liked, although without the sway of skirts it lost some of its appeal for both artist and audience.

"I'm sure you do." Felix caught my hand to stop me. "But that's exactly what I'm talking about. Not exactly a Russian foot stomp, is it?"

"I love the pavane," I told him, to keep him from having the last word. I knew very well that Russian men didn't dance the pavane. They seldom socialized with women, so whom would they partner?

"So do I," Felix said. "Much good it will do us in Moscow. Let's practice making firm statements instead. No hesitation that gives someone else a chance to butt in. No head dipping to undercut your point. And by the rood, no lovely graceful hand motions!"

I groaned. I needed six months, and I had at most six hours.

Chapter Four

"WELL?" I TWISTED AND TURNED, TRYING TO CATCH THE smallest glimpse of the remarkable costume Felix had insisted I don. Crimson hose; a velvet doublet the rich blue of skies darkening into twilight, embroidered at cuffs, hems, and shoulders with geometric designs in gold and extending into a short, full skirt ending at mid-thigh; a cap of the same blue edged with gold; a linen shirt with only the lace cuffs showing beneath the doublet—I had felt less exposed in the loose gauze robes of my masters' harems. "Will I pass muster?"

He laughed, his gray eyes bright. "By the time we get back from Moscow, you will have ruined my reputation. Everyone in the dual kingdom will believe me besotted with beautiful boys."

I touched the pockmarks on my left cheek, for once free of powder, which Felix had insisted I scrub off on the grounds that a man wouldn't wear it. "Boys, perhaps, but not beautiful ones."

"Don't beg for compliments, Juliana. It doesn't suit you." Still laughing, he stood and kissed the cheek I had touched. "The marks will fade, you know, in time. And so long as they remain, they will help conceal your identity—even from the inconvenient husband, we hope."

He handed me the mirror, and I tried one angle after another, surveying as much as I could of the absurd clothes. "I suppose I do look like a young man," I said, not sure in the least. The chin-length hair and marred skin, the narrowness and lines of strain that hadn't marked my face before my illness, and the rather jaunty cap and masculine garb combined to give me an appearance I didn't recognize. The realization jarred me.

"You do," Felix said. "From this moment you become Julian. We must use the name even when we're alone, to avoid any slips."

"From this moment?" I'd reached up to pull the cap from my head, but something in his tone stopped me. "Why should I dress like this before we leave Vilnius?"

"From this moment," he repeated firmly. "We get on the road in an hour, and we want the others in our party to accept you as my young cousin and translator Julian Ossolinski. Those traveling with us on this first stage have ridden in from outlying areas. They have no reason to recognize you, but they will certainly notice if you switch from female to male halfway through our journey. As I promised, you will stay in my room—and I won't molest you, wicked girl, so don't work your wiles on me—but the possibility that you're a woman rather than a man must not enter their heads. That way, they can't betray you. So we make the change now, not in Vilnius."

A surge of rebellion filled me, but I could think of no rational objection. And really, what did a few days matter?

The desire to protest roiled within me regardless. I'd expected more time to adjust to thinking of myself as a man.

As if oblivious to my turmoil, Felix lifted a rapier from a nearby chest and bound it around my waist. It dangled, slapping against my thigh. "Do I have to?" I sounded like a sulky child. "I'll be lucky if I don't fall down the stairs or trip over my own legs. And God help me if anyone issues a challenge."

"Hold it like this." He moved my fingers into place and clasped them lightly until I showed him I understood what he wanted me to learn. "No one will challenge you. The small sword's a declaration of nobility, not an invitation to combat."

I could only hope he told the truth—or that he would have time to intervene if not.

"Come." He placed a hand at the base of my spine and turned me away from the window. "My man packed a full set of clothes for you. We already said our farewells to King Sigismund and Queen Bona, so let's get on the road. You'll do wonderfully, Julian. I have faith in you."

He strode toward the exit. His fur-trimmed cloak puffed out in the breeze as he opened the door. He didn't look back to see if I followed.

With a sigh I picked up the unadorned black velvet cloak he'd chosen for me—sufficiently rich to indicate my noble standing yet designed not to draw attention to itself—swung it around my shoulders, and fastened it. Like it or not, I was on my way to Moscow, a city I hated. And I was going dressed as a man.

What have I let myself in for?

The very first night I learned the advantages of traveling with Felix. As was not uncommon, from what I'd heard, the innkeeper at the tavern where we stopped the first night thought nothing of assigning all four noblemen in our group to a single room.

As it happened, that single room was more of a loft, accessible only by ladder. Quite apart from the discomfort to me personally of sharing a room with three members of the opposite sex, two of them near-strangers, I found it incredible that anyone capable of running a hostelry could imagine the scion of a magnate family—and one who relied on a cane, at that—consenting to such an arrangement. The innkeeper must be the world's biggest dimwit. I awaited Felix's response with a certain anticipatory pleasure.

I didn't have to wait long. "That will never serve," Felix said in a firm voice as the innkeeper, a reedy man who gave little evidence of profiting from his trade, stuttered to a halt. I suspected he might have noticed the stunned expression on my friend's face.

Felix pointed to his cane. "Even if I could scale that ladder, which I cannot, the need to accommodate my injury would cause great inconvenience not only for me but for those who must share the bed with me. We require a room, however small. Preferably one with a trestle or trundle bed for my cousin."

This was a side of him I hadn't seen before. I had to admit it impressed me.

The innkeeper protested, wringing his hands, but Felix stood firm. After a few more ineffectual complaints, the innkeeper yielded to the inevitable. A beckoning hand summoned a strapping lad who looked as if he might be the innkeeper's son. He led us down a corridor and, with the air of a traveling magician pulling a rabbit from a hat, threw open a wooden door.

The room on the other side was more inviting than I'd expected. I saw fresh linen on the bed and clean towels next to a pitcher emitting curls of steam. The strapping lad crossed the room and pulled a low bed from under the mattress. It too boasted newly changed linen. My fears of bedbugs and lice, sparked by the innkeeper's air of poverty, ebbed as I surveyed the room. I wondered if he always kept rooms in reserve for difficult customers or whether the family would sleep in the barn tonight. After his attempt to cheat us, I didn't much care if he slept in the hay.

"It will do," Felix said in lordly tones. "Send my man here at once." The lad bowed and left, drawing the door shut behind him.

"Thank you," I said. "I had no idea you could muster such an air of command. But suppose they'd insisted they had no other room? Would it cause talk if I slept in the carriage?" I was genuinely curious, but appreciative too.

Felix dropped the "royalty must be served" pose he had worn as if it were a second skin. "No doubt it would. We may encounter such a situation again, so we should be prepared. If necessary, I could insist that, as the youngest, you should take the place nearest the wall. Then I'd keep the others away by sleeping next to you and kicking anyone who came too close. At least in a group like that, no one would undress." He pointed at his leg. "A damned nuisance most of the time, but it has its benefits, you see."

I doffed my cap to him. "I suppose so. Thank you again, kind sir." I had already decided I could trust him with my person, yet the narrowness of this escape made me nervous.

What other threats would I face that I didn't even know to anticipate?

On the third day after leaving Cracow, we reached the town of Sandomierz. The castle on its hill looked like a smaller version of Wawel, its stone walls shading into brick and ending with red tiles on the roof. Several other men assigned to the journey met us there, and I was startled to recognize the dark-haired young man I had overheard at the king's birthday celebration. His name, I discovered, was Adam Tarlo. He and Felix greeted each other like old friends, and I soon learned that Adam was the nephew of Samuel Tarlo, whom I'd beaten at chess the day I met Felix.

All of which put me in something of a dilemma. I couldn't blurt out my discovery in front of everyone without endangering myself. I had to worry that Adam might recognize me as I had him. And although I trusted Felix enough to accompany him to Moscow, I didn't know how to assess his apparent friendship with Adam. If I told Felix what I knew, would he believe me? Was my identification even right? I had seen the young man for a few minutes, in profile, almost a month ago. Since I couldn't be certain, I decided to wait and watch before sharing my impressions with Felix.

The military governor and his deputies welcomed us, so for this night I needn't worry about dodging group quarters at an inn. It was, of course, the governor's duty to put up the king's envoys as they passed through, but the eagerness with which he and his men greeted our party convinced me that they also looked forward to news of the court.

I stood behind Felix and bowed when introduced, but otherwise I remained in the shadows, hoping to avoid Adam Tarlo's attention. The strategy seemed to work. To my surprise, so far no one had questioned my disguise. By the time I returned from Moscow, I suspected I would have become quite accustomed to life in doublet and hose, but every time someone glanced twice at me, I still expected them to tear my cap from my head and proclaim me an imposter. Adam's presence increased those fears fivefold.

When the military governor and his staff ushered our party to the high table, I took my seat on the bench at the far end, as required by my position as (nominally) the youngest person present. Felix accepted a place about halfway between me and the military governor, with a pair of princes who had also just arrived, Simon Belsky and Martin Glinsky—from prominent western and southern Russian families in service to Lithuania—to Felix's right. Both of them, I noticed, had sandy hair. They looked quite similar, in fact, although they came from different clans. Perhaps their ancestors had intermarried at some point in the past. Adam Tarlo faced Felix, and two or three less important Polish lords filled the benches between Adam and myself.

That reassured me. I would have felt even more reassured if Adam and I sat on the same side of the table, but at least he had no reason to speak to me directly, and in the dim candlelight my place at the end made me almost invisible. Because Felix and I traveled by sleigh, to spare his leg, while the others rode, I didn't interact much with the rest of our party. So if I could survive one evening in Adam's presence without being unmasked, that would bode well for the rest of the journey.

Compared to the court banquets in Cracow, this group was small: no more than twelve nobles at the high table. Our servants and men-at-arms sat lower in the hall, so they must wait for us to select the pieces that we wanted from each dish before sending the plates down to them. We barely had time to fill our cups with small beer before the servers arrived bearing tureens of borscht, which they ladled into wooden bowls. Behind them men bore platters of salted herring in verjuice and an assortment of pickled vegetables—nothing else being available in Poland in winter. Baskets of wheat rolls and cabbage pirogi followed.

As I ladled soup into my mouth and waved away the unappetizing slab of herring, I studied my fellow diners between bites of roll, pirogi, and vegetables. Not only did my silence encourage them to concentrate on one another rather than me, but the sooner I discovered who was sharing information with the Russians, the sooner I could relax in the knowledge that I had attained my goal of financial independence. So I pretended shyness, listened for hints of disaffection, and strove to recall whom Felix had identified as members of the previous mission to Moscow. Those were my targets, but given our small number, it seemed likely that some of the suspects must be seated on Felix's other side.

Those within my line of sight ranged in age from twenty to fifty and varied in size and in color of hair and eyes. Two had a rotundity that suggested they lived well enough and dressed as if they belonged to the lesser gentry—their mail battered but functional and well maintained, their doublets and hose of warm and serviceable materials richer than those of ordinary townsfolk but nowhere near as grand as the robes of merchants or nobles from older aristocratic families like Felix's.

Up to this point, Felix and I had been operating on the assumption that whoever supported the Russians against King Sigismund and Queen Bona must have made the switch out of conviction. But suppose we were wrong? These less prestigious gentrymen might fall for promises of higher rank and financial gain. Even princes switched sides for personal advantage and to advance the standing of their lineages. Both Simon Belsky and Martin Glinsky had relatives who had fled to Moscow in search of greater power and the economic rewards that went with it. Why assume the same factors would not draw those lower on the social ladder?

With that in mind, I paid particular attention to the three men who sat closest to me, looking for armor that showed hints of rust as well as hard use or whose clothes went beyond serviceable into the land of faded and patched. From what Felix had told me, I felt pretty certain that every one of the three had taken part in that previous journey, so any of them could be a suspect.

The man across the table from me, Bogdan Ostrogski, looked like a potential conspirator—to the point where under other circumstances I would have dismissed him out of hand as a potential suspect. No one could run so true to type as that, which made me think he must suffer from bad fortune. At around thirty, or so I guessed, Bogdan had a long narrow face with green eyes that he flicked at the world like a lizard or a snake. His body, perennially huddled in on itself, stood in stark contrast to the proud and carefree stance of the other noblemen.

Like me, Bogdan didn't trade banter with the group. But he also didn't observe his surroundings. Instead he concentrated on eating—steadily, like an automaton, as if he couldn't recall when he'd last had a solid meal. He ate like that at every stop, although food didn't stick to his lanky frame. Next to Bogdan, I looked chubby. And he definitely seemed to have fallen into straitened circumstances. His leather jerkin had seen better days, as had his scarlet doublet, frayed at the seams. The right combination of lure and threat might turn him from supporter to traitor.

Leon Laski, who sat next to Bogdan, came from a more prominent family but perhaps from a branch that had fallen on hard times. His clothes were neither worn nor ragged, but they were sadly out of date: the sleeves hugely puffed, the doublet open at the neck to reveal the linen shirt beneath. I could entertain the idea that Leon, well into his forties, might prefer the styles of his youth to the current mode. And since he lived outside the capital, he could be behind the times for that reason too. Still, the Polish nobility prided itself on following every shift in Italianate dress, so it surprised me to see one of its members in apparel that had been considered old-fashioned when I first arrived in Vilnius—unless that person lacked the means to replace his clothes on a whim. Other than that,

I saw nothing in Leon's manner or appearance that gave cause for suspicion, but as with Bogdan it would be foolish to draw conclusions solely on the basis of looks.

That left Adam Tarlo. His dark doublet and linen cuffs did look rather shabby, but in a way that indicated carelessness rather than penury. Watching him laugh and joke as he raised his goblet in response to this toast or that, I hoped he harbored no greater tendency to betrayal than the glee with which he dragged Felix's trencher out of the way just as a filet of herring descended on it. If Adam and Felix were friends, the treachery of one would upset the other. I didn't like to think of Felix suffering.

I leaned forward enough to glance at Felix and found him also watching and listening. Good. Tonight we could compare notes.

But it was late by the time the dinner ended, and Felix and I put off our discussion until the next day. While Felix washed his face and hands, I pulled my long nightshirt over my head and undressed beneath it. When my turn came, I washed and brushed my teeth with a stick and a chalky powder Felix's man had provided, then slipped into a narrow bed.

That night I dreamed about the ogre for the first time since my illness. I lay in a familiar dark room—familiar from the dream, that is—lit by a single lamp near the door. The looming man-sized shape appeared, filled with menace. As always, my body froze in terror.

Then something changed. I saw a thornless white rose, its stem broken, lying on the tiles between me and the ogre.

And I heard a woman's voice, singing in Persian, a haunting tune I couldn't place—almost like a lullaby.

The room shook, as if in an earthquake. Shook, and shook again. I heard rumbling.

My legs wouldn't move. My arms lay as if pinned to the bed. I couldn't catch my breath. I would die. I knew it with the dull certainty of horror, just as I had known that the doctor doomed me with his callous assessment of my attack of smallpox and its costs.

Then a man's voice spoke—calm, familiar, reassuring. "Julian," it said. Released from the spell, I opened my eyes on a night-dark room with a man-sized shape outlined against the moonlight that shone through a slit between the curtains.

For one ghastly moment I remained locked in the nightmare. I bolted upright and scooted as far away from the shape as I could get, stopping only when my back hit the headboard and my left shoulder smacked against the wall. I pressed my hand against my throat, where a scream threatened to burst loose, and stared, rigid with fear, at the ogre.

"Juliana, it's Felix," the ogre murmured in Felix's voice. "What's wrong?" He stretched out a hand and caressed my cheek. Only then did I realize he was sitting on the mattress next to me, not on the other bed, where I'd seen him shortly before I fell asleep. The impression of him shaped like the ogre was a trick of the light. He rested one hand on my shoulder, and I realized he'd been shaking me gently. To wake me from the dream, probably.

Still wrapped in wisps of horror, I hurled myself forward and wrapped both arms around his waist. He hugged me close, murmuring the kind of meaningless comfort one whispers to a frightened child. I pressed my eyes tight shut, inhaling his scent of woodsy shaving oil and almond soap.

After a while, I forced my closed lids open, trying to slow my breathing as I looked around the room, forcing myself back to the present.

"What happened?" he asked. "You were whimpering like a cowed puppy and shuddering in your sleep. Did you have a nightmare?"

When I released a gasping breath and nodded, he patted my scarred cheek. "Tell me. It will help."

"It won't," I said. "I've had the dream for as long as I can remember. I'm trapped—in a room, on a bed, a place I recognize, only I never know just where it is—and I can't move, not so much as a finger or toe. Then a fuzzy shape appears at the door and I know it will kill me. Like the ogre in a fairy tale. I want to run, but I can't. I want to scream for help, but the words stick in my throat. I can't raise a hand to defend myself. I wake up with my heart pounding like a cannon attacking a town under siege. The last time I had that sensation was after the smallpox, the day the doctor announced I would live. But I wasn't dreaming then; I really couldn't move, because of the disease."

Felix pulled me tighter. "I'm here. No ogre can touch you. You're safe."

My jaw dropped against his nightshirt, and I hastily closed it. Felix had taken me seriously. He hadn't said a word about how silly it was to get into a panic about ogres when anyone could see I was in a room in Sandomierz with no one scary nearby. I nestled into his hold, relishing the sense of safety.

When I could control my limbs, I straightened. "Thank you," I told him. "Go back to sleep."

"Are you sure?" He stroked my cheek once more. "You had me worried there for a while."

He was a prince among men. I was lucky to have such a friend. And he needed his rest. "I'll be fine," I said. "The dream never comes twice on the same night. I'm sorry I woke you."

He studied me for a moment, as if he would argue further, then returned to his own narrow bed. I lay on my side, my back to the wall, and closed my eyes. The moment I heard the mattress creak under him and the rustle of covers stop, I again stared into the dark, reluctant to give the ogre another chance to attack me, even in dreams.

But as I watched Felix relax into slumber, the image of the broken rose stayed with me. Again I heard the singer's voice. I knew that voice and that song, although I couldn't recall the woman's name or when I'd heard her sing. I knew only that the sound made me inexpressibly sad.

Where had I heard them before? Puzzling over that problem kept me awake for the rest of the night.

Chapter Five

On the Road to Vilnius, February 1542

"I DON'T BELIEVE IT." FELIX TIPPED HIS KING SIDEWAYS, leaned his head against the cushions, and groaned. "Three times in a row. A fiendishly strategic mind you have, my lay—lad. *Where* did you learn to play chess again?"

I laughed, and not only because he had, for the umpteenth time, slipped and almost called me "lady." "I told you, a friend of my father's." The familiar half-truth brought a lump to my throat, and I switched subjects as fast as I could. "How else can we occupy ourselves? It's not much past noon. We won't stop for hours."

"Virgil?" he offered. He was teaching me Latin, which he insisted on calling the lingua franca of Europe. Not of Muscovy, our current destination, but of the many lands I would prefer to visit. I wanted to learn—and to improve my Italian, in the hope that one day I might see Florence.

"Later," I said. "I love listening to you read, but at this moment I feel too restless to study. I wish I could dance, or run." I stopped myself then, realizing he could do neither, and patted his knee. "Sorry."

He shook his head. "Don't be. I'm used to it. If not Latin, then shall we compare notes from last night? We promised each other we would, and there's no better time than now."

Although not the most exciting way to travel, the long hours in the sleigh did have one advantage: we had lots of opportunity to talk without being overheard. We'd spent the better part of the time between Cracow and Sandomierz constructing an elaborate history for Julian Ossolinski, so that no one could trip us up with simple questions about where I went to school or how often I visited Felix as a child. We'd left Sandomierz at dawn, and we could look forward to, if that was the right expression, another two weeks on the road before we reached Vilnius.

"You first," Felix said.

"I didn't hear anything definitive," I told him. "A lot of male banter and jokes. Not from Bogdan Ostrogski—he kept quiet and ate, as he usually does. Adam Tarlo made up for Bogdan's silence. But I noticed that the two of them and Leon Laski seemed less well turned out than the other men. Bogdan especially. I wondered if one of them might have reason to accept payment if the Russians offered it."

Felix directed a contemplative stare at the cunning pocket that held his copy of *The Aeneid*, as if seeking inspiration. "Laski's better off than he looks," he said. "He doesn't like to spend money on clothes, but he has plenty of it. Tarlo can stay with his uncle whenever he wants. Plus those two are Polish Catholics with property on the western side of the country. It's hard to imagine them conspiring with Muscovy."

He had a point. I opened my mouth to tell him I had identified Adam as one of the men I'd overheard at the king's birthday celebration, which was my only reason for suspecting Adam at all, but Felix was still talking. "Ostrogski, though, is not just Orthodox but rather rabid about his faith; his whole family is. And I think he *has* fallen on hard times, although I don't know why. His uncles are prosperous enough. They're also vehemently anti-Muscovite."

I set the news about Adam aside for a moment to follow this new trail. "But if Bogdan has had a falling-out with them, it could explain both his penury and a decision to switch sides. He wouldn't be the first Lithuanian prince to think he'd do better in an Orthodox Christian kingdom." I wrinkled my nose. "It's just ..." I stopped. The thought was too silly for words.

"What?" Felix asked when I didn't continue.

I shrugged. So he'd laugh at me. How bad could it be? "It's just that he *looks* so villainous. Bogdan does, I mean. I almost want him not to be guilty."

Felix did laugh, but he nodded at the same time. "I know. But we have to keep him on the list for the moment."

"Yes, of course," I said. "What about you? Did you see anything odd from your seat closer to the military governor?"

"I did, actually." Felix pulled *The Aeneid* from its pocket and riffled the pages. "I sat with two princes who might well have reasons to involve themselves in the feud between the Russian clans. Simon Belsky comes from one of the families fighting for power in Moscow and may hope that joining them will improve his position. Martin Glinsky, who's a hothead to start with, might take it upon himself to avenge what he sees as the murder of his cousin Elena, the former grand princess—"

I interrupted him. "But she died in 1538. Why now?"

He took the interruption in stride, as he usually did. "For one thing, because he was in Bologna then, at the university. He returned to Lithuania only a few months ago. And for another, the Shuisky clan was losing the Russian conflict from last January to this, and they are the ones Martin blames for his cousin's death. Konstantin, the head of the Belsky clan, managed to get Iosif, the head of the Shuisky clan, sent off to a punishment post in the east, dealing with the Tatars. And Iosif's sixty if he's a day. I doubt even a maniac like Martin would head off to some distant Russian outpost to wreak vengeance on an old man under such circumstances. He was ranting about it plenty last night, though. It seems he visited his cousin when he was sixteen and fell madly in love with her. She was quite beautiful, from what I've heard."

"I never met her," I said. "But you're right. Both Simon and Martin have stronger motives to flee than Adam and Leon, and even Bogdan Ostrogski. But would they attack Queen Bona?"

Felix shrugged. "It's hard to see why, I agree."

I saw my chance and took it. "Remember before we left, when I told you I'd overheard two men talking about the attempt on the queen's life?" Felix nodded.

"One of them was Adam Tarlo," I said. "That's the main reason I included him on my list of suspects just now. The other could have been Simon Belsky or Martin Glinsky or another person entirely; I didn't see his face, so I can't be sure."

I'd shocked Felix. He dropped his book and didn't seem to notice. He stared at me openmouthed, then rallied. "Why didn't you tell me right away?"

"Because I met him last night, at the beginning of the dinner, when we were surrounded by people."

"So why not later, when we went upstairs?"

"Later ..." I blushed. "I probably misjudged this, I know, but you two seemed so friendly. He was teasing you, even. And you'd told me no one would recognize me dressed as a boy, and here was someone who had attended a reception where he might have seen me as a woman—and after my illness, at that. For a while I wondered whether I could trust you to take my concerns about him seriously."

He tapped my nose, a gentle admonition. "You *can* trust me. I promised to protect you, remember? And to protect the king and queen too. I like Adam, it's true. We went to school together. But the threat to our country is serious. I won't play favorites."

"I'm glad to hear it," I said. "Does Adam hate Queen Bona?"

"I wouldn't have thought so. Unless he has something to gain from the Habsburg alliance that she opposes. She's not after the Tarlo lands, for sure." Felix stared, frowning, into the distance for a while before saying, "I should sound him out. You don't know him, so he'd be less likely to talk to you. But how to raise the subject? I don't want to tell him he was overheard. That could precipitate the very crisis we're trying to avoid, because he'd start wondering who overheard him. He might recognize you then, where the possibility of you being a woman hadn't entered his head before."

"And that's another issue. I don't know that he saw me in Cracow, so he may have no reason to expose me, but suppose he knows you have no cousin Julian?" Another thought that had kept me up last night.

Felix fell back against the cushions that lined our seat, his tension dissipated in laughter.

"What?" I asked, astonished at his reaction.

It took him a while to pull himself together enough to answer the question. Even when he did, the occasional chortle escaped him. "You haven't seen my family estate yet," he said. "Adam has. My generation calls it the Rabbit Warren for a reason. The place is huge, and my sisters and sisters-in-law and every other female on the place breed more often than cattle. That's why no one's pressuring me to marry, despite my having reached the advanced age of twenty-eight. For all I—and Adam—know, I have a dozen cousins named Julian. As for the reception, Adam can't have been there for long, because I didn't see him either. If I had, I'd have said something when the issue of your joining the mission first came up. We'll just have to keep our eyes open and hope he had other things on his mind besides the beautiful woman in front of him."

This time pleasure rather than embarrassment warmed my cheeks. A nice thing for him to say, even if it was an idle compliment. "We know he did," I said. "The attempt on Queen Bona's life. What we don't know is why. He seems an unlikely conspirator, I agree, but he did sound as if he had a stake in finding out whether the would-be assassin had talked. He even mentioned that torture didn't yield true confessions, as if he wished to discredit any admissions that came out."

"He's right," Felix said. "People will say anything to stop the pain. But we already agreed that I would talk to Adam. If I don't tell him he was overheard, what's the best way to approach him?"

"I wouldn't mention the assassination attempt no matter what," I said. "If Adam played a part in that, he won't confess it to you or anyone else. I wouldn't ask him what he thinks of Queen Bona either. Suppose you start a conversation about Princess Elisabeth and the forthcoming wedding? He'd be less likely to feel threatened, and you might get a sense of how he views the Habsburg alliance that way."

"Excellent. I had no doubt that so fine a chess player would discover the winning strategy." Felix's delighted laughter filled the sleigh. "I'll try that tonight. And now we need yet another occupation."

"I should have brought my lute," I said, not for the first time.

I saw Felix's lips curve, but he didn't reply. "I know." I supplied the comment he'd already made so often I could repeat it by heart. "My voice is too high for a boy of the age I'm supposed to be. But I could play."

"We'll ask about a suitable instrument in Vilnius," he said. "I'm sure someone at the grand duke's palace can spare a lute. The rest of the journey is even longer, so you'll have plenty of time to practice. But how shall we pass our time today?"

"What about the quotation game?" I offered. I hadn't played it in ages, but Felix should be good at it. And although I hadn't recited much poetry since I left Chorasan, I remembered enough to play, perhaps to win.

"Quotation game?" He raised an interrogative eyebrow.

"I give you a line of poetry—classic or made-up," I said. "Say, 'The moon glows pearl-bright over the night-dark willows.' Then you pick up an image from somewhere in the sentence: night or willows or even pearls, but not moon, because I started with that, and quote a line back to me. The person who can keep going longest wins."

He straightened in his seat, as if challenged. "Hmm. 'In the emerald shade of willow leaves pretty girls scry their fortunes.' Will that work?"

"It'll do for a start." I giggled at the face he pulled when I said that. He looked like a small boy told that his offering of a mud pie wasn't suitable for the dinner table. "See what you can do with this one. 'All day long my heart trembles like a leaf. Yet here I am, alone at midnight. Where did that beloved go?'"

"Ah, now that's charming. Where's it from?"

"Rumi," I said. "One of my favorites. You're stalling."

"I am indeed. I don't know Rumi. How about this one? 'I am the same: Inside my heart, although my vision is almost entirely faded, droplets of sweetness fall like the sun dissolving the snow's crust.'"

"Oh, I like that!"

"Dante," he said, looking smug. "From *Paradiso*."

I ransacked my memory. So many possibilities. Then I recalled the beginning of a poem I had always loved. "'I pull a sun from my purse each day, and at night I loose my pet moon to run at will among the heavens. If I whistle, she turns her head to look at me. If I wave my arms, she runs home wagging a glittering tail of stars.'" I had so wanted a cat or a dog as a child, especially a cat. A beautiful sleek cat with blue eyes and white fur, but it was not to be.

"Nice," Felix said. "Rumi again?"

"No, Hafiz. He and Rumi are our greatest poets."

"Our?" He looked genuinely startled. "You know, I don't think I've heard you express a sense of belonging to a place before. Who are 'we'? Chorasan?"

I felt myself blush. It was true. I had no home, in my own mind. "Persia," I said. "So much of the literature and art I learned in childhood came from there. It's like you and Dante or Virgil; they aren't Poles and you aren't Italian, but they speak to you."

"True. Tell me your line again." When I repeated it, he said, "Ah yes, I heard this one in Padua. You should like it. It's by a woman. 'Lit by all the glory of the heavens, I stand, racked with longing, among the sleeping roses waiting for my love.'" He regarded me with a mischievous gaze that deepened my blush.

"A woman poet?" I asked to distract him. "Really? What's her name?"

"Violetta Cecchetti. Women poets aren't rare in Italy. I met several there." He grinned. "Now who's stalling?"

"I'm not," I said, although I was. The pause had given me a moment to match the sleeping roses. "'I hang the stars with meshes for men's souls; the garden underneath my music rolls. The long, long dawns that mourn the rose away I sit in silence and on anguish prey.'" Only as I reached the end did I realize that I'd opened a pathway I might not wish to tread. The image of the broken rose still tugged at my heart. "It's from *The Conference of Birds*, the book I found in the king's library."

"Lovely, of course, but dark." Felix scratched his nose, as if seeking inspiration. "How about this one? 'O celestial eyes, how you summon me to drown in your depths! Spheres of joy and grief, pride and fury, tenderness and bliss, you inspire me with passion and anguish.' That's a madrigal. You like madrigals. And by another woman, too. Bianca de Luca. But my brain is running dry. I concede the victory, so you supply the last line."

"Eyes." I thought for a moment. "Well, if I don't have to set up another image in the line, I'll go back to Rumi. 'Who is it in my ear that hears my voice? Who says words with my mouth? Who looks out from my eyes?' He means not just who am I, but what am I, as in what makes me a person."

Felix doffed his hat in acknowledgment. "An excellent ending to an excellent game. Let's move on to something else, shall we?"

"Are you sure?" I asked. "You can invent lines too, you know."

"And have you make faces at me again, you heartless wench? But don't get too cocky. I'll study hard, and you'll rue the day you introduced me to this game." He laughed, an absurdly boyish expression on his handsome face.

I couldn't help but join in his laughter. "Well, if you've had enough Persian and Italian poets for one day, how about a Latin one?" I scooped *The Aeneid* from the floor and held it out to him. "Read to me, please. Virgil's tale of war and wandering seems quite relevant to our journey."

At last we reached Vilnius. The stucco walls of the Grand Ducal Palace stood out within the old city, their boxy shape set off by decorations around the highest layer of windows and interspersed with towers topped by black tile triangles.

The sight touched me in ways I hadn't anticipated. Vilnius had been my first refuge within these western lands, the place that had welcomed me and offered a safe harbor where I could recover from the horrors of my arrest and captivity, where people asked few questions but instead accepted me, especially after I attracted the attention of their young grand duke—the same Sigismund Augustus who now spurned me. Even when my detestable husband appeared out of the blue and tried to reclaim me, the Vilnius court rallied behind me. Soon enough, my husband returned to Russia, and I could relax once more. I loved Vilnius every bit as much as I loved Cracow.

However, a certain anxiety did offset my pleasure at seeing the palace once more. As I walked through the main door, faced with gray stone, and traversed the light and airy rooms with their wooden ceilings inset with brightly colored tiles; as I sank gratefully onto a mattress in a room that for the first time in two weeks was entirely my own, so I needn't worry about waking Felix with my nightmares for the next few days, and waited for his manservant to provide warm water, soap, and a towel; and when, refreshed and refurbished in clean linen, I rejoined my friend—throughout the entire short stay, in fact—I watched constantly for indications on the faces of the staff that someone recognized me. King Sigismund the Younger had, thank goodness, remained in Cracow, and as a result his courtiers remained there too. But I had lived in Vilnius on and off for four years as the royal mistress, so it seemed incredible that not one of the servants could identify me by sight.

They didn't, though. Perhaps they couldn't imagine a connection between the acclaimed beauty Lady Juliana Krasilska and a pockmarked boy with scraggly hair, dressed in drab clothes and in the constant company of a somewhat older cousin who walked with a cane. Perhaps they found me so uninteresting that they never glanced at me long enough to mark my resemblance to anyone, let alone a young woman known for her elegant attire and air of fashion.

Either way, it proved a blessing. At last I could stop worrying that exposure lay just around the corner. I even said a silent prayer of thanks for my ruined face.

The morning after our arrival in Vilnius I met the ambassadors. Or, to be more accurate, I stood in line next to Felix as, one by one, each member of our party bowed when the herald called his name. Once my part in the ceremonial was done, I retreated, still at Felix's side, to one of the chairs in the reception room, where I split my attention between admiration for the painted knights who charged across a frieze just below the ceiling and study of the two men who would lead our mission to Moscow. Jan Glebow and Nikodem Tichonowski both represented the landed magnates of Lithuania, and like the two princes who had traveled with us from Cracow—Simon Belsky and Martin Glinsky—the ambassadors seemed to me interchangeable, both with each other and with their Belsky/Glinsky subordinates. Did every Lithuanian male have sandy hair and pale blue eyes?

Once we were seated, Lord Glebow took his place behind a podium set up in front of a magnificent painting of the Madonna in Glory, framed in chased gold the width of my spread fingers and taller than the ambassador himself. He addressed the room—twenty-five or so of us—while I examined him and Lord Tichonowski, assessing what kind of leaders they might be. Although Felix and I had no reason to include them on our list of potential suspects, their conduct would determine the success or failure of the mission as a whole.

Lord Glebow impressed me. He spoke clearly and concisely, and he seemed to know how to present his material to a group of strangers. On the surface, we (that is, the envoys) had a simple task: travel to Moscow, present our kings' offer to renew the truce for seven years, and leave.

"But there are complications," Lord Glebow said. "There always are when dealing with the Muscovites. First, we can expect to wait at least a month before young Grand Prince Ivan receives us. Second, because Ivan is only eleven years old, someone else will be acting in the boy's name, and at the moment we can't be certain who that person will be. For most of the time since Grand Princess Elena died in April 1538, the Shuisky clan—headed at present by Prince Iosif Shuisky—has controlled the government. But over the last twelve months we have heard an increasing number of rumors that Prince Konstantin Belsky, the Shuiskys' main rival, has been ingratiating himself with the young grand prince."

Simon Belsky, sitting to the far left of the front row, where I could see him only in profile, jerked to attention at that comment. Reacting to news of his family, I assumed.

From what I'd learned, Konstantin was not the head of the clan, but he played the most active role in advancing its status at court. If he could influence the grand prince in the way Lord Glebow suggested, it would bode well for the future of Simon's relatives, and by extension Simon himself.

But as Lord Glebow continued, I realized Konstantin Belsky's influence might not last. "Konstantin Belsky even managed to get Iosif Shuisky out of the way by sending him off to the town of Vladimir to fight the Tatars," the ambassador said. "But Prince Iosif has just secured his return to Moscow, and we have every reason to suspect that he will renew hostilities with the Belsky clan. In fact, he has already ordered Prince Konstantin's arrest."

A gasp went round the room at that—including from me, although my gasp had more to do with the possible resurgence of the Shuisky clan, whom I hated for taking me captive almost five years ago in retaliation for my husband's flight from Moscow, than with the information that the war between the Shuisky and Belsky clans continued to plague the Russian lands. It went without saying—to anyone but a Shuisky—that I had not encouraged my husband to flee, so their vengeance against me for an act that was in no way my fault rankled even now.

Simon, however, did not gasp. Perhaps I had misunderstood, and Lord Glebow had already warned him of the danger facing his cousins. That would make sense, surely?

Lord Glebow ignored the interruption. "Therefore, we don't know whether we will be dealing with the Belskys or the Shuiskys or whether either side has the power to negotiate with us in good faith. That means we must vet the treaty closely to ensure that the other side makes no attempt to alter the terms in ways that our king would not approve. And third." This time he paused, whether for dramatic effect or to gather his thoughts I couldn't tell. "Once we cross the border, we must assume that everything we say or do will be monitored by the Russians. Watch your words, watch your actions, and above all, watch your step. The voluntary surrender of information to an adversary is treason, but even an involuntary surrender is undesirable. On the contrary, we want to find out as much as we can about them while keeping them guessing about us."

He couldn't have made his point clearer. I surveyed the room, trying to judge whether his words had a particular impact on our four suspects, but sitting near the back of the room put me at a disadvantage. Was that Martin Glinsky tensing his shoulders, or someone else? Was that a flush of guilt on Simon Belsky's cheek, or just the result of sitting too close to the tiled stove? And what would I see if Adam Tarlo, sitting directly in front of me, turned his head? Felix had chatted with Adam about the Habsburg alliance as promised, but with inconclusive results. Nor did I have a clear view of Bogdan Ostrogski.

Glebow spoke to Tichonowski. "Have you anything to add, Nikodem?"

Lord Tichonowski stepped forward, and as the bright light from the glass-paned window struck his face, I realized that the resemblance between the ambassadors was not as great as I had first thought. Lord Tichonowski was older than Lord Glebow by a good ten years, broader of frame and more corpulent, his cheeks less defined and his nose less hooked. It reassured me that I might find it easier than expected to tell them apart. It might mean that, with a bit of effort, I could learn to distinguish others among the Lithuanians as well—Martin and Simon from the back, for example.

"I have but one thing to add," Lord Tichonowski said. "This is not a game we play with the Russians. The safety of our older king and queen, of the young king and his soon-to-be bride, and of Poland and Lithuania as a dynastic union depend on our keeping our own counsel. Someone last year failed to do that, and we must—I repeat, *must*—ensure that no such incident recurs. Whether it was a mistake or a deliberate breach of confidence doesn't matter. Anyone who engages in such behavior can expect severe punishment. Prepare to leave Vilnius tomorrow morning. Until then, you are dismissed."

The ambassadors left the room in a swirl of silk robes and self-confidence, and in due course the rest of us filed out behind them. In response to Felix's hand on my elbow I accompanied him to his chamber, where we sat side by side on a window seat gazing out over the cobblestoned courtyard. Although not secluded as effectively as during our sleigh rides, we had created enough distance between ourselves and the door that we had only to keep our voices low to foil unwanted listeners. For added protection we spoke in Italian, which most of the servants didn't know.

"He warned them," I said in a not-quite-whisper. "Lord Tichonowski, I mean. Were you expecting that? I thought the idea was to prevent the culprit from guessing that we suspect a deliberate sharing of information."

"I wasn't, no." Felix shook his head. "He issued an effective threat, I thought, but not sufficient to deter a determined traitor, only an unwitting one. And it could backfire if the person we seek becomes more careful and harder to track. But the news disturbed me too. Tell me, why can't the Shuisky and Belsky clans get along? They didn't battle like this five years ago."

"I think because neither side has legitimacy," I said. "Iosif Shuisky and Konstantin Belsky both want power and have enough backing to take it, but neither of them can hold it. In the end the other side has as much right to rule as the group currently in control, whichever clan that is. The best each of them can do is wangle a place next to the grand prince until the other dislodges him."

Felix drew his eyebrows together at this, as if I had spoken in a foreign tongue. "Explain, please. What makes power legitimate in Russia?"

I knew from our many discussions of government, including Machiavelli's *The Prince*, that Felix had a far better grasp of political philosophy than I did. So I assumed he meant that, in his mind, the Muscovites never worried about legitimacy, only about who wielded the strongest fist. Or as the Russians themselves put it, "who beats whom?"

But how best to answer his question? My husband, Fyodor, loved politics, and I'd often heard him explain the basics. Not to me—he regarded me as too light-brained to handle any task outside the bedroom—but to his son-in-law, my former lover Alexei. It didn't occur to Fyodor that a woman in my position survives by turning eavesdropping into a fine art. I strove to remember what I'd overheard.

"From what I understand," I said, "your Machiavelli would love the Muscovite system. It relies on a strong central leader—or at least the perception of such a leader. There's no parliament of nobles like the Polish Sejm."

Felix gave a rueful chuckle. "So much for theory. The Sejm gives Sigismund a pain in his behind often enough, but I'm not sure an autocrat is much of an improvement."

"You're abandoning Machiavelli?" I asked, teasing him. "Didn't I hear you touting his merits just last week?"

Felix acknowledged the hit with a raised hand, a gesture that my time among the Polish aristocrats allowed me to recognize as a fencer's admission of defeat. "He's an Italian. What does he know about tyrants? But go on. If Russia has one-man rule, it shouldn't also have fighting boyar clans."

"The clans fight for the attention of the leader. He needs the nobles to direct his armies and enact his policies," I explained. "So he isn't truly a tyrant, even though he's portrayed as one. The nobles must agree with his dictates, or nothing gets done."

"A subtle distinction," Felix said.

"But an important one." When he nodded his understanding, I went on. "That's where legitimacy comes in. To keep the competition among themselves under control, the great clans have for centuries agreed to accept the leadership of the House of Moscow. No one outside that lineage can rule with full legitimacy."

"Ah, I begin to see the light. And Grand Princess Elena?"

"Yes, she had legitimacy as the widow of one grand prince and the mother of another. Not as much as a man would have, but enough. After she killed her brothers-in-law out of fear that they meant to unseat her and her sons, though, her death left Russia with no ruler except her son Ivan. He's legitimate, for sure, but too young to control the clans." Grand Princess Elena had, in the end, approved my departure for Lithuania. I owed her a debt for that even though she'd also approved my arrest. Remembering what happened to her, I shivered.

"Martin Glinsky's not the only one who thinks the Shuiskys killed her. Is it true?" Felix put my unspoken thought into words.

"It wouldn't surprise me," I said. "They're an ambitious bunch, and ruthless to boot. But whether they killed her or not, they've been squabbling with the Belskys ever since. I suspect each side hopes to knock out the other before Ivan reaches his majority and reins them both in."

Felix gazed at me with an intensity I found disconcerting but at the same time thrilling. "Can we use their squabbling to predict what our traitor will do?"

I gazed at the courtyard, where a surprising number of servants traipsed back and forth, heads bowed against driving sleet and wintry wind, bundles of various sorts clutched in their arms. Could we? "Perhaps. Simon Belsky may be discouraged, if the tide has again turned against the Lithuanian princes, as Lord Glebow indicated."

"Or more inclined to offer himself as an alternative," Felix noted.

"Yes. Martin Glinsky, though, if he is driven by hatred of the Shuiskys, will have an even stronger motive to act. Bogdan Ostrogski is in the same position as Simon, because if he does want to switch sides, he'd do better with the Belskys, who also came from Lithuania, than with an old Russian clan like the Shuiskys." The only suspect who seemed to have no reason to benefit from the victory of one clan leader or the other was Adam Tarlo. I admitted as much to Felix, but that overheard conversation between Adam and the sandy-haired man still bothered me.

"Could the assassination plot have nothing to do with the loss of secret information?" I asked.

Felix raised both hands in a gesture conveying ignorance. "It could," he said. "Although that, too, was secret information that Adam somehow learned and chose to discuss. Much as I hate to say it, I think we have to keep him on our list until we know the whole truth."

And with that conclusion I could only agree.

Chapter Six

Smolensk, Russia, February 1542

"OH, THIS IS BAD," I SAID TO FELIX. LED BY THE TWO AMBASSADORS and accompanied by fifty of the king's mercenaries for maximum protection and impact, the twenty-five envoys—yes, even Felix—were arrayed on horseback not far from the formerly Lithuanian, now Russian, fortress of Smolensk. Not to get caught up in details, we had reached the Muscovite border, where custom required us to wait for a Russian detachment to escort us to the fortress. The great lords Jan Glebow and Nikodem Tichonowski wanted to start the negotiations with the most impressive display they could put on. That meant every member of the mission, no matter how junior or disabled, must mass behind the ambassadors, wearing either full armor or, in my case, my very best doublet and hose.

However, while a small part of my brain pondered how we would get Felix off the horse without toppling the poor man into the muddied snow, concern for him was not what drove me to complaint. The Muscovites had drawn to a halt not far from our envoys. I recognized the banner they carried: a winged horse embroidered in red against a white silk background banded with gold. I had seen that banner shortly before I left Moscow, and I had a long acquaintance with the man who flew it. A Tatar in his mid-thirties, his wavy brown hair untouched by gray, his handsome face unscarred—he hadn't changed much since the last time we met, almost five years ago. He was absolutely, positively, the last person I wished to encounter in the wake of my illness. I had loved him and lost him, a grim reality I had yet to accept completely. Surely Fate would not also force me to watch him recoil in horror at the sight of me.

"Damnation," I said. "There can't be three men in Russia who know me well enough to recognize me in this garb. How in Hades did one of them end up here?"

Felix scrunched his nose, peering at the Russians. The man I'd identified directed his magnificent dark bay Arabian to a point opposite our ambassadors. "Who is he?" Felix asked.

I opened my mouth to reply, but before I got the words out, the Tatar commander spoke. "Welcome to the Russian lands," he said in a clear voice that reached our back row without difficulty. His rich tenor sent shivers down my spine. "I am Tsarevich Alexei Bulatovich, military governor of Smolensk, and I welcome you on behalf of our lord and master, Grand Prince Ivan." He proceeded to list every one of the young grand prince's titles and properties, while the Poles awaited their turn to laud King Sigismund the Old and his son and co-ruler, Sigismund Augustus, in the same exaggerated fashion.

I ignored the diplomatic folderol and focused my eyes on the face of the one man I had ever permitted myself to love. A man who had deserted me out of fealty to his lord, brought me with him when he fled that lord to seek sanctuary in Moscow, and exchanged me for a wife whom he then had the temerity to adore. "He's the one I followed to Crimea," I said quietly to Felix. "It couldn't be worse if the grand prince had sent my detestable husband."

I looked at Alexei again. He hadn't yet noticed me. Perhaps I could keep a steady stream of envoys and servants between us. Felix, although not by any means the most important member of the mission, had sufficiently high rank to merit an introduction, but I was only his young cousin and unofficial translator. Surely the military governor of Smolensk had no more reason than his counterpart in Sandomierz to concern himself with me.

And given that I barely recognized my reflection in the glass, why flatter myself that Alexei would believe me anything other than the boy I pretended to be? Keep out of his direct line of sight, and I could survive my stay in Smolensk without drawing attention to myself.

"Beautiful horse," Felix said in a conversational tone that made me wonder if he'd understood a thing I'd said.

"Yes," I told him gloomily. "His name is Ajdar. It means 'dragon.'"

Which at that moment struck me as a grim jest. Because although not by any definition a virgin, I felt like a damsel chained to a rock, waiting to become dinner for a fiery beast.

Felix handled the dismount better than expected. I passed him his cane and followed him to the room set aside for us. His normally sunny outlook had disappeared behind a dark grumbling cloud, and I assumed the time on horseback had left him in considerable pain. But when I suggested he ask for food to be served in our chamber, he bristled at the very idea.

Men! What is it about them that causes false courage to trump prudence every time?

"Rest, Felix," I pleaded. "That ride must have hurt. The other envoys will understand."

Felix waved his cane. "No," he said, his voice flat. "I'm going to dinner, and so are you."

I agreed, with a loud sigh. "If you insist." Felix hadn't convinced me of anything except that he'd barricaded himself inside one of those ridiculous man-states where common sense hadn't a chance of holding its own against obstinacy. Still, I could hardly tie him to the bedpost, and if he insisted on attending the dinner, I might as well go too. I could help Felix if he needed help, and if not I could watch my former lover from a distance, hidden behind my mask of a plain boy with short hair.

Oh dear, how pathetic that sounds!

Dinner was long and lavish, the hall filled to bursting with Russian troops and Polish visitors, civilian and military. Alexei had traded in his armor for an ankle-length robe of brocade in shades ranging from cream to dark brown and trimmed at collar and cuffs with sable, clothes befitting his status as a descendant of Genghis Khan and the highest-ranking Russian present. He sat at the center table with Lord Glebow on one side and Lord Tichonowski on the other. Nobles of ancient lineage surrounded them, arranged according to status: military governors, leaders of the right and left divisions—Alexei introduced them one after another, and I forgot their positions the instant I heard them. I had enough trouble dodging the endless toasts, each of which required me to drain my cup. I'd be lucky if I finished the evening without collapsing chin-first on the table.

I hoped the dogs appreciated the ale I tipped into the rushes whenever I saw a chance to evade detection.

Here in Smolensk only the ambassadors rated a seat at the high table. As a result, Felix had little difficulty in manipulating the seating so that he and I formed the distant points of a small rectangle, with our four suspects—Martin Glinsky, Simon Belsky, Bogdan Ostrogski, and Adam Tarlo—on the same two benches. Adam sat opposite Felix, with Simon between Adam and me. Bogdan again faced me, as he had at Sandomierz, and Martin occupied the place across from Simon, between Felix and Bogdan.

For quite a while the conversation remained on neutral topics. As before, Bogdan kept silent for the most part, although as the toasts continued, he became livelier, from time to time taking part in the banter between Felix and Adam. This was a side of him I wouldn't have believed existed. He could never wholly overcome that rabbity face and those shifty eyes, poor man, but I did warm to him as I realized he possessed a sense of humor and a talent for word play. Although not a scholar like Felix or a rogue like Adam, Bogdan did have more learning and wit under his belt than I would have credited him with a week ago.

I shared in the others' laughter, as usual eager to avoid drawing attention to myself. But as the toasts went on and the others indulged while I did not (Felix also exercised a certain restraint, I noticed), tensions rose within our group of six. Martin Glinsky became more somber, then more combative, with each round. Simon Belsky's temper visibly frayed in response to a series of jabs about his relatives in Moscow and their inability to hold power. Bogdan retreated again into his shell, regarding the table gloomily as if it could transform itself into a shield if he stared hard enough and protect him from his ever more hostile neighbor. Only Adam and Felix remained cheerful and calm, respectively.

Then Martin said, in a voice with a distinct edge, "So, Belsky, have you already made plans to see your cousins? We travel quite close to your family lands, do we not?"

I blinked. What was wrong with the man that had him spoiling for a fight? Felix put a steadying hand on Martin's arm, but Martin shook it off.

"What are you implying, Glinsky?" Simon half-rose in his seat, hands clenched, but in response to a sharp reprimand from Felix sank back onto the bench. When he spoke, though, I heard his irritation. "You'll seek out your relatives, won't you? You have more than a few in Moscow. They breed like vermin, as I understand."

I hissed at his tone, and Felix said, "Ignore him, Belsky. Can't you see the man's drunk?" in the same sharp tone he'd used before.

Simon paid no attention to either of us. From where I sat, I could see him clutching the hilt of his sword—yes, the same type of sword that Felix had assured me meant nothing more than a declaration of nobility. My stomach tensed.

"Shut your mouth," Martin said with an odd humph. "The relative I wanted to see is dead and gone, and your clan did nothing to defend her. Or avenge her, for that matter, despite its year in power." He leaned forward, elbows on the wooden board, his expression truculent.

"Take his cup, Bogdan," Adam Tarlo put in. "The fool's had too many toasts already. He's picking fights with his own side."

Bogdan reached for the cup, but Martin snatched it away and held it high. A servant promptly refilled it, and Martin glared at Adam, then at Simon and Bogdan, in an unspoken challenge before draining it. The servant filled the cup once more.

"I speak the truth," Martin said. I detected slurring in his speech. "Not my fault the rest of you don't want to hear it. Belsky knows what his clan did, and what they didn't do. Jackasses."

As I watched, he plunged from aggressive into maudlin. Loud but maudlin. "My cousin was a beautiful woman. I loved her, and she was good to me. Even though I was a boy like him at the time." He pointed at me, and I started, but he went on without waiting for a reaction. "And what reward did she get? The Shuiskys murdered her while your relatives"—his pointing finger moved to Simon—"stood by and did nothing. You make me sick."

Simon rose to his feet with a roar, turning over the trestle table and hauling his sword from its sheath. Felix fell backward as the table smacked against his legs. I could hear him swearing, or what I assumed must be swearing since he emitted a string of harsh-sounding Polish words I'd never heard before. Adam grabbed Simon's right arm, and I went for his left. Together we wrestled him back onto the bench while Bogdan extricated himself, then summoned servants to right the table while he went to Felix's aid. Martin lay on his back, mumbling, his arms outstretched. Despite his fall, he still clung to his cup with one hand. A pair of husky men hauled Martin to his feet and supported him between them while he stared at the floor and mumbled under his breath.

Only then did I think to glance at the high table. The heads of every nobleman there had turned in the direction of our scuffle. Including, of course, Alexei, who regarded the scene from beneath brows drawn tight together. I saw him beckon to a man whom I recognized of old as the captain of his personal guard, then deliver an order that ended with a nod in our direction. The captain headed toward us.

As fast as I could, I withdrew into my shadowed corner, thankful that I'd played only a small part in the fight. With luck, Alexei had focused most of his attention on Simon and Martin.

I damned both princes for a pair of idiots and examined Felix as well as I could from my corner. He seemed more angry than hurt. As I watched, he resumed his seat on the bench and said something I couldn't hear to Bogdan. The captain arrived just in time to receive Felix's apologies for the disturbance and assurances that everyone was well. After a bit of prowling and questioning, the captain withdrew. The five of us turned as one to glare at Martin Glinsky.

Martin raised his head and scowled back. Continuing his previous train of thought as if the confrontation with Simon Belsky had not happened, he grumbled, "The whole lot of you make me sick."

Then his hand dropped. Bogdan caught the cup as it fell, and while the rest of us watched aghast, Martin's chin touched his chest and he sobbed like a child. I didn't know what to say, and in fact had little desire to say anything. Despite my vast experience with men, I'd never seen a grown one behave that way.

But Felix reacted with his usual aplomb. He gestured to the servant who had filled Martin's cup twice. "Get someone to help Prince Glinsky to his room," Felix ordered. "He's ready to retire for the night."

At long last the meal ended. After taking a moment to verify that Felix had emerged unscathed from his fall, I left him to head for our chamber as I went in search of a close stool. Finding safe places to relieve myself was the most awkward part of my masquerade, but a fortress, even a Russian fortress, should have some kind of facility I could use. A question addressed to the right servant procured the directions I needed.

When done, I washed my hands in a conveniently placed basin and headed back to the main hall. Which exit led to our room? I turned slowly, searching for a configuration I recognized. I was mentally congratulating myself on a successful evening of deception when trouble struck with the force of storm-fed waves crashing against the Black Sea coastline.

Halfway around, I saw a dark menacing shape in the window embrasure, like the ogre of my dream. Horror held me motionless for one crucial instant, then I let out an odd sound like a small shriek and dashed for the nearest doorway, hoping to escape without ending up thoroughly lost.

Faint hope. Rapid footsteps sounded, and an arm snaked around my waist, dragging me against a hard male body. Alexei's well-remembered voice said, "What game are you playing, Roxelana?"

He spoke in Persian, and that was my undoing. The sound of my native tongue and my former name overwhelmed my defenses, and the amount of ale I'd consumed undermined the little control I had left. I forgot that I was supposed to be Julian Ossolinski, the young cousin of a minor Polish envoy, who spoke nothing but basic Russian and Polish. I forgot that I had lost my looks and that Alexei's identification of me could only be a lucky guess. I even forgot that Roxelana was the name conferred on me by my masters, and therefore less mine than Juliana. I responded out of instinct, as a slave would.

I twisted in his hold and pushed both palms against his chest. It was like fighting with an oak tree, and about as effective. "Let me go," I said, also in Persian. "What I do is no concern of yours."

I spat at him; he snarled at me. You could see we were former lovers.

"Are you joking?" Alexei asked, but he did step back. Now that he'd tricked me into admitting my identity, he switched to Tatar. He released my waist but clasped my wrist in one hand, as if convinced I would flee if he didn't keep a grip on me.

He was right. I would, if I had anywhere to go.

"I'm in charge of this fortress," he went on. "Everything that happens here concerns me. And when I see a woman I know disguised as a man, I want to find out why. *Especially* when that woman is you. What brings you here, dressed like that?"

"How did you even recognize me?" I dragged at the wrist he held, to no avail. My throat ached with grief that he had seen me so damaged—and *identified* me as that damaged person—but I refused to let him know that.

I should have insisted on having food delivered to my room. I should have stayed there like a hermit until the minute the ambassadorial party left. The hell with Felix and his demands!

"Of course I recognized you," Alexei said. "I know you, remember? Rather well, in fact. Now tell me what you're doing here."

I winced at his perfunctory tone. Did he care nothing for my disfigurement? What happened to the man who once yearned for me?

Locked in emotional turmoil, for a crucial moment I stood like a stone, incapable of invention. In the past I would have flirted with him, a trick that rarely failed to turn his anger into smiles, but as Julian I would look more grotesque than alluring, even without the pockmarks. And my friendship with Felix and the promise of financial security had taught me something. I no longer wanted to pander to the fantasies of men. *Especially* this one.

But I couldn't tell him the real reason for my journey, to spy on the envoys and the Russians. Who knew what

Alexei would do with that information? I would betray Felix and everyone who traveled with us.

I'd hesitated too long. "Never mind." Alexei snarled again. "You wouldn't know the truth if you met it in a back alley. Why am I even asking you?"

My unspoken grief blazed into fury. "I don't know," I snapped. "Because you're a hot-tempered idiot? I can't believe I ever cared for you!"

"Oh, did you? You hid it well." His sneer made me long to smack him.

"So did you," I retorted. "You ran off back to the steppe fast enough. And how is your darling Maria? Has she presented you with a round dozen of sons yet?"

"Leave Maria out of this, and answer my question before I order you thrown in chains. Why are you here dressed as a man—and traveling with the Polish envoys, to boot?" Alexei shook my wrist, and I kicked at his shin. He sidestepped me easily.

I swore under my breath. "Let me go, you brute, and I'll tell you."

He shook his head. "Tell me first. And before you decide to lie, let me mention that my service here is done. I'll be returning to Moscow with your ambassadors. Leading their escort. Convince me you mean no harm, and I may permit you to come along."

Fuming, I scuffed a shoe against the stone. One more week, and I could have avoided him altogether.

But I had to say something, and the whole truth wouldn't do. I settled for the only alternative I saw, suggested by Queen Bona herself. "I want to ask Koshkin for a divorce."

"So you can marry your crippled paramour? A bit below your touch, isn't he? What happened to King Sigismund the Younger?"

I gasped with rage. "How dare you? And how do you know about Sigismund?"

"Your husband," Alexei said. "Who else? He told me in one of his rants. You flirted with his replacement right in front of him, and he was furious. Although why you rejected him, I can't imagine. The two of you seem like a perfect fit. He's very prominent in Moscow these days. Definitely a better choice than that naïve courtier you're bedding. Probably a better choice than Sigismund. They say the young king has a roving eye."

His tone was an insult, although he spoke the truth: Sigismund did have a roving eye, and it had roved away from me.

I'd die before I admitted *that* to Alexei. My palm itched to slap him, but when I pulled my arm back, he grabbed that wrist too. I settled for shoving both hands against his chest once more. "Felix is not my paramour. He's my friend. And unlike you, he understands that women have brains too. I swear, I pity your Maria."

"Don't," Alexei said, his voice curt. "Maria has intelligence and sincerity. She's earned my respect. *She* doesn't pretend a passion she doesn't feel."

The bitterness in his tone shocked me. Was *that* what had driven him away from me so many years ago? Why had I never realized it?

I spoke without thinking. "I can't feel it. Before, after, at the beginning—yes, I experience desire. But then it fades, until the act of love ends. Even with you, although

I desperately wanted it not to. It's like I die inside. Pretense is the best I can do." My anger dissolved again into grief, and I blinked, fighting tears that Julian wouldn't shed and I didn't want Alexei to see.

Alexei's fingers tightened around my wrists. I didn't protest. A hidden, quivering part of me welcomed the pain. Pretense had kept me alive, in the most literal sense, but it also raised a barrier between me and those who could save me. Like Alexei. I saw that, far too late.

When I looked up, his expression softened. "That's the most honest thing you've ever said to me," he murmured. "Thank you." He released one wrist to caress my cheek, as he used to do during that brief, magic month of communion, veiled by time. "What happened to your face?"

"Smallpox. A few months ago." I sighed, forcibly reminded that although my outer scars had healed, the inner wounds still bled. I would never see admiration fill his, or any man's, eyes again.

Except Felix's. The thought came unbidden, but it propped up my spirits enough to dull the pain.

"I'm sorry," Alexei said. "That must be difficult. For anyone, but for you in particular. You know Maria and I will help if you need us."

I bit my lip, staring at him and struggling to keep the tears at bay. I didn't want his charity—still less Maria's—although I understood that he'd made the offer as a kind of olive branch, an unspoken statement of forgiveness.

A perverse determination gripped me: to succeed on my own. I murmured my thanks, but I had no intention of accepting his aid.

And in that instant when I again saw in Alexei the man I had loved, I understood at last that I no longer loved him. That in a sense I had never loved him, because love requires openness and acceptance, and at the time neither of us had those to give. We were both injured, but in ways that aroused the worst in the other rather than the best. Each of us needed someone else to help us heal. Alexei had Maria, but I? I had no one.

"Julian." A familiar voice, speaking Polish, interrupted us. "Are you all right?"

Wrong. I had a friend, my first and only friend, for whom I had no need to pretend a passion I didn't feel. "Let me go." I tugged at Alexei's hand. "And promise you won't stop me from going to Moscow. I have no interest in you, or in Maria. I just want a divorce."

"I don't believe you," Alexei said. For the first time since our confrontation began, he sounded like himself—courteous, distant, urbane. My confession had touched him, yet he'd already retreated once more into his shell. "Send a letter if you want a divorce. You don't need to travel to Moscow, especially as a man. Why the disguise?"

"I've sent a dozen letters. Fyodor doesn't reply." That was a lie. As I'd told Felix during our first conversation, I'd never bothered to ask for a divorce. But however much Koshkin had ranted about Sigismund, I doubted my husband had confided the full history of our separation to Alexei, whom Fyodor tended to distrust. "And to travel with the envoys, so he doesn't hear of my journey before I reach Moscow, I do have to dress as a man. Otherwise he'll grab me and shut me up in that house of his, and I'll never be free."

"Oh, very well." Alexei released my other wrist. "If I want to find out what your game is, I suppose I'll have to let you play it to the end. But I'll keep an eye on you, so don't try any of your tricks. Save the seductive wiles for your friend." The emphasis he put on the last word made it clear he didn't believe me about Felix, either.

I didn't care. By then I wanted to put as much distance between us as possible. I'd gladly have turned tail and run the whole way back to Vilnius rather than travel to Moscow in Alexei's company. The click of Felix's cane against the flagged stones of the floor reminded me why I shouldn't offer to do just that. My future depended on convincing Queen Bona that I had fulfilled the task she set me. "You're wasting your time," I told Alexei, still in Tatar. "I'm no threat to you."

Felix reached me. "Has my cousin offended you, Lord?" he asked Alexei in Russian. "I'm sure he intended no harm."

I bowed, flourishing my cap in the style Felix had taught me, and said in Russian more fluent than Felix's, "I hope not. I lost my way, and Tsarevich Alexei kindly redirected me. I bid you good evening, Tsarevich, and thank you again for your assistance."

Alexei regarded us steadily before he too switched to Russian. "As you wish, *Julian*. I leave you to the care of your protector. But don't think I've forgotten our conversation." He spun on his heel without waiting for a response.

"Neither have I," I told his departing back. "Not one word."

When he didn't reply, I went to Felix and tucked my hand into the crook of his arm. "Don't worry. He must have caught sight of me while Adam and I were dragging Simon away from Martin. And recognized me—I don't know how. He wasn't pleased to see me either. Let's go upstairs, and I'll tell you the rest."

Chapter Seven

"I WANT TO KNOW WHAT HAPPENED LAST NIGHT AFTER WE parted," Felix said. "The full version, if you please."

His manservant, Gregor, handed me a wooden board holding several slices of bread, a wedge of runny homemade cheese, and a cup of ale. It was the morning after my confrontation with Alexei, and we were breaking our fast. Felix's board included cold beef instead of cheese, but I couldn't stomach meat in the morning, as the manservant had soon learned. An old retainer of the Ossolinski family and devoted to Felix, Gregor was the only one—other than Alexei as of yesterday, alas—who knew that I was a woman dressed as a man. Felix and I had debated whether to tell Gregor and concluded it was unavoidable. It would be difficult to travel without a servant and impossible for a young man to travel with a maidservant. Felix insisted Gregor's loyalty was unswerving and his discretion assured.

I had to trust that Felix was right about that. If nothing else, although I was often irregular, at some point in a three-month journey I could expect to run my courses. If that happened, I couldn't hope to conceal the truth from the person who oversaw the washing of my linen. Better to swear him to secrecy in advance.

After passing out the food, Gregor left. I spread cheese on one slice of bread, considering what parts of last night's argument I could safely share with Felix. So much of my exchange with Alexei had veered between the overly personal and the offensive, including insults directed at my friend. What little there was of substance I had related before falling asleep. Then I'd had the ogre dream again. Felix hadn't woken me this time, but I suspected he had tried to soothe me in some way, because when I did wake I felt less paralyzed with terror than usual.

"I told you the important parts yesterday," I said. "He caught me off-guard, and by the time I remembered I was supposed to be your boy cousin, I'd already told him in Persian to mind his own business. It was too late for denials. We shouted at each other for a while, but he revealed only one thing of importance: that he's returning to Moscow soon and plans to head the escort for our ambassadors. So it won't be months or even weeks, most likely, before we leave Smolensk."

"Doesn't he need permission from the central government?" Felix asked. "I thought the authorities in Moscow had to approve any travel by envoys."

"They do, but Alexei is a Tatar tsarevich. He might not say so, but he expects clerks to accept orders from him, not the reverse. He'll have sent his own couriers at top speed with instructions not to take no for an answer. He probably dispatched them the moment we crossed the border, before he even set out to meet us. I'm sure he's eager to get home to his wife." Hearing the hint of bitterness in my own voice, I suppressed it. My flash of insight—that I had never truly loved Alexei—stayed with me, but old habits die hard, and I couldn't prevent a twinge of resentment that he so obviously doted on Maria.

Or was it grief? Either way, it made sense to focus on attaining my own goals, which I could do more quickly if I didn't spend weeks kicking my heels in Smolensk.

Felix pierced a chunk of beef with his eating knife and waved it at me, an act of such extraordinary discourtesy from him that I could only gape in surprise. "Yes, I heard shouting." He stabbed the knife, still loaded with beef, into the board, where it quivered. "That's why I came to find you. That and the fact that you'd been gone for ages. I started to worry. But when I got there, you weren't shouting, and neither was he. Why was he caressing your cheek if you dislike each other as much as you say?"

Was he *jealous*? He certainly sounded jealous, but why?

As always, my first instinct was to coax him into a better frame of mind. Old habits die hard, as I said, and the beatings I'd received as a child had burned their way into my bones. "Yes, I blurted out something that for the space of three sentences reminded him that I'm a human being. Then he went back to scowling at me."

Although Alexei hadn't, exactly. He'd remained suspicious, but his anger had dissipated. I gambled that Felix, who couldn't understand Tatar, had missed that nuance.

"What?" He pulled the knife out of the board, leaving the beef behind. "What did you say?"

I stared at my own breakfast, my appetite destroyed by the memory. "I'm sorry, Felix. I can't tell you that." I blinked back tears. "Nor do I want to share the other things he said, most of which were rude."

"Yet you love him." Felix stabbed another piece of beef. His tone made it clear that he was not asking a question. "And don't try to please me. I hate that."

I abandoned my attempts to coax. If he wanted honesty, I'd pour a bucketful of it over his head. "Will you stop waving that knife around? You're scaring me. What has you so riled up, anyway? If I didn't know better, I'd think you were jealous of Alexei."

He dropped the knife but not his aggressive stance. "Why wouldn't I be? You love him. He *had* you. And he's not a cripple."

A cripple? That's what had given him a fit? "I told you I don't care about that."

He smacked his hand against the table. "And I've told you, more times than I can count, that I don't care about the pockmarks on your face. So stop cooing at me as if I were a grumpy old sheikh. You're better than that."

"Then stop acting like a grumpy old sheikh," I snapped.

For a moment he glared at me, and I returned the glare in full measure. Then, unexpectedly, he began to laugh. "I was, wasn't I?"

"Yes," I said. Relief flooded me at the return of his usual good humor. "You were. It's so unlike you, too."

He produced an elaborate shrug. "I'm sorry. When I walked in, it looked to me like the pair of you were having second thoughts about your separation. I can't compete with a man like that. Rich, titled, handsome, whole—"

"And completely uninterested in me," I interjected. "I can't speak for him, but the only second thoughts I had were why I'd ever loved him in the first place. I don't understand, though. If you want me enough to be jealous, why do you withdraw whenever I flirt with you? I thought you must be repelled by my looks but too polite to say so."

I held his gaze with my own as I waited for him to answer. He'd deny it, because he really was a kind person, but if I watched him, I could divine the truth.

Felix sighed and reached for my hand. "Of course I want you, Juliana." His voice, throbbing and intense, held a note I'd never heard from him. "I'm a man, not a saint. I dream about making love to you a hundred times a day. I'm not repelled in the least. You're far more beautiful than you think."

"Then why?" I stammered, unsure I could believe my ears.

"Because I want a woman I can share my life with, not someone who's convinced she has to placate me so I won't assault her. I've watched you, sweetheart. You coax and seduce out of fear. When you're comfortable with someone, you're adorable: clever and funny and enchanting. But let me show the slightest hint of interest, and I can see the panic in your eyes. I withdraw so that you'll feel safe again. Whatever you believe, the question isn't whether I love you. It's whether you dare love me. And for God's sake, don't yield because you think doing so will please me. That's the last thing I want."

I stared at him, stunned—and yes, scared—by his declaration.

He was right. Wasn't that what had ruined Alexei's love for me? That I'd yielded to please him, as my masters had trained me to do, even though my own desire died as soon as he moved beyond a kiss?

"It's true," I said slowly. "Only I'm not scared of you. It's something else. Something in me. That's what I'd just told Alexei when you found us. That I can't feel desire. Can't sustain it, I mean. It's as if I go dead inside."

"Dead," Felix said, his tone and expression thoughtful. He paused, and I waited for several breaths before he added, "You know, sweetheart, I think you need to hunt down that ogre of yours."

"But he'd kill me." I heard my voice, high as a frightened child's. The terror of the nightmare flooded my senses. Again I felt my eyes widen and my heart pound.

"Listen to yourself, Juliana. You sound like you're about eight years old. I didn't mean hunt down the man, if there is one. I meant understand the source of your nightmare. You had the dream again last night, didn't you?"

I gripped the cloth of my doublet with my free hand, trying to slow my breathing, get my voice under control. "I did, yes." I didn't ask how he knew; I must have whimpered and thrashed as I had before. "I'm sorry I disturbed your sleep."

Felix waved my last sentence away. "That's of no importance. You were so terrified the last time I didn't want to take the risk of waking you again. I talked to you and stroked your back until it stopped. Was it the same as before?"

"It's always the same." I shivered, remembering. I'd even seen the white rose and heard the singing. New elements, but they were repeating too.

"And you remember every detail?"

"Yes. Always. It's more like a painting than a dream. Only I'm part of it. I can call it up in the middle of the day if I try." Indeed, I could see it now: the tiled room, the blurred shape, the broken flower. "But I don't try, because I hate feeling so helpless."

Felix pressed the hand he still held. "That's not usual, sweetheart. I have dreams as well, even nightmares, but not the same dream over and over. Most of the time I don't remember them clearly. There's something going on there, although I don't pretend to know what. Would you like to tell me some of that past you prefer to keep to yourself?"

I shook my head, shuddering at the very idea. "I can't."

"Are you sure? I won't judge you, you know."

My throat tightened. He said he wouldn't, but he would. How could he not, once he learned the truth? It would change his whole opinion of me. "Not today. I can't bear to think about it."

"Not today, then," Felix said. I heard a note of resignation in his voice. "Soon, I hope. I think it would help."

I wanted to believe him, but it was an easy claim to make when he hadn't heard my story. Look how Alexei treated me, and he knew less than a quarter of the whole—and that the most tolerable part. "I've disappointed you," I said instead.

"No, you didn't. It's not your job to please me. Remember that." Again Felix tightened his fingers on my hand. "Someone hurt you. When you were quite young, I'd guess. That makes me angry. Only a beast hurts someone too small to fight back. It's like pulling the wings from a butterfly or tearing the petals off a flower."

A flower. The broken rose. I hadn't told him that part of the dream, yet there it was. Tears pricked at my eyes, and I fought the urge to give in, to weep, to spill the whole truth into his lap like the petals of his metaphor. But some barrier held me in check. Once I told him, there would be no going back. In my mind I heard the singer's haunting melody once more. The words hovered just out of reach.

I took another gasping breath and pushed the sensations down into their deep and hidden vault. In some part of my brain I understood I'd probably pay for that tonight, but I wasn't ready to confront the significance of the song. The risk was too great. I couldn't even have said what the risk was. Death? Destruction? A truth about myself that I couldn't face?

"Thank you," I said. "I'll tell you one day, I promise." One day meaning never. "But not yet. Let's talk instead about what to do next. I can't stop Alexei from watching me, but I can watch him at the same time. He will be surrounded by Russian noblemen—a Tatar or two, maybe, but mostly Russians. I can listen to what they say."

"Is he caught up in this fight among the noble clans, your Alexei?" Felix wrapped a piece of beef in bread and ate it, accepting my change of subject. On the surface, in any event. I suspected he would circle around and ask me about my past another day.

Eager to escape the demons of the dream, I sipped ale. I had yet to eat a single mouthful. I'd learned from experience that if I concentrated as hard as I could on the dry facts, I could keep the roiling emotions at bay. "I doubt it. As a descendant of Genghis Khan, he outranks every prince—Russian, Lithuanian, Tatar, the lot. Everyone except the grand prince himself. Alexei learned from his father to stay out of squabbles among the clans as a general rule. But he monitors what goes on, and the other men in the escort will be involved—not his personal bodyguard but the rest of them."

"Will he talk to you, then, when he calms down?" Felix asked.

I'd recovered enough to pick up my slice of bread and take a bite. The cheese had a fresh taste and smell that I enjoyed, and the consistency was just right. "He may," I said. "I wouldn't count on it, though. Like my husband, Alexei thinks I'm a featherbrain. But I'll give it a try. You can come along. Maybe he'll deign to share his thoughts with a man."

Felix patted my shoulder. "Let's finish our meal. Then we'll launch a foray into the fortress and see what we can discover."

But when we made our foray, we discovered that Alexei had wasted no time. He must indeed be anxious to return to his Maria. I'd been right about the couriers, too. They galloped into the courtyard, howling like devils, before we reached the top of the stairs. Warriors raced through the open doors, scrolls in hand, and passed them to their leader as we descended to the main hall.

Alexei scanned the documents and returned them. "Tell the ambassadors to prepare," he said to a Russian standing nearby. "We leave tomorrow." The Russian bowed and departed, pushing past us to reach the large room where we'd eaten the night before. I assumed the ambassadors must be inside.

Alexei turned away. I thought we'd escape his attention altogether, but a tip of his chin acknowledged us. "You heard that," he said. "Tomorrow morning. Be ready, *Julian*, or I'll set off without you."

"Oh, I'll be ready, Tsarevich." I gave him my best false smile and widened my eyes like the innocent he knew I was not. "Felix and I will both be ready at first light, won't we, Felix? Don't you worry about us."

Alexei's mouth quirked at the corners, and I saw the glint in his eyes that signaled amusement. We were back on the old terms: light teasing, but without the former attempts at seduction. That pleased me. Better than imagining him lurking in corners waiting to pounce on me, for sure.

The gleam brightened when Felix scowled, so I placed my hand on my pretend cousin's arm and directed him toward the room that appeared to contain the ambassadors. "Until tomorrow," I said.

Felix echoed my words. His voice maintained its usual even tone, and the scowl vanished, although the arm beneath my hand still felt tense.

Alexei nodded in reply, and Felix and I withdrew. "Ignore him," I murmured once we were out of earshot. "He's decided to let me travel with you. That's what he wanted us to know. The rest is just him needling me."

"So it is," Felix said. His muscles relaxed in my hold, and he grinned. "And it's good that I don't have to smuggle you into Moscow. I suspect your Alexei is a difficult man to sneak past. I'll be glad to get out of Smolensk, too, although I could wish for a different escort."

"I'd guess that he's caused as much trouble as he plans to," I said. "He wouldn't let me come along otherwise. And if nothing else, we can be sure he'll leave on time!"

And so it proved. Our ambassadorial mission had arrived in Smolensk on a Monday afternoon, and by Wednesday morning we set off for Moscow under Alexei's supervision.

As before, Felix and I shared a covered sleigh, but this time the entire group traveled in sleighs as well. Winter still enshrined the roads in snow, and the horses, eager to reach a resting place as soon as possible, dashed with amazing speed from one posting station to the next. According to Alexei, now more preoccupied than surly, we would reach the Russian capital in less than a week. At first I didn't believe him, but as we raced past miles of forest, stopping at regular intervals but driving through the night, I came to see how such speed was possible.

"I can't wait to get there," I told Felix. "Even if it means dodging my detestable husband. I'm so tired of sitting in a sleigh I could scream." It was evening, and we curled together on the seat, fully clothed under a fur robe that draped us both. Our conversation in Smolensk had established a new level of comfort between us. I enjoyed the sensation of his arms around me, the softness of his cloak against my cheek. Best of all, his presence seemed to keep the ogre at bay: I didn't have the dream once during that part of our journey.

At the same time, I longed for a bath. Washing more than face and hands was out of the question when we left the sleigh only long enough for necessities. Felix was in no position to complain, but still the situation irked me. I valued cleanliness, in myself and others.

Driving through the night served purposes other than speed. Unlike Poland, Muscovy had no inns, so remaining on the road with fresh horses provided a suitable alternative to lodgings as well as shortening the time spent on the journey. As a result, though, those posting stations offered the only opportunity for Felix and me to engage with any of our fellow travelers. From a positive standpoint, I experienced little difficulty in dodging Alexei, who hardly had time to concern himself with me while ordering the disposition of so many diplomatic pawns. But the conditions under which we traveled did little to advance our mission for Queen Bona and my hopes for a better future.

We reached Vyazma, which according to Felix put us about halfway along this last stage of our journey to Moscow, at dusk on the fourth day after leaving Smolensk. I had finished washing whatever I could reach without revealing my female body to the world and entered the main room when two sights caught my eye, one expected and the other meriting investigation. Ahead of me, near the door, Felix waited with both hands on his cane, his man Gregor next to him bearing a basket—of food, I assumed. But off to one side, as if trying to avoid detection, Adam Tarlo and Bogdan Ostrogski stood nose to nose, as if in the midst of an argument.

I raised a hand to Felix and jerked my head to my right, where the two men faced each other outside Felix's line of vision. Without pausing to see if he followed, I moved as swiftly as I could toward my quarry. My felt boots made little sound as I crossed the room, and I had no difficulty ducking behind a door that allowed me to overhear the two men's conversation. From that perspective I could see Felix heading my way, but he walked slowly, placing the cane with care at each step to avoid making noise.

"I wish you'd stop pestering me," Bogdan said as I arrived. He sounded more aggrieved than conspiratorial. "I've told you I'm getting along fine with my Uncle Damian, except that he keeps pushing me to marry some dog-faced girl. Why you think that would cause me to switch sides and join the Russians I can't imagine. Don't they have dog-faced girls they're desperate to marry off?"

Felix squeezed into the space next to me, and I touched a finger to my lips. He gave a quick nod, and I dropped my hand, concentrating on the voices from the other side of the door.

"I wasn't talking about your uncle's marriage plans for you," Adam said in a low tone he probably considered reasonable but which to me sounded almost as peevish as Bogdan's. "I wondered how much he monitors the situation at the court in Cracow—and Vilnius. There's a fair amount of unrest among the nobles, from what I hear."

"And you think my uncle the general confides in his uncooperative nephew whom he's busy consigning to destitution until I cave in to his demands?" Bogdan's voice sharpened with annoyance, its pitch rising to the point where Adam emitted an audible "shh."

"You must have rocks in your head," Bogdan finished. "I'm tired of you cornering me to ask the same stupid questions over and over when you refuse to believe my answers." And with that he stomped into the main room.

I glanced at Felix, but with impressive presence of mind he had stepped around the door, a point from which he could block Adam's escape. I followed in time to see him spread his arms wide, their draping sleeves making an effective screen.

For a moment I thought Adam might charge Felix and knock him down. I ducked under Felix's left sleeve and positioned myself in such a way that Felix could rest his hand on my shoulder for support if he needed it. I did my best to look formidable. I don't think I succeeded too well at that part, but with Felix at my side I did create an effective barrier.

"Oh, the cousin." Adam scowled at me, then Felix. "What are you up to, Ossolinski?"

"The very question I planned to ask." Felix reached for Adam's elbow. "Our sleigh is waiting. Please ride with us as far as the next posting station."

Although Felix phrased his last sentence as a request, the way he gripped Adam's arm seemed to leave no doubt in that young man's mind that it was more of a command. I stepped back, giving them room to maneuver, although I stayed close enough that Adam wouldn't imagine that he might shove us both aside and get away.

But in fact Adam showed no sign of wanting to make a break for the main room. Felix was taller and older, if only by two years, and the imperious air he had demonstrated with the innkeeper that first evening of our journey gave him a chilly calm that apparently convinced Adam that violence wouldn't serve. He stopped looking like a bull ready to defend his field and allowed Felix, gripping Adam's elbow as if he needed it for balance but in fact preventing any escape, to lead him to the doorway. I followed them to our sleigh, curious to find out what would happen next.

We had barely settled ourselves on the seat before the coachman released the reins and the horses took off on their usual mad dash. I sat on the side farthest from the door, with Felix to my right and Adam facing us. I applauded Felix's aplomb in recognizing that here we had a place where we could discuss and, if necessary, probe without having to worry about who might overhear. Other than the coachman, perhaps, but unless we pounded on the carriage roof and shouted at him, the rushing wind and cantering hooves rendered his chances of catching what we said in a foreign tongue unlikely.

As the sleigh picked up speed, Adam regained his pugnacity and launched the initial attack. "Why did you meddle? I've been chasing that dolt Bogdan for weeks. Now what am I supposed to tell Sigismund Augustus? That I almost unmasked his traitor but Ossolinski got in the way?"

I gasped. "You're working for Sigismund Augustus? To find the man being wooed by the Russians?"

Adam leaned forward, elbows on his knees, so he could turn the full force of his anger on me. "That, yes. And whichever bright spark convinced certain members of the gentry that assassinating Queen Bona would advance their interests."

I stared at him, at a loss for words. Felix, however, smacked his forehead and burst into a guffaw that caused Adam to regard him as one would a lunatic.

"What is *wrong* with you?" Adam demanded. "I swear, you must be possessed by demons. You wreck an investigation, and all you can do is split your sides?"

His indignation sounded sincere, and under the circumstances I couldn't blame him for thinking Felix quite mad. I waited for Felix to respond, and after a while he stopped chortling, crossed his arms over his chest, and caught Adam's eye.

"You'll laugh too when you hear," Felix said. "There's nothing else *to* do; the whole thing's ridiculous. I gather King Sigismund Augustus didn't bother to check with his father before charging you with this mission of his? If he had, he might have discovered that King Sigismund the Old sent Julian and me on the exact same quest. We could have been working together. Instead you've been high on our list of suspects since Sandomierz."

"You're joking me." It was Adam's turn to smack his forehead. I spared a moment to wonder if I'd need to spend the evening explaining that the two of them hadn't acquired bruises from punching each other, only themselves. "And you were on mine, the pair of you acting as shifty as you were." He pointed at me. "Especially him, hiding in the shadows like a common pickpocket." I bridled at the implication, but he was staring at Felix.

"I'm not joking," Felix said. "You, Simon Belsky, Martin Glinsky, and Bogdan Ostrogski. Leon Laski, too, although we eliminated him early on. But you did find out what's driving Bogdan, it seems. We owe you a debt for that, if only because Julian was quick enough to spot trouble and follow you. Otherwise, I suppose, we'd still be working at cross-purposes."

It didn't escape my notice that Felix withheld both my true identity and the real cause of our suspicions—that I'd overheard Adam's conversation at the king's birthday celebration. I appreciated his restraint. I didn't want Adam to know those things, which would increase my own chances of exposure or even place me in danger if Adam turned out to be lying.

"You didn't believe that claptrap, did you?" Adam said—referring to Bogdan's explanation of his diminished wealth, I assumed. "Bogdan's guilty as sin. Look at his face. Did you ever see a more obvious villain? One of these days I'll break down those barriers of his and get him to talk."

Hmm. But Bogdan too had sounded sincere, and his statement that an autocratic uncle was using his control of the purse strings to force his nephew to marry the young woman selected by his elders rang true. Truer than Adam's willingness to blame a man based on the shape of his eyes. "It seemed like a plausible explanation to me," I said. "At least as plausible as yours."

Felix said, as if taking Adam's claim seriously, "What drives Bogdan, then? Belsky has relatives fighting for power in Moscow. Glinsky has a murdered cousin to avenge, and his yearning for vengeance doesn't depend on whether it really was murder. Bogdan has neither."

"No, but he hates Catholics and doesn't much like being ruled by Poles." Adam announced this opinion as if no sane person would question it.

He could be right. We had thought the same. Still, that didn't make it the *only* possible explanation.

"Enough to kill the queen? To ally with the Russians?" Felix's skepticism drew a snort from Adam. "Perhaps. I think it would take more than an unwanted bride to overcome years of learning to detest the Muscovites, but one never knows. We should keep an eye on him, for sure. But let's not ignore the others. What else have you learned?"

"Doesn't that cousin of yours speak?" Adam countered.

His tone rankled. I leaned forward to glare at him. "Of course I do," I said. "Didn't you hear me say I thought Bogdan's explanation was as plausible as yours?"

Felix chuckled, and I leaned back, satisfied that I'd managed to score one point. While I listened to Felix and Adam speculate about the rest of our party, I debated the merits of Adam's story. It made sense that Sigismund Augustus, with the arrogance of a twenty-one-year-old royal prince (his crowning as king and grand duke didn't change the reality that in relation to his father he remained a prince), had decided that he could do a better job than the old man of protecting the queen. And that it hadn't occurred to Sigismund Augustus to check with his father even to prevent duplication of effort fit with his age and personality too.

I sent a silent protest to the heavens. Because Sigismund Augustus wanted to outshine his father, the three of us had run around in circles for weeks instead of cooperating. Was that fair? Was it right?

Getting no answer to my questions, I consoled myself with the thought that having Adam on our side should make my task for Queen Bona easier. But had he told us the truth?

We stopped next in Mozhaisk, where Adam departed without so much as a goodbye and Alexei announced that we would reach Moscow in about a day and a half. Refreshed and back in the sleigh, I tackled Felix at once. "Did you believe Adam's story?"

He made a "so-so" gesture with his left hand. "The tale itself fits, by which I mean I can imagine Sigismund Augustus appointing Adam and Adam agreeing. The role of investigator or even spy suits his temper better than that of traitor."

"His suspicions of Bogdan too." I'd thought about this aspect while listening to Adam converse with Felix. "Adam is straightforward—at least he seems that way—but inexperienced. He might fall for the man who looks like a villain and ignore the stronger motives of others."

I paused before adding the one element that still troubled me. "But if he was already collecting information for Sigismund Augustus at the birthday celebration, why didn't he admit that? Identify the man he was questioning? That wasn't Bogdan I saw talking with Adam. It could have been Simon or Martin or someone else altogether, but the coloring and physical shape were both wrong for Bogdan. The voice too."

Felix rested his elbow on the side of the seat and touched his thumbnail to his teeth, concentrating. A slight frown creased his brow. After a while he said, "I'm inclined to trust that Adam's telling the truth as he sees it. But not to share with him everything we know. He mustn't find out you're a woman. I don't want him to learn that you overheard him—not until we know who the real traitor is. His sincerity troubles me less than his tendency to run at the enemy without stopping to think. This is a game of shadows, and like his master Adam is too direct for subtlety. That's why the old king appointed us."

"I agree," I said. "We should tell Adam enough to convince him that we're his allies and nothing more. That way, with luck, he'll share with us what he finds out, even if he fails to understand its importance. As with Bogdan's reasons for falling on hard times. That story I do believe."

"Yes," Felix said. "But we should continue to watch Bogdan too. Like you, I tend to accept his story about the uncle and the dog-faced girl. It sounds right to me, not least because I know his uncle—as great a tyrant as any ruler of Muscovy, I can assure you. But let's not sacrifice our pawns until we have the knights and bishops cornered."

And with that, we returned to our usual pursuits. For the next day and a half, when not sleeping or stopping at this posting house or that, Felix and I conversed in Latin and Italian, I played the lute he had purchased for me from one of the musicians in Vilnius, we matched wits over the chess board. At times we discussed our destination, the ceremonies and dangers that awaited us, the opportunities for information gathering we might create.

What we never discussed was my husband. I chose to believe Felix's assurances that Koshkin couldn't touch me. Worse, I convinced myself that just because Alexei had recognized me despite my illness didn't mean that anyone else in Russia would.

I should have known better, especially when it came to that last part.

Chapter Eight

Moscow, March 1542

ON THE FIRST DAY OF MARCH WE AT LAST REACHED OUR destination. Our sleighs entered the residential area of the city, known as the Kitaigorod, through the St. Barbara Gate. Our carriage, a kind of box on runners with blurry panes inset in the upper half of the door, didn't permit a clear view of the city, but I had a general sense of massive brick walls surrounding us, then opening to reveal a kind of architectural cacophony that I recalled all too well from my time living here: rows of wooden houses packed so close together that the windows of one would permit spying on the bedchambers of the next, planked streets cleared for the most part of snow, churches and bell towers.

And people, visible wherever I peered through the flawed window. Again memory allowed me to interpret the far from clear scene outside. Nobles in elaborate dress rode amid peasants carrying goods for market and artisans on their way to or from work. Black-robed monks and white-robed priests wandered amid the throng, stopping from time to time to answer the pleas of the faithful.

Shopkeepers set up impromptu stalls at corners, fighting off beggars who importuned the passersby, plagued also by pickpockets and thieves. Even the occasional noblewoman drove past, invisible beneath her veil. Hard to believe that for six months that was my life.

Animals, too, roamed amid the crowds: chickens, geese, and ducks; slinking cats and dogs in search of handouts; and, of course, horses of every size and description, leaving their excrement on the streets as they went by. In the hubbub our formerly rapid progress slowed well below a crawl.

"What a mess," I said to Felix, sitting opposite me. "After so much time away I'd forgotten what Moscow's like."

"Cracow's not such a madhouse." He too peered through the window. "If Rome were made of wood, it might look like this."

"You've seen it before, though. Or did I misremember?"

"I have." He gave me his charming smile, the one that crinkled his gray eyes at the corner and warmed my heart. "Last year, when we came to deliver the king's request to send his plenipotentiaries. But like you I forget the full effect when away from the chaos." As he spoke, our sleigh made a sharp turn to the right, throwing me against him. He caught me round the waist.

For a long moment, the idea of pulling away didn't enter my head. I didn't experience the flash of fear that had plagued me at such moments ever since my illness. I stared into his eyes, sensing my own widen, my lips part. I thought he might kiss me. I *wanted* him to kiss me, I who had never experienced desire—except briefly for Alexei.

But Felix wouldn't kiss me, because he wanted me to feel safe. He'd said that in Smolensk. Testing the waters, so to speak, I touched my lips to his. They parted, warm and welcoming, like Felix himself. His arms tightened around me, his mouth moved on mine. A timeless, precious instant of perfect communion.

Then the sleigh jerked again, passing through another set of gates. The clamor outside stilled. With a sigh, Felix released me. "We've arrived," he said, his voice unsteady. His hand caressed my cheek.

I looked past him and saw the outline of buildings—some close to the ground, others several stories tall and flanked with covered staircases—surrounding an open courtyard devoid of humanity in the chill winter air. An urban estate, with kitchens well away from the main house to protect it from fire and storerooms for various types of food: I remembered the layout well. My husband's homestead followed a similar plan.

"Yes," I said, fighting a strange reluctance. "We can't be seen in each other's arms." I straightened and pulled back as the sleigh stopped. Felix lowered his hand, but he continued to stare at me, his eyes warm.

"Are you sure about this, Juliana?" he asked. He kept his voice low. We had minutes, at most, before someone came to inquire what kept us inside when we had reached our destination.

"Not entirely," I admitted. "But I did enjoy it. Can we talk about it later?"

"Of course," Felix said. Then the corners of his eyes crinkled. "I'm glad you liked it, though, because I did—very much."

I blushed and didn't respond, since I had no idea what to say. Yet as I scrambled out of the sleigh, my legs cramped from so much sitting, the memory of my response to Felix sent tingling tendrils into the depths of my mind.

When did I last yearn for a man's kiss?

And the answer rang like a bell. *Not for a long time.*

Alexei identified our lodgings as a private residence, generously donated for our use by the family that normally occupied it. I saw at once that the estate lay at the extreme end of Varvarka Street, right next to the Kitaigorod wall. The rough brick triangle loomed over the estate buildings, and we could see the gleam of spears and helmets between the machicolations, the slitted windows above the St. Barbara Gate that would bristle with artillery on the side that faced away from us. The whole effect lowered my spirits, a reminder of the ever-present menace of war.

What had happened to the estate's usual residents after their generous donation, Alexei didn't bother to mention. When I asked Felix, he shrugged. I interpreted that to mean he didn't know rather than that he didn't care. The Foreign Office had moved them to a different property, I guessed, either within Moscow or outside the walls—maybe to a different town altogether. In my limited experience, the Russian government tended to treat its servitors with a callous disregard for their comfort.

Nor did it worry overmuch about its visitors' comfort. It shouldn't have surprised me when Alexei lined us up and explained the rules, but it did.

"You will remain in the compound," he said, "until the grand prince summons you. Servants will bring food and drink each day. Ask them if you need anything. My men will guard the estate, and no one enters or leaves without their approval. You needn't fear for your safety. This will be your home for the duration of your visit."

Home? Read jail.

A babble of questions and exclamations greeted this announcement, but Alexei paid them no heed. He dipped his head in the direction of the ambassadors and vaulted onto Ajdar's back. As he passed me, he slowed the horse, leaned sideways in the saddle with that aplomb so characteristic of Tatar riders, and said in his own language and a voice pitched solely for my ears, "I'll warn Koshkin to expect you, shall I?"

I hissed at him, but he had already resumed his upright stance. He rode off, laughing, while I muttered curses that he, blast him to a pile of embers, couldn't hear.

And as if Alexei's gibe weren't bad enough, I turned my head to find Felix glowering at me. "What was that about?" he demanded.

Our easy rapport from the journey, the pleasure of that kiss, destroyed by a single jab from Alexei. I longed to pitch both men into the sea. Instead, I touched Felix's elbow. "Let's go inside."

Felix didn't budge. "Answer me," he said.

My patience, sorely tried, scuttled into the woods and vanished. I dropped his elbow. "The bastard offered to tell my spouse to expect me." I spoke in Italian, which I hoped the Russians and Tatars wouldn't understand. Although half the Poles probably would, so I kept my voice to a hissing snarl. "And you're doing the grumpy sheikh thing again. I promised you he's no threat to you, so stop it." Without waiting for an answer, I stalked off toward the staircase.

"Julian," he called.

I pretended I hadn't heard him. Let him find his own way into the house.

"I'm sorry," Felix said. "You're right."

Damnation. I turned. He was leaning on his cane, holding it with both hands. "I'm sorry," he repeated.

With a sigh I went back and took his arm once more. "Behave yourself," I said. "Don't we have enough complications without you acting as if you're a dog with one bone? Let's go upstairs, and we can talk about how we're going to do the task we were sent here to do when the Muscovites have ordered us not to leave the estate."

With harmony restored (sort of), we walked slowly toward the house. I wasn't sure how Felix would navigate the outside staircase, although he must have been confronting such obstacles for years, but the first floor almost certainly contained only storerooms, and the servants' stairs would pose a much greater challenge than the formal entranceway to the house. Even if I asked for a storeroom to be cleared and a bed set up there, as people did for weddings, Felix would still have to climb the stairs to eat and to meet with the rest of our group.

In fact, he outdid my expectations, although climbing the stairs took him a long time. I matched his pace, keeping him company with idle chatter about the house and the city. By the time we reached the top, he was sweating but smiling, his usual sunny demeanor restored. I was quite glad, by then, that he wouldn't need to tackle the stairs again until the Muscovites deigned to receive us.

But I had no intention of waiting inside the building for the grand prince's summons. A quick change of clothes, and I would head for the courtyard. Not to visit Koshkin either, whatever Alexei thought.

Felix and I had a mission to perform.

I waited until Felix fell asleep before rummaging in my bags, which Gregor had delivered while we negotiated the stairs, for the set of Russian men's clothes I had hunted down in Cracow the morning after I received my first set of doublet and hose from the queen's tailor. A pair of homespun trousers tied with a cord, a homespun linen shirt with high collar and tight cuffs, felt boots scruffier than those I wore as part of my masquerade, and a worn rabbit's fur cap and coat with a wide sash where I could tuck my hands to keep them warm—with my short hair and undistinguished face I could pass for any Russian artisan's lad. Satisfied with my appearance, I left Felix a note to stop him from wondering where I'd gone and slipped out the door.

I didn't intend to challenge Alexei's guards on this excursion, although if I saw a chance to get by them I'd take it. What I wanted was a clear sense of the estate, its exits and entrances, the size of the staff, ways that I could leave if I needed to and—just as important—return unnoticed. It stood to reason that if one of the envoys wanted to negotiate an exchange of information or allegiance with the Muscovites, either he would have to leave the compound to talk with them or they would have to visit him here.

But if the Russians came here, then everyone on the Polish side would know that such a meeting had taken place. So a secret exit and return struck me as by far the better choice for our would-be conspirator, whether that person turned out to be Adam, Bogdan, Simon, or Martin. And it wouldn't do to wait until the man we'd traveled so far to intercept disappeared from our midst before working out how best to follow him. I needed to identify the possible exits and entrances as soon as possible.

With that goal in mind, I explored alternative means to reach the storerooms on the ground floor with the idea of heading for the stables. Because of my Russian clothes, with luck the guards would think me a member of the household—a groom, maybe—and pay no attention to me.

My six months as Koshkin's wife paid off. I had no difficulty locating the inside path the servants used. When I reached the storerooms, I found the main one almost bare. When I lifted the lid on the one large chest, it was empty.

That surprised me. Where did the household store its goods? I saw no tools, no forgotten furniture, no insignia-draped coffers overflowing with armor and weaponry, no round traveling trunks or buckets, no coats of mail hanging from pegs attached to the wall, no clay pots or iron skillets or chased goblets large enough for three—none of the detritus of everyday life that had cluttered the storerooms at Koshkin's house. The maids would live in the attics, the horse tack fill a side room in the stables, and I felt certain the servants had distributed the food among the ice house and cellars, the pantry and buttery. Even so, the absence of the familiar trappings of domestic life struck me as strange.

Still pondering what I'd learned, I left the almost empty storerooms and ventured into the courtyard. In March, evening arrived early. The glow of sunset was fading, and the encroaching dusk would make my movements more difficult to detect. I skirted the stables, adjusting my original plan. I checked the storehouses and found them as devoid of provisions as the rooms on the first floor of the main house, another surprise. Then I surveyed the wooden fences that surrounded three sides of the compound. Alexei's warriors patrolled them, which would inhibit any attempt to escape or return that way. The brick of the city walls completed the rectangle, running behind the house where the ambassadors lodged. Hiding under the overhang, I investigated.

The distance between the house and the wall couldn't be much more than the length of my foot, but a slender person might make it through. I tested this notion, walking crabwise the whole width of the house and encountering (no surprise there) neither windows nor doors nor any other openings. When I reached the far end, though, I did discover a wood-paneled doorway. I pushed at it and found it barred from the inside, so I went back the way I'd come. A quick mental calculation based on the position of the staircase had convinced me that the window of the room assigned to Felix and me opened right over my head, and if Felix woke up and looked out onto the courtyard, I preferred that he not see me roaming around in my disreputable garb. He might not recognize me if he did, and I had every intention of confessing when I returned, but I liked the idea of completing my self-appointed mission without interruption.

My last stop was the kitchen, which should be humming with activity at this hour of the day. I approached with caution, eager to avoid a challenge from the only group of people on the estate who could swear that I was not one of them.

But the kitchen was silent, the fires unlit, the ovens cold. Although the lack of supplies in the storerooms should have prepared me for the absence of servants throughout the estate, I nonetheless felt my jaw drop as I stared at the empty room, unable to believe the evidence of my own eyes.

Where are the cooks?

I turned to leave, intending to slip back into the house and share my observations with Felix. The sound of heavy footsteps sent me instead under a table, where I crouched behind an empty barrel. My insides churned, and my hands shook. If this turned out to be one or more of the missing cooks, I'd have some explaining to do. I'd have done better to stay out in the open, where I could claim confusion if challenged. Instincts honed by years of dodging, often unsuccessfully, masters with discipline or non-conjugal bliss on their minds didn't always serve me well in this adult world.

The entrance of two pairs of legs clad in long dark hose and flat shoes, however, reassured me that in this case my instincts had not let me astray. The shoes, fine leather and close-fitting, belonged to nobles, not servants—and certainly not Russian cooks. The exposed legs in their tight hose also didn't match the style of Muscovite boyars, who wore boot-length robes even with their armor.

The voices spoke Polish. I recognized one voice as Adam Tarlo's. The other had the liquid fluency of a native speaker and didn't match any of Felix's and my three remaining suspects. No one in our party, in fact. Something about it, though, tugged at me. A nuance in the tone, the words, or the phrasing matched that other voice, heard so briefly at the king's birthday celebration.

The Russian agent at King Sigismund's court?

The man I'd overheard that day, though, didn't sound Russian. Nor did this man. Prickles ran down my spine and along my arms, the kind that people describe as meaning that a goose has walked over one's grave. Eerie, ominous, and as yet dimly understood.

I heard Adam talking about the difficulties of living under King Sigismund and, especially, Queen Bona. The usual complaints: the king indulged her overmuch; she wasted a fortune on finery and adornments for the palace; she had forced her son on the magnates during his own father's lifetime, instead of respecting their traditional right to elect the next monarch; she expropriated lands that belonged to others and bought up estates that fell vacant to provide further support for her spendthrift ways, not caring that she bankrupted the nobility by doing so.

"We did our best," the unknown speaker said in soothing tones. "Next time our assassin will succeed. And this one maintained his silence, as I understand. He managed not to implicate us, despite the torture, and that ended after the first session. We gave him poison in case he failed."

"Yes," Adam said. "He took it, or so my informant told me. You have nothing more to share? I had hoped for more information. Or an offer, but if your master can't make up his mind ..."

Is he disloyal after all, then?

I bit my tongue to avoid crying out. Discovery now would doom me in ways I didn't want to think about.

Again I heard the odd note of eagerness or anxiety in Adam's voice, the same note that had struck me during that earlier conversation. Yet a moment's thought convinced me that Adam might have other motives for eagerness or anxiety besides disloyalty. If he had set up this meeting to smoke out the Russian agent, he might anticipate a moment of discovery, of success. I'd thought him too straightforward to make a good actor, and Felix agreed. It made sense that he might find it difficult to conceal his emotions.

"I'll remind him of your interest," the Russian—because he must be a Russian, must he not, if he had a master here?—said. "He can always use good men, but you understand, treachery works both ways. If you would betray your lord today, we must ensure you don't betray ours tomorrow."

"I see," Adam said with studied indifference. "Well, tell him not to delay too long. Other countries have their own spymasters, although most don't pay as well as yours."

Is Adam chasing the spymaster, then, as Felix and I are?

I wished I knew the answer, but both explanations seemed equally credible: Adam angling for an offer, Adam seeking information. I couldn't tell.

"I'll convey that news to him as well." The Russian spoke with a certain impatience. "Meanwhile, if you will excuse me, I have an appointment elsewhere."

I wouldn't have another chance to identify the Russian. Taking care not to make the slightest sound, I slid from behind the empty barrel and lay flat on my stomach. From that angle I could catch a glimpse of the speakers without pushing my head past the edge of the table, although it was a tight fit and if either man glanced down, he might meet my eyes.

Fortune continued to favor me. The two men in Polish dress, at least one of whom didn't serve the kings of Poland, had already reached the door. Adam faced sideways, just as he had that day in the royal reception rooms at Wawel Castle, his gaze fixed on the man with his back to me.

Again I couldn't see enough of the man's face to identify him. But I recognized the build and the stance. And I couldn't fail to notice the color of the hair that showed under the rim of his velvet cap.

It was sandy.

As soon as Adam and his companion left, I extricated myself from my hiding place. I needed to reach Felix as soon as possible, but not at the risk of letting Adam find out I'd overheard his conversation with the Russian spy. While I waited, considering how long I should stay here before making my move, I pondered what I'd heard.

This was a new development, and a disturbing one. How had Adam managed to set up a meeting so soon after our arrival? For sure, he hadn't confided his plans to us, any more than we had confided everything to him. So while we might be working on the same side, the three of us were still not working together.

Indeed, after what I'd heard, I was no longer convinced that the three of us *were* on the same side. We could be, but I couldn't ignore the possibility that Adam had decided to play both ends against the middle, as they say.

What could the Russians offer that might cause him to betray his homeland and his king?

By the time I decided I had given the men sufficient time to get back to the main house, I stood half-frozen in the frigid air of the unheated kitchen. With due caution I opened the door, surveyed the scene before me, saw that the sky had darkened to the point where only the occasional lantern hanging from this structure or that would make it possible to cross the courtyard without stumbling, and ran as fast as I dared toward the door from which I had exited what at that moment seemed like a lifetime ago.

Chapter Nine

FELIX WAS AWAKE WHEN I RETURNED TO THE HOUSE. "Where did you go?" he asked as I crossed the threshold into our shared chamber. When he got a good glimpse of me, his eyes widened and his eyebrows rose. "And where in the wide world did you find such abominable clothes?"

"In Cracow," I said, stripping off the rabbit hat and tossing it into the chest where I'd found it. I pulled off the jacket too, leaving only the coarse linen shirt, pants, and boots. The furnace in the corner kept the room balmy as a day in June. I fought the temptation to wrap my arms around it. The shivers from my time in the kitchen had yet to abate. "If I went out dressed as an envoy, I'd attract the guards' attention." I grabbed his arm and shook it. "Felix, listen. I found out something important!"

"If you'd waited, I'd have come with you," he said.

I couldn't point out the impossibility of his navigating the servants' stairs or the likelihood that the two of us lurching across the courtyard would have alerted the guards. I'm not that cruel. But even without my telling him, I saw he'd reached the same conclusion. He slumped onto the nearest chair. "You went alone because I'd slow you down." He smacked his hand against the settle. When I reached for him, he shook his head. "Don't say it."

"It doesn't matter, Felix," I said anyway, to remind him that his limitations didn't count with me. "We're friends and partners." His smile warmed my heart, and I thought of the kiss. With everything I'd done and discovered since I arrived at this house, I hadn't had time to ponder my reactions—why I'd done it, what I'd expected, how I'd felt. Whether I dared try it again.

I took the seat opposite him, my palms curled in my lap. On my way across the courtyard, I'd decided to start with the least controversial information and build to that unexpected and disturbing conversation between Adam and the unknown speaker who was, most likely, a Russian agent. Otherwise I might leave out something that might later prove to be more important than I considered it right now.

So with that goal in mind I said, "Felix, listen. Alexei told us this house belongs to a private family. But the storerooms are empty. I saw no servants outside the main house. I didn't enter the stables, but I didn't hear any horses. The kitchen is deserted. What happened to the staff? And why would the family take all its possessions, even things like buckets and brooms? We won't stay that long. A month or two at the most. Something doesn't add up."

He leaned forward, his eyes alight with excitement. "You're right. It doesn't. Perhaps they took the horses so we have no choice but to stay put, but since the Russians are supplying our food, they have to send someone to cook it. Surely they don't plan to transport it through icy streets. I assume they have servants to spare?"

"By the score," I said. "In Russia, even more than Poland, servants are everywhere. At Koshkin's house you couldn't toss a stick for a dog without hitting three of them. The wealthier a family is, the larger the staff. It shows how rich the masters are. The Foreign Office can summon as many people as it needs. Besides, if the Russians plan to eavesdrop on us—and we must assume they do—servants are perfect for that task. With so many of them around, you soon forget they're lurking in corners, listening to every word."

"Brilliant." He caught my hand and kissed it. "I would never have thought to check the storerooms. I knew you'd prove your worth, Master Julian, and you've not been here one whole day."

I laughed and accepted the compliment. I'd planned to move on to Adam and his odd behavior when the bell rang indicating that we should prepare for supper, although where the supper would come from remained unclear.

Still, I couldn't attend a meal with the ambassadors looking like a scruffy artisan from the trading quarter, and it would take time to restore my appearance to the level of remotely respectable. The news about Adam and his mysterious contact must wait.

"I'd better change back into my ambassadorial clothes," I said. I reclaimed my hand and headed for the area behind the screen where I'd left my doublet and hose. "I'm hungry, and the great lords won't let a ruffian like me in their dining hall!"

The missing cooks arrived as I finished changing my clothes for something less likely to get me thrown out of the supper room. A clatter in the courtyard sent me rushing for the window, only to remember when I reached it that the Russians still used mica in their panes rather than glass—here pale yellow flakes that obscured everything but the roughest outlines. With a quick apology to Felix, I slapped my velvet cap on my head and dashed for the platform at the top of the outside staircase.

An astonishing sight greeted my eyes. A long procession of gentry in full court dress trailed by an equally long train of less exalted servitors bearing covered platters and steaming bowls crossed the courtyard, heading for the buildings I had previously identified as the kitchen. The whole lot of them crowded inside, and before long, smoke rose from the holes at the center of the roof.

I shivered. I'd forgotten my cloak, and the March air was freezing. Although I'd stood in the cold for a time too short to measure, the tips of my ear lobes burned and my hands felt chilled. I darted back inside the main house and went to find Felix. "One question answered," I told him as we set off for the dining hall—on the same level of the house as the quarters assigned to us, a converted former meeting room and thus a concession from the ambassadors to Felix's injury that I much appreciated. "The servants came with the food. And an entire retinue of gentry led the way. The cooks are cutting up and reheating our meal, I guess, since they haven't time to prepare one from scratch. Besides, those dishes looked pretty hot to start with. They must have been cooked almost next door."

"Nothing unusual after all, then," he said. "We need to worry about eavesdropping, but no more than that."

"It seems not," I agreed. But as I listened to the steady tap-tap of Felix's cane against the floor, I wondered. Perhaps the cooks would stay now that they'd appeared, and I had exaggerated dilatoriness into evidence of ill intent because I so disliked Moscow.

But my instincts said otherwise. I sensed the presence of too many tangled threads. Now that it was dark, I should grab the opportunity to spy on Alexei's guards. I might learn nothing of value, but men love to talk—every bit as much as women do, whatever they say. And what else would occupy them on such a chilly night? They had no reason to hold back, especially since they would assume no one in the delegation spoke fluent Tatar.

Yes, I'd leave the dining room as soon as I'd eaten my fill. I could dream up some excuse. I had an inkling that the success of my mission for Queen Bona might depend on what I found out.

An hour or so later, fortified by a hot and filling supper served by the gentrymen who arrived with the cooks, dressed from head to foot in black, and warmly wrapped against the chill night air, I slipped out of the room I shared with Felix and made my way down the inside stairs and into the darkened courtyard. This time I hadn't bothered to leave a note; I intended to return before he finished his post-dinner conversation.

So far, everything had gone according to plan. I'd pleaded a headache and left the banquet hall as soon as I finished the main course. To attempt my reconnaissance mission against Alexei's guards I needed a free hand, and a few hours with everyone else on the mission preoccupied with food and drink offered the perfect opportunity. Even the guards should have relaxed their vigilance, believing their quarry confined to the dining area.

Despite the cold, a dozen or so warriors manned the walls. Others clustered in groups of four around Tatar-style metal braziers—one group beneath each of the three wooden platforms that together barricaded the estate from the city outside. The brick fortification surrounding the Kitaigorod had its own regular force, but I had no plans to sneak up on those sentries, who would be ordinary troops unlikely to worry about ambassadors nearby. Instead I crouched outside the closest circle of fire. I slowed my breath and stilled my body, using techniques that had worked for me as a child, when my safety depended on learning the whereabouts of my master and his friends so that I could avoid any summons from them. I thought some phrases in Tatar to remind my ears of the sounds, then listened, blending into the night, imagining myself no more substantial than the wisps of smoke that had wafted from the kitchen roof before supper.

At first I heard nothing useful. Men's jokes about a curvaceous cook, crude comments on what the warriors considered the effeminacy of Polish dress and the ridiculousness of Polish manners. Huddled behind the scarf that concealed my pale brown complexion while protecting my cheeks from frostbite, I sensed ice forming on my eyelashes before I heard one of the guards mention the word "sultan."

I perked up. I assumed he meant Alexei, who like any son of a khan bore the Tatar title of sultan. It was natural that the men would discuss their own commander, strengthening the bonds among themselves by trading stories—and complaints, no doubt. And they did exchange a few remarks about Alexei being in a right tear ever since these Poles reached Smolensk—more complimentary than disparaging in tone, as if a good commander *would* drive his men with ruthless efficiency and irritation.

Then one of them mentioned a young lord he'd been ordered to watch. I gripped my upper arms and hunched even further into myself, if that were possible, barely daring to draw breath lest I attract their attention. Alexei had made his distrust of me clear. Had he also warned his men about me after our confrontation in Smolensk? I trembled, not from the cold.

"Good thing, too," one of the guards said. "One of ours reported to the sultan that he heard the meddlesome lad tell his cousin there were no cooks. Means the boy was roaming about the courtyard where he'd no business being, and we didn't notice. Got into the storerooms, too—don't know how he managed that, never mind why. Then realized the family's goods were missing: can you imagine? What odd sort of lad even thinks about such things? Anyway, the sultan was furious. Swore himself blue at me for letting the boy give us the slip within an hour of the Poles' arrival. So keep an eye on the youngest. You don't want the sultan getting into one of his tempers, do you, and you the cause of it?" With that he shuddered, as if the memory pained him.

Amid the chorus of denials I slipped into the darkness and made my way to the main house as quietly and quickly as I could. At some point—after Alexei left but before the Russian servants arrived—one of "ours" had overheard my private conversation with Felix and reported it. How was that possible?

My heart pounded, my hands trembled, and my throat hurt as I realized the narrowness of my escape. Thank the saints on high that I hadn't had time to discuss with Felix what I'd learned in the kitchen. I could have doomed our entire mission and not recognized the damage I'd done until too late. Then I'd have had more to worry about than failing Queen Bona. I'd have placed our lives at risk—mine and Felix's.

Adam's too, if he remained loyal to Sigismund Augustus. This game of shadows, as Felix called it, required a steely spine I wasn't sure I possessed.

But Adam had chosen to walk his path alone, so I couldn't waste time worrying about the effects of my behavior on him. I needed to concentrate on myself and Felix, on fulfilling my task for Queen Bona, and on finding out the name of this agent who boasted about arranging the queen's assassination, as well as that of the unknown spymaster.

That meant discovering, among other things, who had heard Felix and me talking. Even Felix's man, Gregor, had not been present at the time, so how had the Tatars learned what we said when we were alone in the room? Not that I had any reason to mistrust Gregor, but his absence relieved him of all suspicion.

Last, I had to find a way to share what I'd learned with Felix while ensuring that any future discussion remained private. Including the information about Adam.

By the time I heard the tapping of Felix's cane in the passageway, I'd stripped off my black outfit and replaced it with the long nightshirt that preserved my modesty in the cramped quarters we called home. Particularly cramped in this instance, because although the proportions of the room were sufficiently generous, it contained but one large bed. I constructed an impromptu barricade from an extra coverlet, arranged it down the center of the mattress and took the side nearest the wall. Given my history as a concubine with six masters, two lovers, and a husband, I couldn't help but consider the barricade something of a joke. But since our conversation in Smolensk I understood why Felix insisted on it. He wanted to remind me that my presence on this journey came without obligations, especially in bed. I respected his self-restraint.

After the kiss earlier today I appreciated the barricade more than usual. I had initiated the kiss, and I was happy with my choice. But Felix and I had had no chance to discuss it since, and I wouldn't bring it up tonight—both because my masquerade as a boy was threatened by the Russians' ability to overhear whatever Felix and I said in this room and because I hadn't yet had time to decide what it meant to me. Had I kissed Felix because that was what I wanted or because I imagined it would please him? I thought the first, but I wouldn't risk repeating the mistake I'd made with Alexei. I needed time to ensure that I could follow through on any implicit promises I made.

When Felix came in, unsteadier than usual due to an excess of hospitality, I sat up and touched a finger to my lips. He raised his eyebrows, especially when I held out a piece of paper. "Good evening, Julian," he said as he walked toward me, propped his cane near the wall, pulled his cap off, and placed it on the small table next to his side of the bed. "I trust your headache has improved." He took the paper from me, handling it in such a way that it made no sound.

"Yes, thank you. I needed only some peace and quiet, it seems. I hope you enjoyed the rest of your evening." I drew up my knees, tucking the nightshirt around my legs, although the covers hid everything below my waist.

"Martin Glinsky got drunk again," he said. "I thought Adam and I would have to separate him and Simon by force. Not the most pleasant ending, but until then the conversation went well enough."

"I'm glad I escaped it then," I said. "What a fool Martin is, to be sure."

He murmured agreement, but his eyebrows drew together and his eyes flashed as he read my account of the conversation I'd overheard in the kitchen and my trip outside after supper. I knew when he reached the crucial point because he immediately twisted the paper into a tight cylinder and held it to the candle flame. Then, raising a finger as I had done when he entered the room, he retired behind the screen we used to change clothes. I lay down, straightened the nightshirt once more, closed my eyes, and waited.

After a short while, the candle went out. Soon I felt the mattress dip as he joined me. He pushed the highest part of my manufactured barricade down and pulled me against him, so close that his beard tickled my cheek as he spoke in a near-whisper into my ear. "Don't think me unappreciative, Julian, but can't I leave you alone for a moment without you sneaking out of the house and risking your neck?"

A thrill ran through me at his touch, and I clasped my hands loosely behind his shoulders. "I had to. I'm the only Tatar speaker among the envoys. The only one you can trust, that is."

"I know." He sighed, a soft warm breath against my cheek. "And you learned something vital both times. I can't run such risks myself, and I wish I could. As I said, I appreciate it. But I'm attached to you, sweetheart, and I'd prefer to see you keep a whole skin. Will you at least talk to me next time before you slip off? Suppose you get in trouble and I have no idea where to look?"

Sweetheart. He'd called me that in Smolensk, too, during that long conversation where we'd begun to reveal our hidden selves to each other. And he was attached to me. A soft glow ringed my heart, tinged with fear that I would repeat the patterns of my past, that I would drive him away. I trembled in his hold.

But I owed him an answer. "Yes," I said in the same near-whisper he'd used with me. "I'm attached to you too. I won't go off again without leaving word."

More was at stake, though, than my affection for Felix and his for me. "We need to talk about what I heard," I told him. "When can we do that, and where?"

"Not here and not now." Felix confirmed the conclusion I'd already drawn. "Nowhere in the house is safe until we find out who reported our conversation and how he heard it in the first place." He turned his head long enough to kiss my nose. "Get some sleep. You'll need it if you're going to help me down those hell-born stairs tomorrow."

"Down the stairs?" But the words had no sooner left my mouth than I understood what he meant. "Yes," I said. "The courtyard. It's the only place we can prevent listeners from coming too close."

"Or at least see them in time to change the subject. I have information to share with you, too, but we'll discuss it in the morning." Felix moved to kiss my nose again, but I forestalled him by tipping back my head so that he could touch his lips to mine.

This time he didn't hesitate. He pulled me close and kissed me with a passion that surprised me, given his usual self-control.

At first I responded in kind, cherishing not just the experience itself but the response it evoked in me. I had spent so much of my life ministering to men's sexual urges, whether I wanted to or not, that desire had long since vanished from my calculations as to whom I wanted to embrace and under what circumstances. Even when I yearned for Alexei, it didn't occur to me to think about what it meant that I couldn't open up to him. But Felix's hands, Felix's mouth ... well, I'm sure you can understand why I stopped thinking altogether for a while.

Then he pressed against me. In response, dread flowed through me, displacing desire. The ogre hovered in my mind, and I sensed a door looming behind him. I didn't want that door to open. I couldn't bear for it to open. What lay behind it would destroy not only what I felt for Felix but everything that mattered to me, the life I'd built since childhood, the person I'd become, my soul.

As I pulled back, I remembered that the Russians could hear everything we said and did in this room. "People are listening," I murmured. I couldn't talk about the door. I would sound as if I'd lost my mind. But this was an acceptable excuse, one that would stop Felix without discouraging him.

His hand, which had wandered up from my waist, fell. He rolled onto his back and groaned. "Yes, of course," he told the ceiling. "Damnation."

"I liked it," I said into his ear. And I had, until the dread drove the pleasure away. I should tell him about that too, so he would understand, but I couldn't. Nothing said here would remain private. I couldn't speak without revealing too much to the listening ears. And even if I could speak in confidence, I wasn't ready. Because the dread led to the door, and to what lay beyond.

Felix turned toward me and stroked my face. "So did I," he said softly. "Someday, when we get out of this room."

I nodded, although I was still unsure. The ogre and the dread gave me pause. Suppose that happened every time? Suppose what lay behind the door drove Felix away?

I was being absurd, fantastical. Nothing that lay behind an imaginary door guarded by an ogre could harm me. I should stop behaving like a child. I was twenty-seven, for goodness' sake.

"Good night, sweetheart." Felix kissed me once more, a gentle brush of the lips. "Pleasant dreams."

"Good night, Felix." I closed my eyes and let my cheek rest on his shoulder.

I felt warm, at peace, and, yes, safe in his arms. The cloth barricade stayed folded back for the rest of the night, but the ogre still haunted my dreams.

Getting Felix down the stairs the next morning took somewhat less time than going up the day before, probably because he could transfer his weight to the uninjured leg more easily. Even so, I found the thought of having to do this every time we needed to engage in an important conversation daunting. Felix didn't complain, but I had to believe the prospect troubled him as well.

Still, we made it to the courtyard without incident. Bundled against the cold, we could escape easy identification, although our clothes, as ever, marked us as Polish envoys. The Tatar warriors were different men this morning, but about the same in number. The kitchens and some of the storehouses showed evidence of use: servants going in and out of them, steam rising from the smoke holes, the smell of meat and onions scenting the air. Otherwise, we had the courtyard to ourselves.

The air, although not as icy as during my excursion last night, remained chilly enough that we wasted no time. Our need to avoid any possibility of Russian eavesdropping prohibited huddling against a building or taking refuge in one of the unused storerooms, so we had only our warm cloaks to keep the wind and cold at bay. "Tell me what you noticed at supper," I said to Felix. "After I left but before Martin got drunk."

"Him and Simon Belsky," Felix said. "Chatting with a third man I didn't recognize—sandy-haired and broad of frame, like the one you saw at the king's birthday celebration and in the kitchen yesterday afternoon. He arrived after you left. When I strolled over to join them, Martin introduced him as his cousin Lev Mikhailovich, a resident of Moscow. He spoke flawless Polish, this Lev, and I assume flawless Russian as well, since he has presumably lived here since childhood, like the rest of the Russian branch of the Glinsky clan."

"That would fit with what I heard. And it sounds like Simon and Martin were getting along then, although they argued later." I scrunched up my face, trying to line up the different pieces of information. "Did Lev say why he came to visit? Or Martin?"

"To see his cousin, he implied. I didn't ask directly. The three of them talked for some time about conditions in Moscow, the struggle between the Belsky and Shuisky clans, the chances of the Belskys again coming out on top. I listened for nuances, but they talked in generalities. Clearly they had an interest in the topic, which suggests it has some meaning for them, but I heard nothing that pointed to the kind of personal involvement we're looking for."

"They wouldn't express that in a public setting," I noted. "And what of Adam? Did he also talk with this Lev Mikhailovich?"

"No," Felix said. "They behaved as if they neither knew each other or wanted to. It's too bad you didn't stay a bit longer. You might have been able to confirm whether Lev Glinsky is the man you saw."

"That's true, but then I wouldn't have found out that the Tatars can overhear us. We would have shared our secrets in a room where nothing we say is private." I caught Felix's arm. "One of the guards is heading this way. Let's stroll about a bit."

Without glancing at the guard or acknowledging my comment, he moved with me in the general direction of the stables. "Yes, it's an odd time of the year to be stretching our legs," he said when we'd again put a sufficient distance between ourselves and the guard. "We need to go back upstairs soon. I still tend to think that Adam is in fact working for Sigismund Augustus, that he's trying to trap the man you saw into an admission or a crime, and that he doesn't trust us, anymore than we trust him. But it doesn't matter, because he's our link to those we too need to uncover. And the sudden arrival of Lev Mikhailovich, native in Polish and Russian and at least of the same general appearance as the man you saw, strikes me as rather too much of a coincidence, relative of our envoy or not."

"Yes, and if Martin and Simon in fact wanted information from Lev about the Belsky clan's prospects for regaining power in Moscow, then we need to keep them under watch until we find out how serious their interest is." I saw we had come close to the stables and turned. "Let's go back. Did Bogdan Ostrogski express an interest in this Lev as well?"

"No," Felix said in a contemplative tone, as if weighing the possibilities. "He stayed apart from the rest except when eating or chatting with the ambassadors, as he usually does. We'll keep an eye on him too, just in case, but my guess is that one of the others is our man and Lev acts as that man's contact."

I pondered that statement as we crossed the courtyard. We had almost reached the bottom of the stairs when the last part of Adam's conversation with the man who might be Lev Glinsky came back to me.

"Let's not forget the unknown spymaster," I said to Felix. "Whether Adam wants to switch sides for real or not, the person he spoke to is not the man in charge. Adam was waiting for an offer, remember? He dangled the possibility of selling his secrets to someone else, although he didn't say whom. The Habsburgs, I suppose. That was part of our mission too: to identify the man pulling the puppets' strings, so we can figure out his goals and take steps to prevent him. The man who spoke to Adam referred to another assassination attempt against the queen, for example. Who can convey that information to Cracow?"

Felix stopped in his tracks to stare at me. "You're right. If we can find the spymaster as well as the agent, we will have done King Sigismund and Queen Bona a great service." His eyes sparkled like a mischievous boy's in the morning sunshine. "As for getting information to Cracow, I think it's time I introduced you to invisible ink."

"Invisible ink?" What an extraordinary idea. "What is it made of?"

"I'll show you when we get back to the room."

We had reached the staircase. I stepped onto the bottom stair and held out my arm. "Here, see what happens if you put your good leg up first and balance yourself with the cane and the banister while you move the other. I can support you to take the strain off the injured one."

Felix reached for me, and it did seem to help. We progressed, not fast but faster than the day before, up the stairs. "Thank you, Julian," he said as we approached the top, and from the look in his eyes I knew he wasn't talking only about my assistance with the staircase.

"My pleasure," I said, and meant it. But my thoughts remained with the invisible ink. Clearly Felix had even more experience with this spying business than I'd thought. It made me wonder what had really taken him to Florence. More than buying art for the king—he'd indicated that much the day Queen Bona assigned me to this mission. I realized now that I'd never asked what he meant, despite his promise to tell me later.

But those questions would have to wait, because we had returned to our room, where someone—the Russians, the Tatars?—had the ability to overhear everything we said.

For the same reason, I couldn't ask Felix outright about the invisible ink. I watched with interest as he took a scrap of the paper we kept nearby and jotted a note, which he passed to me together with a larger sheet of paper, a quill pen, and a bottle of black ink. The note said, "Write out the Lord's Prayer in Latin, leaving space between the lines."

Hmm. I thought of the manuscript prayers I had seen and wrote "*ater noster*," leaving a space at the beginning of the line that raised Felix's eyebrows. I wrinkled my nose at him and held up a hand signaling patience, then filled in the rest of the prayer, aligned to the left in neat lines as far apart as they were tall, but with the first three indented.

When I reached the end, I sanded the ink and waited for it to dry before sketching a big splashy P in the space I'd left and topping it with an angel blowing its trumpet. I added a flourish below the prayer. Then I pulled the box of colored inks that I'd brought from Cracow from its chest and highlighted elements of the P and the angel in red, blue, and gold. By the time I handed the paper to Felix, his eyes were as round as a child's on the Twelfth Day of Christmas. I reached for the notepaper and wrote, "You want it to look real, don't you?"

Felix nodded. He left the room for a short while and returned with a small clay pot that turned out to contain honey, as well as a spoon made of horn. He diluted the honey with water, reached for a clean quill and, while I watched, wrote three or four lines in Italian in the middle of the prayer, in the spaces I'd left, warning the recipient to expect another attack on the queen or her husband. As he wrote each word, I saw it fade on the page until it blended into the paper as if it had never existed. By the time he finished, the paper looked exactly as it had when I drew the final flourish.

I looked a question at him, and without speaking he picked up the smaller piece of paper and wrote something on it with the honey solution. He beckoned to me, and I followed him across the room, where he held the paper above a candle. Like magic, words formed on the page before my eyes.

I felt my jaw drop. No doubt I now looked like a child at Christmas. I had never seen such a trick or imagined it, and the sheer mystery of it delighted me.

Felix held out the slip of paper, and I read the faint brown script. *Next we look for a pious merchant leaving for Cracow.*

"How?" I wrote back in black ink. "We can't leave the estate."

Felix repeated his trick with the honey and handed me the result. *Leave that to me.*

Which told me nothing whatsoever, but I decided not to argue, especially when I couldn't say a word aloud. Instead I held the note over the candle flame and watched it curl into ash.

Chapter Ten

FOUR DAYS PASSED, MORE OR LESS WITHOUT INCIDENT. When not strolling around the courtyard, Felix and I continued to communicate our suspicions and speculations in writing, burning each message before we left the room. He told me on one of these excursions that the ambassadors, by means and methods undisclosed, had succeeded in smuggling our prayer page with its hidden message to a good Catholic merchant on his way home. Otherwise we strove to speak normally, to allay any possibility that we would ourselves become the object of suspicion and speculation—more than we already were, I mean, given Alexei's professed distrust of me and my motives. Under the circumstances, my long years of watching every word that left my mouth stood me in good stead.

On the morning of March 5 the ambassadors gathered the entire delegation for a long explanation of the protocol we could expect to encounter when the grand prince at last summoned us into his presence. They had received word that this boon might be conferred on us soon. Although not the most scintillating of subjects, the protocol discussion proved enlightening in terms of whom I could expect to encounter, how to stay in the background if necessary, and under what circumstances I might enjoy freedom of movement. The meeting also gave me a chance to verify that no Russian servants stood within earshot and confirm that the ambassadors still sought to extend the treaty of 1537 without changing the terms.

That last should limit the scope of any would-be mischief makers, or so I hoped. Our suspects had already shown an alarming capacity to establish contacts with the Russians, and Felix and I still had insufficient evidence to settle on the true culprit. Martin had a cousin who might well spy for Russia in Poland; Simon had connections with one of the warring clans; and Adam's motives and goals remained as murky as ever. Plunging the three of them into the heart of the Russian Foreign Office should offer us a chance to separate the innocent from the guilty, but it would also give our traitor an opportunity to complete his plans. Our mission for Queen Bona was entering a new stage.

As the only beardless "boy" among the envoys, I didn't venture to speak. But I did listen as Lord Glebow listed the gifts he planned to offer various dignitaries—one of them, alas, my detestable husband, so I must take care to avoid his notice. My thoughts drifted during Lord Tichonowski's review of the clan alliances, since he included no one whose allegiances I didn't already know, until a mention of my husband's name jerked my attention back to the present. Koshkin, it seemed, supported the Shuisky clan—a surprise, given the role they had played in his disgrace and my arrest. I pondered the implications of that without setting off a single flash of enlightenment, then stashed the information in my brain for later consideration.

I made only one more foray into the courtyard—with Felix's knowledge, as I'd promised—in the late afternoon after the meeting. Dusk was setting in, but the weather had warmed from freezing to cool; in the middle of the day I had sensed the first hint of spring. So in that sense this expedition proved more comfortable than the last. Again I wore the disreputable artisan's clothes, but this time I avoided the kitchen and the stables, instead heading in a roundabout fashion for the platforms where the guards marched back and forth. Hearing nothing of interest, I slipped back into the house through the empty storerooms on the ground floor.

Halfway across the main storeroom I heard voices. I ducked behind the door that led to the inside staircase and held my breath, praying that the speakers had no reason to enter the room where I hid, which contained nothing of value. Surely the servants—for who else could they be?—would move on soon enough.

But the voices didn't fade, and after a short, stunned silence I realized they were speaking Polish, not Russian. A moment more, and I identified the speakers: Felix and Lord Glebow. I heard no sound of a cane, and I felt certain that Felix had not left the floor above. He couldn't possibly be standing outside the storeroom door.

A breath of warm air touched my cheek. I looked up. And that's when I saw it. A small vent, bordered in metal. No, a set of vents, five or six in each corner of the ceiling, that allowed anyone standing where I was to listen to what went on in the conference rooms above. If I hadn't heard the voices, I would have assumed they were heating vents.

Assessing them, I wondered whether every storeroom in the main house contained such vents. They must, I thought. Otherwise the Russians would find it difficult to keep the different conversations straight. But it would be dangerous to explore any more this evening. I'd have to try again another day.

And where were the eavesdroppers? The rooms had been empty and the doors unlocked the two times I'd come here, and surely the spies wouldn't want envoys or even scruffy artisans walking in on their sessions.

I walked about the room, testing the boards with my feet and doing my best to make no noise. I found more vents in each corner, and off to one side, partly covered by an ancient rug, a line in the floor felt rough against my fingers when I bent to investigate it. Hardly daring to breathe, I traced the outline of a trap door. Where the listeners lurked?

As fast but as quietly as I could, I replaced the rug and padded to the doorway. There I pulled off my ragged hat and coat, slipped through the door, and dashed up the stairs before anyone from the household could see me.

Now I knew how the guards had learned about my conversation with Felix. And why the servants could arrive at the house after we did, because servants were not the only way the Russians gathered information. I also understood why the storerooms lay empty, since their main purpose appeared to be providing a listening station for the unknown spymaster and his men.

I guessed, too, that Felix and I had just spent the better part of five weeks chasing our tails. Here we'd scrutinized every member of the delegation, wasted hours in speculation, and read meaning into words and phrases that could be every bit as innocent as they appeared.

Not everything we'd uncovered met that definition, of course. Adam, whether a loyal agent or a dissatisfied would-be conspirator, had a good deal of explaining to do. The plot against Queen Bona was real, as was the information about Russian attempts to promote unrest. And Lev Glinsky, if he was in fact the person who spoke native Russian and flawless Polish and traveled in both courts as a nobleman of their lands, definitely merited investigation. The unknown spymaster we should discover as well, if we could. But if the Russians routinely used such technology in ambassadorial residences—and did they?—they possessed means other than suborning a Pole or Lithuanian to acquire information they shouldn't have.

It hurt me to think about how deeply Alexei and his men must be involved in spying on us. Despite my prickly exchanges with him since I ran into him in Smolensk, I'd considered him a man of honor. Since my life had left me with no choice but to listen at keyholes, I made a virtue of necessity and took pride in my subterfuge. Koshkin, I felt certain, would not hesitate either. But Alexei was a warrior. I'd expected better of him. More fool me.

What I didn't know was how much the Russians had overheard. Or how, since they clearly had reason to protect both their listening center and their secret, they had twice let me into and out of the storerooms.

Is it possible they don't know I'm here?

But I would soon discover that they knew a lot more than I thought.

The next morning Alexei's guards arrived to escort our party to the Kremlin. I'd expected Alexei himself, but I interpreted his absence to mean that the task fell below one of his exalted standing. The leader—a handsome young Tatar, fluent in Russian, who gave his name as Mansur—confirmed this supposition by announcing that the tsarevich attended the grand prince in the Kremlin and would greet the ambassadors there. We hurriedly changed into our most illustrious clothes, donned outer garments of fur designed to proclaim King Sigismund's wealth and generosity, oversaw the loading of the ambassadorial gifts, and mounted the richly caparisoned steeds provided by the escort.

The journey, although short in terms of distance, took the better part of the morning to complete. Felix and I rode near the middle of the ambassadorial party, surrounded not only by our fellow Poles but by Mansur's Tatars and a growing escort of Russians. Seeing the grim cast to Felix's mouth and imagining the discomfort he suffered, I kept quiet as we traversed the narrow Moscow streets and passed the marketplace, where crowds of ordinary townspeople milled even though the shops and stalls were closed. Every few streets groups of gentry servitors, then Moscow nobles and princes—each delegation higher ranking than the last—stopped our convoy, engaged in long ritualized exchanges of courtesies, then replaced its predecessors as leaders of the procession until itself yielding to the next group in the invisible chain.

At the fifth of these stops, I murmured to Felix in Italian, "I hope you're enjoying the game. They strive to impress us, and we strive not to be impressed. Surely both sides have made their point by now."

Felix grunted. He must be in greater pain than I thought. But then he said, "By my count we have three more rounds to go before we reach the palace."

And halfway through he would have to dismount and walk. No wonder he looked grim.

But he didn't complain, so I also refrained from mentioning his injury. "Oh joy," I said instead. "We'll be lucky if we see the grand prince before sunset. Please tell me we don't have to repeat the whole performance tomorrow." At that he smiled, and I managed to produce enough lighthearted chatter to distract him for the rest of the ride.

Again Felix dismounted with minimal fuss, using my shoulder as a support. His cane restored, he walked slowly but purposefully in the ambassadors' wake. I maintained my position at his side and kept an eye out for my husband, a task complicated by my being shorter than most of the other envoys and Koshkin not much taller than I. Still, if I couldn't see him, it stood to reason that he couldn't see me, so unless the ranks cleared all at once and dumped me right in front of him, even an imperfect survey should suffice.

My luck held throughout the formal reception. As promised, Alexei awaited us within a pretty Italianate palace. Its diamond-shaped tiles gave it a lightness and grace wholly contradicted by the dark interiors with their fat, squat Muscovite-style pillars looming in the center of the chamber into which our escort, diminished since we dismounted in the courtyard and most of the hangers-on rode off, ushered us.

I caught my former lover's sardonic gaze on me from time to time, but neither of us did anything to call attention to the other. After a while I stopped worrying about him and focused on the room itself, which displayed a strange mixture of western and eastern tastes—rather like Muscovy itself. Walls, ceilings, and pillars were pale blue, covered in paintings of hunting scenes and flowers, giving the room an unexpected liveliness. A half dozen slender, arched windows added to the perception of light, although little actual sunlight found its way past the mica panes.

In contrast to the walls, the other decorations in the chamber proclaimed oriental splendor. Richly patterned carpets in shades of red covered the floor, and benches draped in scarlet satin lined the walls. Noblemen dressed in matching robes made from cloth of gold, with black fox-fur hats the length of my arm on their heads and high-heeled boots with curled-up Tatar toes on their feet sat in rows along the benches. Alexei stood beside them, closest to the throne and farthest from the door.

I didn't see my husband. A few black-wrapped clerics sat in a row by themselves, and four young noblemen, armed with pikes and wearing white robes and hats, had arrayed themselves to either side of the throne. Another red-covered bench sat ready for the ambassadors, who positioned themselves in front of it but did not sit. The rest of us lined up behind them, arranging ourselves by rank before two more long benches. Our escort formed a semicircle at our backs. I glanced at Felix, wondering if the presence of so many armed men within a sword's length of our necks disturbed him too. Seeing no sign that it did, I did my best to quell my anxiety, with indifferent success.

The boy who occupied the white ivory throne at the center of the far wall regarded us with disinterest. Attired in robes so elaborate he resembled a doll more than a child, he struck me as handsome and sturdy, with dark eyes and reddish hair. But I didn't doubt that the true sources of power in the room stood to the right and left of the young grand prince. This pair of massive, middle-aged noblemen introduced themselves almost at once as Prince Dmitry Belsky and Prince Iosif Shuisky. And there it was, the court rivalry, right out in the open for anyone to see.

Prince Belsky took two steps forward from the grand prince's right and delivered the opening speech that the ambassadors had warned us to expect.

The ceremony was underway. I stood and sat with the others, but my mind was elsewhere. A position to the right of the ruler indicated higher status than one to the left. Which suggested that the Belsky clan was holding its own, if not to the extent where it could exclude the head of the Shuisky clan from the diplomatic reception altogether.

Alerted by the existence of senior members of both warring clans, I subjected the ranked nobles seated on the benches to closer examination. As a woman, I hadn't spent time with boyars and princes outside my husband's family except at my wedding and Alexei's. That placed me at a disadvantage, since I couldn't identify most of those in the room by name.

But I did recognize a few on both sides, enough to ascertain that Belsky supporters clustered to the right of the grand prince and Shuisky adherents to the left. I pulled back as I identified Prince Ilya Shuisky, nephew to the head of the clan. After almost two months of captivity and abuse in his house, I still couldn't look at him without shuddering.

It didn't escape my attention that Alexei had managed to create a gap between himself and both groups, as if proclaiming his neutrality—and his status, as he stood almost on a straight line with the young grand prince.

That was when I caught sight of my husband in the upper third of the Shuisky-aligned group. He looked very much as I remembered him, sleek and self-satisfied, in his own way elegant. He must have reached his early forties by now, but he looked younger. The streaks of gray in his dark hair gave him a certain distinction. I understood why I'd agreed to marry him, despite his being fifteen years older than I. I'd seen him as sophisticated, self-assured, astute—not someone I could love, perhaps, but someone I could trust and respect. Someone who knew what he was doing, not a young man who would change his mind on a whim. I'd miscalculated, for once—and not only in marrying him. I'd failed to grasp the depths of his passion, aroused his jealousy when I'd have done better to reassure him, toyed with him when I should have coaxed and flattered instead.

He was a good man in his way. When I made him angry, he didn't beat me as my masters had done. I don't think he even sensed, as Alexei had sensed, that I only pretended to share his desire. But perhaps he did, without knowing it. Perhaps that explained why he left me behind when he fled.

I also saw what Alexei meant when he told me that Koshkin had prospered in the years since I left him. His current robes, like those of every man in the room, came from the Treasury, but he had a smugly comfortable expression that contrasted with the haggard look I remembered from our last meeting in Vilnius.

None of these thoughts made me want to return to him. Alexei had seriously misjudged me in that regard. I pulled back, using Felix as a screen to block Fyodor's line of sight. When Felix sent me a questioning glance, I mouthed my husband's name and ducked my chin in Fyodor's direction. "One-third of the way down, short, dark hair, gray streaks," I said in Felix's ear.

Again I rejoiced in the pockmarks that had destroyed my beauty. Please God they would keep my husband from recognizing me. So long as Alexei did not betray my secret.

I stared at my former lover, willing him to keep silent. He didn't return my gaze but instead watched the interplay between the princes Belsky and Shuisky, the Russians and the ambassadors, with his usual calm but distant courtesy.

I couldn't wait to get out of there.

With the first round of ceremonial completed, the young grand prince ordered us into another room to continue the discussion, then back to the first chamber for a formal dinner. Using Felix as a shield, I succeeded in completing the transit both times without drawing my husband's attention. Again my junior status among the envoys worked in my favor, and I sank with relief onto a bench a good distance from both the high table, where the grand prince sat in a kind of protected space between Prince Dmitry

Belsky and Prince Iosif Shuisky, and the smaller table facing that one set up to honor the ambassadors. Alexei and two other Tatar khans' sons also had seats at the high table, and Koshkin, although closer to me, remained far enough away that I needn't fear him leaping to his feet with an indignant cry to denounce me and drag me from the room. That should have quieted my anxiety, but alas, it did nothing of the sort.

The feast, lavish and filled with everything from chunks of roast swan to royal toasts delivered with goblets of brandy, dragged on interminably. My stomach rebelled at the procession of meats, so I limited myself to bread and soup. The toasts were harder to ignore, but once the brandy gave way to mead and beer I found it easier to satisfy each salutation with a sip. I hoped the Muscovite nobles would either not notice my abstemiousness or consider it evidence of my youth—or some strange Polish custom that defied explanation but would not cause offense.

It didn't escape my notice that Felix had positioned himself on one side of Martin Glinsky while Adam took the other side. Somehow the two of them managed to keep Martin from descending into that state of maudlin intoxication that had twice caused trouble, although Martin still seemed to imbibe a good deal.

I decided that when we left the tables, I should probably keep an eye on Martin as well. I had trouble imagining a bigger scandal than Martin, officially a Polish envoy, attacking his self-proclaimed arch-enemy, Prince Iosif Shuisky—either the most or the second most powerful man in Russia, depending on the relative position of the clans this week—for the murder of Martin's cousin Elena.

Yet there they both were, Martin and Shuisky, in the same room.

As the evening wore on, those nearby lost interest in me, and my fears subsided, although I still yearned for the meal to end. To occupy my time, I listened to the conversations around me, but so long as the profusion of dishes continued to arrive, I lacked the freedom of movement needed to overhear anything interesting.

At last we rose from the tables, although it seemed we could not yet depart. I left Felix to his own devices and circled among the company, striving to appear innocuous and ignorant of Russian. The ambassadors hadn't introduced me, so only those who sat next to me during the meal knew my name. To everyone else I appeared to be a young Polish nobleman, of no threat or interest whatsoever.

That, at least, was my hope. As I moved about the hall, I took care to avoid my husband. What I wanted was information to take back to Queen Bona. Enough that she would decide I had earned my promised reward.

I observed three points of interest, not least because I was on the lookout for such things. The moment Simon Belsky left the table, he attached himself to his cousin Prince Dmitry and remained at Dmitry's side for the rest of the evening. When I drifted by, my eyes fixed on the wall paintings as if I had no other interest in that part of the room, I heard them singing the praises of the family lands north of Vyazma, the town where we stopped just before Felix and I learned that Adam Tarlo claimed to be working on behalf of the younger King Sigismund. From Prince Dmitry's account, I learned that the family had regained its lands after leaving Lithuania for Russia. He sounded like a merchant haggling in the market, doing his best to sell the person in front of him a bale of cloth or a haunch of beef. From the nostalgia in Simon's musings, I had the impression Dmitry might be close to making his sale.

Martin Glinsky talked for a while with the man whom Felix had pointed out to me before dinner as Martin's cousin Lev. Adam Tarlo joined them, and Martin departed to converse with Prince Ilya Shuisky instead. With gratitude I noticed Felix approaching them, Bogdan Ostrogski on his heels. It took no persuasion whatsoever for me to decide they could handle that discussion. I had every intention of keeping as much distance between myself and Prince Ilya as possible. If there was one person in Russia I wanted to re-encounter less than my detestable husband, Prince Ilya was that man.

Instead I took the opportunity offered to duck between a pair of large boyars unknown to me and position myself so that I could survey Lev from the back without attracting Adam's attention. Sandy hair, broad shoulders, the kind of stance that eats up space—yes, he fit my mental image of the man I had seen that day in Queen Bona's reception rooms.

I kept a variety of Russian noblemen between me and my quarry as I circled closer. As soon as I could confirm that the man was in fact Lev Glinsky, I blended once more into the throng and strove to appear disinterested as I found a place where I could distinguish his and Adam's conversation from the many others in the room.

Alas, I couldn't get near enough to hear their words without forcing myself on their notice. I did recognize Lev's voice, though. He again spoke Polish, as he had on those two previous occasions. And his accent was flawless, as I'd expected. All of which suggested that when I first encountered him he had, in fact, been serving as a Russian spy in Poland.

But not, apparently, the Russian spymaster, on whose behalf Lev had spoken to Adam. Was the spymaster present? Could I identify him?

With reluctance, I decided I couldn't. Not from what I'd seen so far. Simon and Adam had done more or less what I might have expected of them. Bogdan's behavior was even more innocuous; he remained in the ambassadors' vicinity or, when they stopped to chat with this senior Russian or that, clung to Felix like a homeless pup.

I assumed Felix didn't appreciate that, since he had investigations of his own to conduct. But since he was perfectly capable of getting rid of Bogdan if he wanted to, I spent my time surveying the room, wandering from place to place so that no one would feel obliged to talk to me or think it odd that I lingered nearby but listening to as many exchanges as I could in the hope of learning something useful, although I wasn't sure what that might be.

I did catch more than a few conversations hinting at who backed whom among the Russian nobles. Some of the information was new—or different. I concluded the clan alliances must change quite often. I tallied each response in my head so that I could commit the alliances to paper once we returned to the Kitaigorod house.

After a while, I noticed Martin had left Prince Ilya Shuisky's side. Felix and Bogdan also abandoned Prince Ilya in favor of the Belsky princes. Adam still chatted with Lev.

But where was Martin? After a good bit of searching, I saw him prowling the hall behind the older Shuisky prince—Iosif, the head of the clan. Exactly as I had feared he might.

Launching an attack in this crowded hall would be suicide, of course, but everything I'd seen of Martin suggested he was sufficiently reckless and hotheaded—or intoxicated—to take the risk.

Again doing my best not to attract attention, I wended my way toward Felix. When I reached him, I managed to draw him away from his conversation long enough to mention my concerns about Martin.

He nodded understanding and, trailed by Bogdan, moved off to track Martin down. "You blend in," he said just before he left. "If there's a scuffle, I don't want you in the middle of it."

I didn't want that either, since my lessons in acting like a boy hadn't stretched to include fisticuffs and a wound or even torn clothing might reveal the very secret I sought to conceal. At the same time, I wondered how capable Felix might be at self-defense, given the injury to his leg, so I followed him at a discreet distance. I couldn't fight beside him—not in any way that would convince the company of my manliness—but I could yell up a storm if needed.

No scuffle broke out, though. Perhaps the arrival of Felix and Bogdan provided the deterrence that the roomful of Russians had not. Perhaps I had an over-active imagination. But once I satisfied myself that Felix and Bogdan had cornered Martin and somehow chivvied him away from the elder Shuisky, I relaxed and returned to monitoring the exchanges of those around me.

At least one of these conversations concerned my husband. I learned that he had indeed repaired his fortunes, that he stood with the Shuisky clan but (or so this particular speaker believed) had some kind of hold on them, which they naturally resented and which might backfire on him one day, although it hadn't yet.

That piece of news stopped me in my tracks until I realized I should move on before one or more of the diners wondered what had me frozen like an ice statue in the middle of the room. The last time I'd seen Koshkin, I'd given him belladonna to use on Ilya Shuisky. My husband had claimed he wanted revenge on Ilya, a goal I applauded.

But Koshkin himself had indicated a desire to give the poison to Grand Princess Elena, who in fact died not two months later. Many people, including Martin Glinsky, blamed the Shuisky clan for her death. Had Koshkin given the poison to them? Or come up with some still more nefarious scheme to dispatch Elena, whom he blamed for his disgrace and his flight?

I came back to myself in time to realize that while lost in this unexpected train of thought, I'd moved uncomfortably close to two of the three people in the room I sought to avoid. I stepped behind the nearest pillar just as Koshkin said, "Are you *sure* that pretty Polish boy is not Roxelana in disguise? He certainly looks like Roxelana to me. Not the face so much, but the body. Take a look at him from the back. I couldn't mistake my own wife, could I?"

Mother of God, I was sunk. How had I let my guard down for an instant so long as I remained in this nest of vipers? I must have been mad to come here, even though I had no choice if I wanted to fulfill Queen Bona's demands and win the prize I so desperately needed!

I dared a swift glance around the pillar, seeking an avenue of escape. I caught a glimpse of my husband's head and beyond him, a tall, slim figure in magnificent robes. Alexei. Fortunately, Koshkin faced him, but that meant Alexei stared straight at me.

Hell and damnation. I looked the other way, trying to decide if I could reach the door before he caught me. Because that had worked so well in Smolensk.

I turned my head back toward him, my gaze pleading. Then, to my utter astonishment, Alexei smiled and said, "You've had one too many goblets of brandy, Fyodor Mikhailovich. That young man looks nothing like Roxelana to me. And I think I know her at least as well as you do." And while my husband sputtered his rage at that last, no doubt deliberately provocative remark, Alexei winked at me over Koshkin's head, grasped Koshkin by the upper arm, and led him to a far corner of the room.

Chapter Eleven

I WAS STILL STRUGGLING TO UNDERSTAND ALEXEI'S ODD behavior as I rode beside Felix back to the Kitaigorod house. By now evening had set in, and with it the bitter wind. I had drunk little and eaten almost nothing due to the anxiety that had roiled me since I first learned that my husband would attend the diplomatic reception. Even before that, I'd worried about Alexei choosing to expose my masquerade in some way. Instead, he'd protected me—from Koshkin, at that—and I had no idea why. When we argued in Smolensk, I'd claimed that asking Koshkin for a divorce was my sole reason for traveling to Moscow, and Alexei hadn't believed me then. Just five days ago he'd gone out of his way to threaten, if in a teasing way, to reveal my presence to my husband. What changed his mind?

Perhaps the combination of hunger and turmoil explains why I didn't consider the consequences of confiding in Felix—that and the reality that we'd become so much closer in the last few weeks. It never occurred to me that he might still see my former lover as a rival. And since we could hardly discuss what we'd observed about the members of our own party while riding among them, I naturally took the opportunity to share the topic foremost on my mind. As quietly as I could manage given the noise made by hooves and the escort's weaponry, I told my friend in Italian what had happened.

Before he even opened his mouth, his glare told me I'd made a mistake.

"Perhaps he means to keep you in his debt," Felix said in the nastiest tone I'd ever heard from him.

"What? Why should he do that?" I nearly dropped the reins in shock. "I have nothing he wants."

"Except yourself." Having delivered this barb, Felix stared straight through his horse's ears as if I didn't exist.

This struck me as the outside of enough. "You have bats in your belfry." I kept my voice as low as possible to avoid attracting attention from the rest of the envoys but otherwise stood my ground. "I've told you before. Alexei doesn't want me. He *had* me, and what did he do? Ran off to the steppe, then came back just long enough to trade me in for a wife he loves. If she hasn't given him half a dozen sons yet, I'm sure it's not for lack of trying. The question is: given that he doesn't want me, why did he go out of his way to help me?"

Right then, the answer came to me. "Oh, of course," I added before Felix had a chance to respond. "Because he dislikes Koshkin more. They may be connected through marriage, but they get on about as well as a tiger and a wolf. Less well, probably."

"What a charming family," Felix said, his voice still acid. "So he doesn't want you. But for someone who insists she doesn't want him, you spend a lot of time worrying about him. I'm starting to wonder who you were kissing the other day. Or do you think the cripple is too stupid to notice?"

I stared at him through narrowed eyes. Hunger and stress had frayed my temper to the breaking point, and I was damned if I would put up with any more nonsense from Felix. "You just insulted both me and yourself," I told him. "I *trusted* you. I *kissed* you. I've told you a dozen times I don't think of you as a cripple. Yet every time Alexei looks at me, even when he's behaving abominably, you act like a bear with a sore head. Well, I won't tolerate it. Not from you, not from any man. I have *had* it with male arrogance and male possessiveness. I can't believe I considered you a friend."

"Then that makes two of us," Felix said with a chilly indifference that forced me to dig my heels into my horse's sides to keep from kicking his beast into a gallop. "I'm sure if you exert yourself, you can win your handsome Tatar princeling back to your side."

Too furious to speak, I urged my horse to a trot. The estate lay right ahead, and the front of the ambassadorial procession had already entered the courtyard. I rode straight to the stables, left my mare with the nearest groom, then rushed up the stairs to grab enough extra bedding to set up a temporary nest for myself in the most distant of the ground-floor storerooms.

I hoped it wasn't part of the Russians' listening network. Once I reached it, I decided probably not, because unlike the larger storage areas no one had bothered to clear it, and the usual clutter prevailed. But either way, at that moment I couldn't make myself care. If anyone had plans to eavesdrop on the ambassadors from my location, that person was out of luck. They'd have to haul me away in chains before I agreed to share a bed with Felix.

And since I'd taken most of his covers, I hoped he would freeze before morning.

Instead, I was the one who almost froze. The bedchambers received heat from the furnaces that lined each room. The storerooms were not completely unheated, because they collected warmth from the surrounding chambers, but on an icy March evening the drafts had me ruing my argument with Felix long before dawn. Not enough to go back, and certainly not enough to apologize: he'd insulted me, after all. But enough to wish that we could have waited until July to have our falling out.

As a result, I woke up early, unrefreshed and even hungrier than the night before. I left my stolen bedding in the storeroom and headed for the kitchen in search of bread, cheese, and small beer. As I left, pulling the door closed but having no way to replace the bar from the outside, I realized this was the doorway I had discovered on that first day, at the corner where the main house met the Kitaigorod wall.

I could guess that I looked my worst. Fingers through my hair had taken the place of a comb. My otherwise fine clothes, worn for the reception, had crumpled as I tossed and turned and acquired some unidentifiable stain from the storeroom floor. And if my cap sat straight on my head, that was a miracle achieved without benefit of mirror. But the Polish style of dress differed enough from the Russian that even the dimmest kitchen boy should be able to identify me as a member of the delegation.

Except that I never reached the kitchen. I hadn't crossed a third of the courtyard before a quartet of Russian warriors rode through the gate and surrounded me. When Alexei's guards protested, the Russians announced that I was under arrest for spying, a charge that outraged me given that I knew what they themselves had done. While I waved my arms and expostulated in three languages, they grabbed me and tied a rope around my wrists and a cloth around my mouth. Then one of them tossed me onto a pony, swung onto the saddle behind me, and the whole group rode out of the estate without further explanation, leaving Alexei's guards shouting questions that the Russians ignored.

Although furious, I didn't dare struggle. It would be too easy for the guard whose mammoth arm clenched my waist to realize that my hips were too wide for a man, and bad as the consequences of exposure to the envoys might be, the thought of a contingent of Russian warriors discovering I was a woman in disguise terrified me. I'd be lucky to escape group rape.

But who were they? Where were they taking me, and for what purpose? And why had they paid no attention to Alexei's guards, who were supposed to be protecting the Polish envoys?

The longer I remained on the horse, the more terrified I became. The chances that I could survive arrest and imprisonment in a Russian jail without my masquerade being exposed seemed less likely with each house we passed. Whoever had ordered my arrest cared nothing for Alexei's fury when he heard that someone had countermanded his orders, let alone the indignation of the Polish ambassadors at the disrespect shown to even a junior member of their delegation and the impact that indignation might have on the peace talks. Which meant that the person in charge must occupy a high enough place in the Russian government that he needn't worry about the reactions of others.

And he, whoever he was, had accused me of spying. I didn't know the Russian penalty for spies, but I feared the worst. I would be convicted, and I would die. The ogre would win, and I would never see Felix again.

And why should I want to, after the way he behaved?

I did, though. I knew him well enough by now to guess that he already regretted his outburst and would apologize the next time he saw me. And except for his inexplicable insecurity regarding Alexei, Felix was a good and loyal friend. He would have to overcome his jealousy, for sure, before I dared entrust him with my heart, but if the Russians killed me for spying ...

I left the thought unfinished as I blinked back tears. I didn't want these ruffians to catch me crying.

As my captors turned a corner and rode into a familiar courtyard, the truth dawned. Hauled off the horse, my gag removed (although not the rope around my wrists—maybe the scowl I directed at the Russian captain convinced him I'd claw his eyes out if he gave me the chance), and dragged into a house I'd hoped never to see again, I was angry enough to spit by the time my illustrious and impeccably attired husband strolled into the study where the guards had pulled, then carried, and finally dumped me in a corner.

I sprang to my feet at the sight of him and held out my wrists in a silent reproach. "You!" I said with loathing. "You should be ashamed! How dare you send your men to drag me here?"

To my annoyance, he remained quite unperturbed. "My dear," he said in oily tones that inflamed me further. "What a remarkable coincidence. I order the arrest of a nosy young Pole, only to discover that the spy in question is my own deeply missed spouse. And to think that last night I questioned my son-in-law about that very possibility, and he swore it couldn't be you. Fortunate, isn't it, that I didn't believe him? Quite remarkable that you still have sufficient hold on him to persuade him to lie for you, but I suppose I don't need to ask how you convinced him. Do I?"

Too angry to speak, I thrust my bound wrists toward him once more. Did *every* man I knew believe me to be Alexei's whore? "I want a divorce," I said through gritted teeth. "What I do doesn't concern you, because I will no longer live as your wife."

"But I respect my marriage vows, even if you don't. I have no interest in a divorce. I've waited five years for you to come to your senses. I want you by my side, where you belong and where you promised to stay." Koshkin raised his eyebrows in a supercilious stare that only fed my urge to violence. "Although I must say, you can't afford to be so picky these days. Despite your fervent assurances the last time we met that Alexei cares for no one but Maria, the man must be besotted to fall for the wiles of a bedraggled would-be youth whose charms have, shall we say, diminished since I saw you last. What happened to your face?"

The same question Alexei had asked me in Smolensk, here delivered as an attack. I responded in kind. "None of your business." I shook my wrists again. "Release me. I don't know why you forced these men to bring me here, but you won't get me to cooperate by tying me up."

"Not yet, my dear." Koshkin nodded at the captain. "There is a room on the floor above, near the end of the passageway. It has a door that bolts from the outside. You'll know you've found the right one because it will contain a pallet on the floor, a set of women's clothing, and bowls for food and drink. When I finish speaking with my wife, take her there, release her bonds, and lock the door behind you. Take care she doesn't make a dash for the exit. Or try to woo you into lowering your guard. She has a gift for deception."

The captain said, "Yes, Lord." He sounded wooden, stolid, the way a man would who understood that Koshkin considered him incompetent.

"Not yet." Koshkin raised his right hand, signaling the man to wait, then crossed the room and gripped my chin with his left. Forced to meet his eyes, I glared defiance at him.

"You will change into clothes suitable for my wife," he said, his voice colder than the ice outside. "Your maid will burn this monstrosity you're wearing, and once you convince me that you're willing to resume your place in my household, I will consider allowing you to do just that. But make no mistake. Julian Ossolinski and the Lady Juliana are both dead to the world. You are my wife, Roxelana. Don't forget it, or I'll keep you shut up for the rest of your life."

"You can't force me to live as your wife," I said with as much bravado as I could muster. But beneath the anger, fear clutched my chest and set my knees to trembling. Although a better fate than the one I'd anticipated during that infernal ride here, it was not *much* better. Because I knew Koshkin had every right, according to the laws of this land, to confine me in his house for as long as he liked. To use me however he liked. The priests might protest, if I could reach one, but by then it would be too late.

I couldn't bear to return to my childhood, when I lived locked away from the world, at the mercy of one master after another, raped night after night, my sobs and screams ignored or punished with fists and the whip. By shutting my memories away, cutting myself off from my feelings about what was happening, I had managed to survive those early years, then my more recent captivity by Prince Ilya Shuisky and his nightly attacks. I had endured the years between, even if my inability to experience passion had lost me Alexei's love. Which had in turn destroyed my friendship with Felix.

I couldn't go through that again. I *would* not go through it. I would kill myself first. Or better, my husband.

Neither Alexei nor Felix knew where I was. No one would speak for me. I was alone, as I had been since the moment my father sold me. The Russians wouldn't lift so much as an eyebrow to secure my release from my husband's house. I couldn't even finish my commission for Queen Bona unless I regained my freedom without sacrificing my masquerade.

I had suffered low moments in the past. But as the Russian captain and his men shoved me ahead of them up the stairs and into the room selected as my prison, I felt that I'd plunged into the abyss.

The guards departed, leaving me unbound but barred from escape. Trying to make the best of a terrible situation, I checked the clothes set out for me and found them acceptable. I wasted no time, changing my man's outfit for the more enveloping women's robes typical of the Muscovite style. No need to give Koshkin reason to stare at my legs or my rear end, a sight that seemed likely to arouse him. I combed my short hair and covered it with veil and headdress, but I ignored the pots of cosmetics. Let every pockmark do its work of repelling my unwanted spouse, unimpeded by thick white powder and rouge.

Once suitably covered, I went straight for the bowls of food and drink. I sipped rather than gulped to prolong the pleasure of sating my hunger after so long. Once done, I wrinkled my nose at the empty bowls. In dire straits, I shouldn't have an appetite, should I? Only the reality of disaster somehow caused less anxiety than the prospect of it, and I had gone too long without food. If my husband read something into my willingness to eat that I didn't intend, let him.

Fed and clothed, I conducted a thorough survey of my luxuriant painted cell. I found books and a lute that I remembered from before my arrest almost five years ago, although I had no interest in playing music right then and doubted I could focus my mind on prose—or even poetry. I explored the drawers in the dresser and opened the room's one chest but found nothing but a chamber pot. I checked the door and discovered it was in fact bolted from the outside. No key that I might push from the lock, however small the chance that I might then find a way to drag it under the smoothly fitting door frame.

I didn't bother to tap the walls for loose panels or hidden entryways; I knew Fyodor Koshkin too well to believe he would leave open such an obvious means of escape. He had, after all, picked a room lit by windows with small, square, yellowed panes inside an iron setting, as if he could imagine me punching them out one by one, wresting the setting from its frame, then dropping three stories straight down to the courtyard below.

Thwarted, I retreated to the mattress on the floor and pondered my situation. I was in trouble. Big trouble. The Muscovites *should* advise the ambassadors before arresting one of their party. I had no reason to think, though, that any official other than Koshkin himself had played a part in bringing me to his house. Most likely he wanted to punish me for staying abroad these last five years, although this could be an ill-advised attempt to lure me back to his side.

That left Alexei, who had no reason to intervene between a husband and wife. None of the other Poles or Russians had any incentive whatsoever to exert himself on my behalf.

Not since I'd quarreled with Felix last night. So much for his vow to protect me.

I was lost indeed. Realizing the full extent of my predicament, I burst into tears.

Chapter Twelve

SOMETIME LATER—I HAD NO IDEA HOW LONG—I LAY ON MY back, staring at the painted ceiling, where improbable birds flitted among large, sweeping roses and peonies with more foliage than ever seen on a living plant. Only the damp cloth next to my cheek and (I assumed) streaks on my face attested to the recent bout of tears. With luck, Koshkin would find me blotchy as well as pockmarked and would realize for himself that I was no longer the woman for whom he yearned.

How was he different, really, from the masters who had made my childhood hideous? Kinder, perhaps, so long as he got what he wanted. But the security I'd traded my freedom to attain hadn't lasted six months. At the time, I hadn't understood the price he'd exacted: in my mind every man wanted a woman to fulfill his fantasies and make no demands of her own. Only in Vilnius and Cracow had I realized that was not always so.

Even now, I struggled to remember that some men valued traits other than a desire to please. Not many, to be sure. Felix, or so he said. Alexei, it seemed, since he loved his hot-tempered Maria. The rest of the men in his family, every one of whom had married a strong-minded and outspoken woman. King Sigismund the Old, because Queen Bona definitely had a mind of her own, yet he seemed to care for her. I could think of few others.

I understood why I'd made Fyodor angry. He must think I'd reneged on our bargain, and he was right. But it had been a bad bargain to begin with. Renewing it on his terms wouldn't make it better. Not for me, in any case.

But how to convince him of that? Here I lay—the supposed mistress of manipulation, calculation, and seduction—staring at a ridiculously verdant ceiling without a useful thought in my head except to request a visit from Father Spiridon, or whoever the current Koshkin family chaplain might be. The priest wouldn't demand my release, because he owed his livelihood to my husband, but he might put enough fear of God into Fyodor to prevent a descent from verbal to physical persuasion.

That last possibility made me shiver in the overheated room. The ogre who haunted my nightmares flashed briefly before my eyes, and I curled into a ball on the pallet, hugging my knees with my arms.

I had to think of something. If I didn't send for him, promising submission, Fyodor would seek me out. When that happened, I needed a plan.

Sure enough, Fyodor appeared not long after a surly maidservant whom I didn't recognize from my time as mistress of the Koshkin household had removed my empty food bowls and left a clay jug of fresh water. The maid had resisted any attempts at conversation, so I couldn't be certain what time of day it was. The yellowed panes allowed enough dim light to penetrate that I could perceive shapes, identify visitors, strum the lute, and—with the aid of a lantern that so far remained unlit—read, write, or draw. They didn't permit swift analysis of the weather outside or the time of day. Sometime in the afternoon, I guessed.

I sprang to my feet when my husband entered, eager that he not put me at a disadvantage. At least he didn't tower over me like Alexei or King Sigismund Augustus, but I didn't want to confront him while gazing straight at his thighs. I held my hands clenched at my sides, trying to look as warlike as possible. The amusement on his face suggested I hadn't succeeded.

"Much better," he said in tones of approbation. I assumed he referred to my women's clothing. I didn't give him the satisfaction of asking for an explanation.

He didn't so much as blink at my lack of response. "Use the cosmetics as well next time," he said. "The marks aren't that bad. A little paint, and you may resemble the woman I married."

The very thing I sought to avoid. "I need to send a message to the Polish ambassadors," I said in the firmest tone I could muster. Recalling my lessons with Felix, I stared straight into my husband's eyes and left no opportunity for him to interrupt or question my sincerity. Keeping my voice from shaking took more effort, but I managed that too. "Arresting an envoy without authorization or notification could undermine the negotiations, don't you think?"

Fyodor shrugged. "Suppose it does? I handle security. The diplomats do the talking. If the Poles want peace, fussing over the misbehavior of one inquisitive boy will hardly deter them."

I narrowed my eyes at him. He handled security. *As in listening devices?*

Obviously I couldn't ask him outright. If he didn't double up laughing at my stupidity, he'd lie through his proverbial teeth. But it made so much more sense that my shifty, unscrupulous husband would have found a way to listen at keyholes than to ascribe such a plan to Alexei and his Tatars, known for their straightforward and unsubtle—not to say singleminded—approach to extracting information.

I set the thought aside for later consideration. "Then let me speak to Father Spiridon," I said. "Have you no concern for my immortal soul?"

He did laugh, then—not an outright guffaw but a dismissive chuckle. "You, concerned for your immortal soul? Besides, didn't you tell me you became a Catholic? What could Father Spiridon do for you, other than persuade you to give up your heretic ways?"

When I didn't respond, he came close enough that I could smell onion on his breath and stroked my pockmarked cheek. When I flinched and twisted away, he grabbed my right arm above the elbow and snarled. "I'm your husband, dammit. If I want to touch you, I will."

I dragged my arm free. "You won't! What kind of bully are you? For shame! After you boasted about being a cultured man!"

"And you swore to remain a willing wife! What happened to your 'dearest' and your smiles? The days when you yielded to me willingly?" The anger on his face made me flinch.

I wriggled inwardly, suppressing any outward show of discomfort. I refused to give him what he wanted, but enraging him further also would not serve. "You left me, Fyodor," I reminded him. "I've told you that before. I know you believe I broke our bargain, but so did you. You broke it first, in fact. I don't trust you anymore. Give me the divorce and let me go."

"Trust can be rebuilt," he said. "I've regained my position at court. I have the support of the Shuisky clan and the friendship of the Belsky clan. I can offer you a good life."

I sighed. How to explain to him that his definition of a good life no longer suited me? That I had never loved him or even desired him? He wouldn't believe me—or if he did, most likely, he would do something worse in an attempt to persuade or punish me. I didn't want to think about what forms his revenge might take.

I shook my head. "You betrayed my trust, Fyodor. I don't want amends. What's the point of living with a woman who hates you? Give me the divorce. I'll go back to Poland and not trouble you again."

"Never." He bared his teeth, giving him the look of a rabid dog, then turned and stalked from the room before I had fully absorbed what he'd said. I heard the bolt slam into place, and I was alone once more.

Despite exhaustion caused by my inability to sleep the night before due to rage and cold, heightened by hours filled with wild swings between despair to fear and hope to despair, I fought to keep my eyes open as evening—or what

I thought must be evening—approached. The surly maid arrived with a tinder box for the lantern and supper but no more conversation than during her last visit, leading me to wonder if Fyodor had chosen her because she couldn't hear and therefore could resist suborning by me. I forced myself to eat, because I would need strength to fight my husband and, if possible, escape. But every time my head nodded against my chest, anxiety jerked it upward again. Even when I lay down and did my best to convince myself that Fyodor had not shown any previous tendency to indulge in physical attacks, whatever he threatened, my tired brain refused to concede.

I missed Felix. For most of the last two months we had spent much of our time together, and I'd become accustomed to his presence nearby during the night. I'd spent the last ten days sleeping in his arms or right next to him, and he'd helped me with the nightmares. His tendency to jealousy troubled me—I'd already endured that with Koshkin and had no desire to repeat the experience. But when not jealous, Felix was a charming and reliable companion, a man who valued me for my thoughts and interests more than my face, who pushed me to become my best and most outspoken self. Could he not understand—or be convinced—that I valued him for more than physical perfection as well?

At last I must have fallen asleep, because I tumbled into the ogre nightmare again, but not as I had experienced it so often through the years.

I lay curled on a soft mattress in a room lined with white tiles decorated in swirls of blue and gold. Carpets spread over the floors and covered the mattress beneath me. My long, straight hair fell unbound about my childish shape—breasts as yet barely budding, waist the slightest of indentations—revealed by swirls of gauze. I couldn't move, because I was paralyzed with terror. I waited, still as a mouse glimpsing a cat's pointed ears outlined against the edge of its hole. The door, cracked ajar, would open, and disaster would stride in. I couldn't prevent it. I couldn't elude it. The end of the world lay at hand.

I whimpered, pleading silently for my mother to rescue me, but she was far away and didn't care. Had never cared. I saw that now. She used to sing to me, a haunting lullaby that I could hear reverberating in my mind, the words soft and filled with love. But her protestations of affection rang hollow. When I needed her, she didn't defend me. Not when my father forced her to weigh my welfare against the health and happiness of her sons.

One lamp stood in a corner by the door, emitting a soft light. The rest of the room lay in darkness, which wrapped around me like a shroud. I sank into it, wishing I could disappear, but however far I fell the light from the lamp kept the night at bay.

As I lay there, unable to move, the inlaid wooden door opened—slowly, like water flowing down a window. I couldn't breathe. I squeezed my eyes tight shut, but not in time. I had seen the ogre limned against the room beyond, seen it bend to retrieve the lamp, which it raised to survey me. My throat hurt as I heard its monster steps shuffle across the room. I wanted to run, but my arms and legs pressed heavy against the mattress. I knew my last hour had come, although I was not yet twelve years old.

"Look at me," the ogre said in a gruff voice. But I lacked the strength to lift my lids. Tears ran from my eyes as I felt the monstrous hand push the gauze away, felt the warmth of

the lamp pass over my quivering skin. The ogre fell on me, and I screamed, but his mouth covered mine and no sound came out.

Then he devoured me, and I died.

I came to. At first the paralysis of the dream lingered, because I wasn't quite awake, but soon I managed to curl back into the position of an unborn infant and pull the covers over my head. I had endured that dream more times than I could count, and its clarity had always set it apart from the normal type of dream that Felix had described and I had also experienced, but the depth of detail and the immediacy were new. Nor had it ever reached the endpoint before. I shook until you'd have thought me a reed in a gale, wave after wave of tremors I couldn't control. I felt sick to my stomach; my throat ached; I couldn't bear the thought of returning to sleep.

As the trembling abated and my strength returned, I rolled into a sitting position and gripped my forehead with both hands. Only then, thinking back over the dream—still clear as a storybook and twice as terrifying—did it occur to me that I recognized the room, and even the ogre, despite not having seen his face. I knew the song my mother sang. I'd heard the man's gruff voice before. I remembered those tiles. Despite the dark, I could identify the color of the gauze, a soft rose pink. That evil man, my first master, had chosen it to mark the moment when he would deflower me. The pink was a parody of my true name: not Juliana, not Roxelana, but the name my mother had given me: Nasrin, the Wild Rose.

Five years he had supported me without any return, he said, and he would wait no longer. Although not a woman yet, I would become one soon enough. And if I didn't want his attentions—but I was a child, so how did I know whether I wanted them or not, or even what he had in mind?—I should not have become so beautiful, he told me.

My face. Always my face. Since birth it had been my greatest asset and my greatest liability. I accepted then that the damage done by smallpox, which even Fyodor described as not so bad, might be as much a blessing as a disaster.

Because the ogre was not a dream. He was a memory. A memory of the fate into which my father had sold me, his only daughter, at the tender age of six. And to which my mother, although she often claimed to love me, had abandoned me. Families need sons, not daughters—thus my mother had taught me—and she'd sent me away at six because she, like every other mother in Chorasan, expected to relinquish me soon anyway. Daughters are mouths to feed, raised for the benefit of other families and sent off to their new homes as soon as possible so that they can, God willing, produce sons of their own. And given the poverty in which my parents lived, she might have convinced herself that my father did me a favor: I would live as a concubine, but I would not want for food or clothes.

I had heard the message my whole life. In that moment I grasped how it had warped my mother, who in turn warped me.

The one object I didn't see in the dream was the broken rose. But after a while I understood that as well. *I* was the broken rose, which symbolized that past I had almost forgotten, because so virginal a name had no place in the life I had constructed at such great effort to conceal the chasm left by the loss of my true self. The loss of Nasrin, the Wild Rose.

I understood, but I did not forgive. Instead, I wept a long time for Nasrin—dead at the age of eleven, replaced by the slave Roxelana, who had learned so well how to please and obey that even her eventual husband couldn't tell the difference between the fantasy and the woman beneath it.

Assuming there was a woman beneath, that any of Nasrin remained. Assuming I remembered who Nasrin was.

I wasn't sure that I did—remember, that is. How formed is a child of eleven at the best of times, especially one raised in conditions of such terrible poverty and degradation, despised for no other reason than being born female, valued for nothing but the money her parents might get in return for finding a rich older man to prey on her beauty? There might be nothing left to discover.

Yet as my tears lessened, I made a vow to myself. However small the seedling of my true self, I would nurture it. I would not submit to Fyodor's demands. I would find a way to escape. If it took the rest of my life, I would free myself of Roxelana forever. One day, if I was lucky, I would find a man who could love Nasrin. And if no such man existed, I would live the rest of my life alone.

Chapter Thirteen

MY FIRST SIGN THAT SOMETHING HAD CHANGED CAME FOUR days after my capture. To occupy myself, I strummed my lute, singing every melancholy Italian ballad I knew. I'd begun setting my Persian poetry to music, starting with the poem by Hafiz I had quoted to Felix that day in the carriage after we left Sandomierz. By working on ten lines at a time between each breakfast and supper, I could keep track of the passing days.

By then I had given up hope that anyone outside Koshkin's house knew where I was or cared. The woman who brought me food and water, removed my chamberpot and returned it cleaned, substituted fresh linen for dirtied, and in general took care of my body's needs clearly either suffered from deafness or produced an excellent imitation of it. I had ruled out any chance of talking her into helping me, but that didn't stop me from scheming.

Each time Fyodor made one of his periodic attempts to undermine my will, which he did at least twice a day, I had to fight the temptation to give in to his demands long enough to lull him into a false sense of security. I'd lived that way for years, after all, so what did a few more weeks matter? But hard as I tried to convince myself that deceiving him, if I had no other feasible course of action, wouldn't kill the tiny seedling of a new person growing in my heart, I still hesitated. What had made sense as a child, when I had no option but to submit, repelled me after five years in relative freedom and several months as Felix's friend. Even if Felix no longer felt his self-proclaimed attachment to me. Even if his silence meant that he never had.

When I first heard the voice it was, by my calculations, mid-morning, because the deaf maid had carried off my empty bowls some time ago. I was sitting on the pallet that constituted my only resting place, pondering the disagreeable possibilities I faced for the umpteenth time, when a woman spoke in the hallway, not far from my door. "What about this one? I don't think anyone has used it for years. It would be a perfect place to keep a set of armor outgrown by a child—or any other household goods of that sort."

I startled at the sound. The voice, a beautiful clear soprano speaking Russian, caused my ears to perk like a cat's. I recognized it at once as belonging to my stepdaughter Maria, my husband's oldest child and therefore not more than two years younger than I.

What brought her here? Can I use her to make my escape?

I cried out, as loudly as I could, and heard her quick response. "What's going on in there? Have you shut someone up inside?"

"An insane maid." Another voice, also familiar, deep and male. Not my husband but his steward, Dimka, who had once taken orders from me. "Come away, Tsarevna Maria. You'll not find your brother's armor in there."

"He's lying, Maria," I called. "It is I, Roxelana."

"Poor thing," Dimka said, his false sympathy giving his tone a rough edge. "Thinks she's the former mistress. Otherwise we could let her roam free as a holy fool. Can't stand by while she casts dishonor on your clan among the townsfolk, though, can we?"

How could he? He'd served me well as steward, always treated me with respect. I'd never have believed he could play me false like this.

In truth, I'd never thought he had the brains for deception. Shows how wrong a person can be.

"I suppose not," Maria said. "Very well, we'll look somewhere else. Perhaps it's downstairs after all. You go on ahead, and I'll make a quick check of the other rooms up here before joining you. It can't take much longer. We've searched everywhere else. Tell my escort to saddle Kumai and meet me as we arranged."

I slumped to the floor, keening, as the tap-tap of her heels against the wood marked her retreat.

So I was completely unprepared when, in less time than it takes for a parched man to gulp down a cup of water, I heard the bolt draw back and the door swing open. I looked up to see Maria standing in front of me with a long, dark hooded cloak. She ran forward and threw the cloak around my shoulders. "Get up," she said, speaking barely above a whisper. "We haven't much time."

I stumbled to my feet, befuddled as if I'd drunk an entire day's ration of ale in one swallow, and clutched the cloak around my neck. "Where are you taking me?" I stammered. "What's going on?"

She grabbed my upper arm and pulled. "Just come. I'll explain later. And don't talk. We're going down the back stairs as fast as we can." She tugged me from the room, pulled the door closed behind us, and slammed the bolt into place. "We have to get you out of here before Dimka wonders where I went."

I shook my head, not in denial but in confusion.

She answered by tugging at me again. "Come," she repeated. "We have no time to lose."

I went. Thoughts pummeled my brain so fast I couldn't have spoken if I tried, and I certainly didn't want to get in the way of my own escape, if that's what it was. Why Maria had come, what she intended, where we were going, and how she expected to get away with the whatever it was—let alone why she might want to help me when we'd seldom gotten along without spats and insults—remained a mystery. But if it meant even the smallest chance of my getting out of my husband's house without having to submit to his carnal desires, I would run halfway to Cathay without making so much as a peep.

We had a brief scare halfway down. Maria hauled me into a window embrasure and stood in front of me as we listened, doing our best not to breathe, to Dimka hauling his ponderous bulk along a passageway one floor below. Then a door creaked open before closing again. The sound of Dimka's tromping feet quieted, and Maria and I were running again, light as house spirits down the stairs. I realized she must have removed her shoes, because the heels no longer clacked. I wore soft slippers, since in Koshkin's view I had not earned the right to leave my room. So only the soft hush of cloth-bound feet and silk skirts disturbed the silence.

We reached the outer door, and she flung it open. Outside, a Tatar warrior waited on horseback. An inexplicable fear pinned my feet to the floor and set my heart racing until I took another look and realized I'd seen him before. He was the man who'd escorted us diplomats to the Kremlin.

"Mansur," Maria said in Tatar as the man rode to meet us. "Take my stepmother back to our house." She pointed to her right. "Go out that way and circle around the estate walls. Watch for my father on the streets; he must not see her with you. And move fast. The sultan is counting on you to succeed. I'll meet the rest of your men in the courtyard, as agreed, as soon as I complete my task. Kumai is saddled and ready?"

When he nodded, she replaced her shoes, turned on her heel, and walked at a rapid pace into the house. Mansur leaned sideways in his saddle, hauled me up in front of him, and before I even realized the horse was moving—and at top speed—we were in the Moscow streets. I pulled the hood closer around my face, but the crowd scattered before the galloping roan, and no one spared me a glance.

Maria had saved me. I didn't know why, and I had no idea what to expect. Yet my heart glowed with gratitude.

I hadn't been abandoned. Someone in Moscow cared about me. Someone, somewhere, was worthy of my trust.

Mansur lowered me from the horse onto the bottom step of an outside staircase and rode off with no more than a wave of his hand in acknowledgment of the profuse thanks I poured on him.

He hadn't said where we were, and I didn't recognize anything except for the general outline of a Russian noble estate and a wooden building at the other side of the yard that in its decoration resembled a Muslim prayer hall. But Maria had told Mansur to bring me to her house, so this must be it. I'd never visited, because her marriage to Alexei upset me, so I refused to call on them for several months. Then my husband fled, and the grand prince's troops arrested me, and I went straight from captivity to Lithuania, then on to Cracow. There I remained until a fit of insanity, combined with the desire to help Queen Bona and attain my own dearest goal, sent me back to Muscovy.

However, I would find no answers in the courtyard, so I lifted my trailing skirts in one hand and climbed the staircase. At the top I hesitated. Where to go from here?

A chill breeze from below sent me through the door and into another world. If the exterior of the house differed little from Koshkin's, the interior looked like nothing so much as Alexei's palace in Crimea, where I lived for two years while he roamed the steppe in service to his renegade lord. From the inlaid wood on the doors to the sparkling glass window panes with their intricate colored patterns, everything I saw flooded my heart with waves of nostalgia. I'd forgotten the beauty of Islamic decor, its exquisite lines and proportions, the comfort of cushioned sofas and rooms heated with clay pipes. Even the glories of Wawel Castle couldn't compare.

A plump woman in servants' dress—about my height but, I guessed, close to twice my age—appeared at the end of the passageway where I stood. "May I help you, Lady?" she asked in Tatar. "I am Tanya, Tsarevna Maria's housekeeper." I must have looked puzzled—although I understood her well enough, I had yet to grasp the reasons behind my change of fortune—because she repeated the whole thing in Russian. Her name and the perfection of her accent told me that *she* was Russian, but no one I'd known at Koshkin's house. How she came to be serving the son and daughter-in-law of a Tatar khan remained a mystery.

I didn't ask. I had more important concerns. "Tsarevna Maria sent me here," I said in Tatar. "I am Lady Juliana. She will join us soon, she said. Please show me where to wait for her."

Tanya had no chance to reply before a door halfway down on the right opened as if under its own power and Felix said in Polish, "Juliana? By the rood, where have you been? We thought you held captive these four days by your villain of a husband!"

I had never heard him sound so astonished. You'd have thought I'd materialized from the nether regions in response to a chanted spell.

"Never mind," I said to Tanya. "I'll wait with Lord Ossolinski. Be so good as to tell the tsarevna where to find me." I left her in mid-bow and crossed the short distance between Felix and myself as fast as I could. When I reached the door, I slipped past him without touching him and stopped in the middle of the room. Only after I heard the door close did I turn. Anger gripped me, mixed with the mingled fear and sorrow that had made my days confined at Koshkin's estate so hideous. But his presence there in Maria and Alexei's house, his obvious amazement, his words—none of it made sense, just as Maria's unexpected assistance, welcome as it was, made no sense.

"I *was* held captive by my villain of a husband," I said. I had no idea which of my roiling emotions had worked its way into my voice, although I heard a certain gritty edge that suggested rage had won. "If you could deduce that, why did you leave me in his power for so long? I told you he would grab me if he saw an opportunity. Didn't you care that the only reason he refrained from forcing himself on me was because he hoped I'd submit of my own free will? I couldn't leave. He locked me in an upstairs room, and except when he stopped by for another round of persuasion, I saw no one except a deaf maid. I even heard his steward announcing that I was an insane servant who thought she was his wife!"

The injustice I'd suffered brought tears to my eyes, and I blinked them back angrily. But Felix must have seen them, because he left the doorway and put his arms around me. I resisted for the space of a few breaths before his murmured reassurances and warm hug overwhelmed my indignation and I sobbed against his shoulder.

"Sweetheart, I'm so sorry," he said. "For everything, starting with my behavior the night before your husband's men came for you. I swear I'll conquer my jealousy. As for why we left you there, it took a while to figure out where they'd taken you. And *who* had taken you, for that matter. At first we thought it was an official arrest. That's how your husband's men presented it to the guards. For spying, no less—pretty bold, given their treatment of us. But when Tsarevich Alexei's inquiries went nowhere, we guessed Koshkin must have you. We've been determined to find you, but we had to make sure we were looking in the right place. Tsarevna Maria went off to question her father and his servants, but her husband and I expected her to come back and share what she'd learned. We always intended to come after you. I didn't expect to see you right in front of me, that's all." He led me to the nearest sofa and pulled me down beside him. When I sat, he produced a handkerchief from somewhere and dabbed at my cheeks. "I'm delighted, of course. How did you get away?"

"Maria," I said, hiccuping. "I have no idea what's going on. I stared at her like a looby when she threw open the door. Next thing I knew, she'd flung this cloak around my shoulders and dragged me down the servants' stairs. Mansur was waiting at the door, and he hauled me onto his horse and galloped through the streets like a madman while artisans and peasants fled for their lives. I couldn't wait to get out of that house, but I'd given up hope. And what are you doing here?"

"When I got up that morning and couldn't find you," Felix said, "I went to question the guards. The captain was nowhere to be seen—I discovered later that he came here to make his report, and quite apprehensive he was, too, for having lost track of you—but one of the other men told me the court bailiffs had arrested you for spying. I went to the ambassadors and demanded they investigate, but even though they promised to look into it, I didn't get the impression they were taking the issue seriously. I couldn't explain to them that you were a woman and letting you be taken into custody would put you in much greater danger than if you were a man, so when I couldn't persuade them to act quickly, I decided to approach the one other person in Moscow who would understand the gravity of the situation."

"Alexei," I said. Of course, I should have figured that out myself. I hadn't—why? Because my brain was muddled, for starters. But also because I'd sensed the tension between Felix and Alexei. It must have cost Felix a lot to swallow his pride enough to seek his adversary's help.

"Yes," Felix confirmed. "I talked to the guards, and one of them brought me here."

The news warmed my heart, because why would he have made that gesture if not out of affection for me? "Thank you." I took his hand in both of mine and kissed his cheek. "I felt so abandoned in Koshkin's house. I had no idea the three of you were trying to free me." I shivered. "It was terrible there. I was scared the whole time."

He caressed my face with his thumb, and I shuddered, remembering Fyodor doing the same. It had felt much different, though. I pressed my cheek against his hand, banishing the memory of my unwanted husband. I still couldn't quite bring myself to believe I'd escaped.

A rush of footsteps and the sound of mingled male and female voices gave way in short order to Maria and Alexei in the flesh. She was flushed and triumphant, her brown eyes sparkling; his frowning brows signaled irritation or concern, but his expression cleared as he caught sight of Felix and me together on the sofa. "You're safe," Alexei said. "I'm glad."

"What happened, Tsarevna Maria?" Felix pulled his hands from mine and rose, balancing himself with the cane as he bowed to her in greeting. "Words can't express my delight at Juliana's safe return, but I thought you were only going to confirm her presence in your father's house."

"Exactly what I was saying," Alexei put in. I decided that must explain his frown. He was upset that Maria had placed herself in danger. Felix's voice had the slightest edge to it as well, as if they assumed a woman couldn't perform a rescue as well as they.

Maria darted across the room in a swirl of silk skirts and kissed me on both cheeks, Russian-style. "How dreadful of Papa to do such a thing. And Dimka! What possessed him to tell that awful tale? Especially after I'd heard your voice. I could smack them both! You weren't harmed, I hope?"

From the earnest glance she sent my way I realized she had no illusions about either her father or what he'd wanted from me. "No," I told her. My voice trembled, which embarrassed me, but my whole body was trembling. Only then did I truly feel that I was safe or grasp the extent of the threat I'd so narrowly escaped. Because of Maria, who had risked incurring her father's anger to save me. "Thanks to you," I said.

"Yes, but why?" Alexei dipped his head toward me. "Don't misunderstand. As I said, I'm glad you're safe. And we would have freed you as soon as my wife returned." He frowned at Maria once more. "But we did agree that you would collect information and bring it to us, did we not? From your father, if possible, but mostly from the servants, as I recall. So that Lord Felix and I could confront Koshkin. That was the plan. Suppose your father had confined you too?"

Maria faced him, her hands clenched at her sides and an expression every bit as annoyed as his on her face. "You wouldn't ask your sister or your stepmother why," she said.

"Nor your sister-in-law. You'd take it for granted that if you sent them to help, they'd do whatever they deemed necessary. What makes me such an idiot that I can't think up a plan and carry it out? As it happens, I saw a chance to get Roxelana away, so I took it."

"Juliana," Felix said quietly. Among those present, he knew best the reaction my slave name evoked in me. And indeed, I'd been unable to repress a wince. Although I wouldn't have corrected the woman who'd saved me right at that moment, I sent him a look of gratitude. He responded with one of his heartfelt smiles.

Maria acknowledged his interjection with a nod. "Sorry. Juliana, of course."

Alexei ignored the byplay. Still scowling, he mirrored her pose. "The other women have nothing to do with this. We had an agreement. So stop trying to deflect me and answer the question. Suppose your father had caught you halfway through?"

"Papa wasn't there." Maria returned the scowl in full measure. "I made sure of that before I did anything. Then I told Dimka I wanted to borrow David's old chain mail, the set he had when he was five, for Alexander. We searched every storeroom in the house except the one where I knew it was kept. I guessed she'd be somewhere in the women's quarters, so when Dimka told me his ridiculous story about a mad girl in a locked room, I sent him downstairs and got her out. I'd already told Mansur to meet me at the back door if I sent a message instead of coming in person to order him to saddle Kumai. What was the point of leaving her to suffer so you could be the ones to rescue her? Assuming Papa would have meekly turned her over because you asked!"

She gave an angry shake, like a cat coming in from the rain, and turned to me. "Do you mind if I use your name? I promise I'll try to get it right. That whole stepmother nonsense seems even more absurd if you don't want to stay married to Papa."

I stood and hugged her. "I don't mind one bit. And whatever the men say, I'm more grateful to you than you can imagine." I released her and looked at Alexei, whose scowl had vanished in laughter. I wondered if the mention of his tempestuous sister, who would have not only engineered an escape but stormed the estate amid a hail of arrows, had sunk in, changing his mood, or whether the credit went to Maria herself. From the way he bent and kissed her temple, I guessed the latter.

"I'm allowed to worry about you, *kaderle*," he said.

Kaderle. It meant beloved, darling, sweetheart. I'd never heard him use that word before. Had never seen him so openly display emotion, in fact, except briefly on that evening in Smolensk.

In the warmth of Alexei's expression as he gazed at his wife, I saw again how much he cared for her. From the arrested look on Felix's face, I guessed he'd grasped that point too. That he might at last understand what I'd been trying to tell him since Smolensk.

And somewhat to my own surprise, I realized that the sight of my former lover and his wife together no longer hurt.

One day, I hoped, someone would love me that way. The real me, still a tendril, a plant unfurling in the sun. Perhaps Felix, if he could keep his oath to overcome his jealousy. He, after all, *did* call me "sweetheart."

A commotion sounded outside the door, and Maria said, "Oh, that will be the servant delivering the armor. After Mansur left with Rox—sorry, Juliana—I found it in the downstairs storeroom, exactly where I left it eight years ago." She wrinkled her nose at Alexei, but she was smiling. "I had to distract Dimka while they made their getaway."

She left the room, only to return almost at once with a chain mail coat and helmet about half as long and wide as those I'd seen on full-grown warriors. She held out the helmet to Alexei and hung the coat by its shoulders, measuring it against her own body. "It'll do quite nicely for Alexander, won't it?"

"Amazing," Alexei said. I didn't think he was talking about the armor.

"He's right," I told Maria. "You are amazing." I reached out a hand to Felix, who clasped it. "You too," I said. "If you hadn't asked them for help, I'd still be Koshkin's captive."

Felix raised my hand to his mouth and brushed his lips across the back, not a formal salute but a real embrace. "Sweetheart, after letting you fall into your husband's hands after promising I never would, asking Alexei and Maria for help was the absolute least I could do."

He gave Maria the benefit of his delightful smile, and she looked at us both and giggled. "We're both forever in your debt, Tsarevna," he told her.

"Oh, tosh," she said, waving the mail shirt. "You'd have found some way to rescue her if I hadn't come along."

Felix still held my hand. I squeezed his. "You're all marvelous," I said. "But would it be possible for me to speak with Felix in private for a bit?"

Chapter Fourteen

MARIA SHOWED US TO A ROOM THAT I GUESSED FROM THE vast array of books and papers must be Alexei's private sanctum. "I'll send Tanya to let you know when the midday meal is ready. You'll join us, won't you? I have an idea to propose."

Felix and I agreed with thanks, and she ushered us in and closed the door. I looked around, trying to decide where best to sit—and yes, what to say. Between my revelation about the dream, the hint Koshkin had dropped about his role in security, my experience in his house, and my observations at the ambassadorial dinner, which I'd never had a chance to relay to Felix, my problem wasn't a dearth of information but a deluge. Where to start?

The room reminded me of the library at Wawel Castle, despite the Islamic design. I selected a carpet-covered, padded bench near the window and extended my hand in invitation. "I missed you, Felix," I said when he sat next to me. "I was afraid you'd abandoned me to my fate. I'm sorry about my part in our quarrel, but I hope you see now that I told you the truth: Alexei loves Maria. And you know, I don't mind anymore. I'm happy for them, that they found each other. So no more jealousy, agreed?" I bent forward enough to kiss his cheek once more, and he caught me around the waist and turned his head so that our lips met. I wriggled closer and pressed against him, wrapping my arms loosely about his neck. It felt like the touch of sunshine in early spring.

"Yes, I did see that," he said after a while. He didn't let go of me, and I made no attempt to free myself. "And I swear, I'll learn to trust you when you tell me you don't care about my leg." He stroked my pockmarked cheek. "You trust me as well, all right?"

When I nodded, he added, "I missed you too. I was quite frantic, in truth, when I couldn't find you. Tell me what happened to you. Tell me everything."

I pulled back enough to concentrate on details, without the (otherwise welcome) distraction offered by Felix's closeness, before giving a short description of my captivity and Koshkin's demands that I return to him, his absolute refusal to consider a divorce. Then I related much of what I'd learned the last few days, including the information from the diplomatic dinner that I'd never had a chance to share. I didn't know how much time we had before Maria's Tanya returned, and the dream that was in fact a memory and my determination to nurture whatever remained of my childhood self were at once the most important and the most difficult things to talk about, because of the emotions they churned up whenever I thought about my past.

"I think we need to push our suspects into revealing their true natures," I said as I reached the end of my recital. "We've given them plenty of opportunity to incriminate themselves, and we still know little more than we did the day we left Sandomierz. Even Adam remains on our list, because we have only his word for it that he does act on behalf of King Sigismund Augustus. In retrospect, we should probably have sent a message to Cracow when he first told us what brought him here, but it would take too long to get an answer now."

"We didn't find out until Vyazma, but you have a point." Felix frowned at his clasped hands. "As for tricking the suspects into revealing themselves, I agree with you that it's a good idea. Easier said than done, though. Perhaps we could manipulate Lev Glinsky somehow? I'd need to give some thought to how best to do that. Bogdan I believe to be innocent—indeed, he may suspect me, given the way he leashed himself to my side throughout the ambassadorial dinner. The others have expressed suitable shock at your arrest, but not in a way that clarifies their own involvement. 'I wondered what possessed the king to assign him to this mission, and now I know' and 'I didn't think him capable of spying' mark the limits of their reaction."

I studied an exquisite porcelain vase in a corner, considering what Felix had said and struggling to pin down my vague sense that our four suspects might respond to pressure and, if so, what kind. I thought Felix was probably right about Bogdan, since the other three had at least chatted with Russians at the dinner, whereas Bogdan hadn't left Felix's side. But the test, if it worked as designed (and if I could in truth design it), would show his innocence at the same time as it confirmed the real traitor's guilt.

I had yet to settle on so much as a suggestion to share with Felix when Tanya pushed the door ajar and announced that she was ready to serve the midday meal. As we followed her out, I admitted to a certain curiosity as to what Maria would propose.

If today had done nothing else, it had revealed the extent of my stepdaughter's intelligence, kindness of heart, and abilities.

Meanwhile, telling Felix about the dream and my childhood self must wait.

Tanya stood back to usher us into the room. More than an hour had passed since my arrival in the house, and I could feel myself relax. Based on Tanya's message, I'd expected to see the meal laid out, but instead Maria's sister Lyuba, now eleven, arrived from the nursery with four-year-old Alexander, clad in armor that he refused to remove. Behind them came a nursemaid bearing his two-year-old sister, Dosya, who headed straight for her father's lap, where she ensconced herself like a queen on her throne.

Again I saw a side of Alexei that I hadn't imagined existed. Warrior, lover, leader—yes. But devoted husband and doting father? I dimly remembered that he had a son in the horde now ruled by his younger brother, a son he'd abandoned when he left for Crimea with me. I didn't see the boy here, but he must have reached the age for fostering. That was the usual custom for Tatar khans and sultans beginning at the age of twelve, and the boy, as I recalled, had been about six in 1534.

I decided not to ask. If Alexei had in fact never reclaimed his son, I could only create unpleasantness at a time when I wanted to do exactly the opposite.

Lyuba at first gave me a wide berth, I noticed with a flash of remorse. I'd treated her more sternly than I should have when I first married, because the sight of her reminded me of how different my life had been at six. But watching her interact with Alexander and Dosya, I sensed a sweetness of temper in her that I'd missed before.

A pretty redhead, not tousled as she'd so often been when younger, Lyuba had an innocent fire that fit my memories of Nasrin, the childhood self I sought to revive. She carried a small book that, when I questioned her, turned out to contain *The Conference of Birds*, as exquisite in its miniatures as the copy I'd found at Wawel Castle. On the frontispiece it bore the signature "Timur," the name of Alexei's older son. So it seemed that a reunion had taken place after all.

I asked Lyuba, who said, "Yes, Timur lives with his uncle, learning to become a khan. We see him sometimes." A wistful expression dimmed her gray-green eyes.

"You miss him," I said.

She turned a startled face to me, as if she hadn't expected kindness or understanding, intensifying my regrets over my past curtness toward her. "I do," she said. "Alexander and Dosya are too young to ride or read or talk with me, although it's fun to tell them stories. I like that."

"I like stories, too." I pointed to *The Conference of Birds*. "This book is my favorite."

After that, we got along beautifully, trading lines and swapping tales and exclaiming over the pictures while Maria watched from the other side of the room like an indulgent parent when not being called to admire Alexander's chain mail shirt and helmet.

From the large embroidery frame in one corner, I guessed this must be the room where Maria sewed. She had always demonstrated an extraordinary skill at embroidery, and the frame held what looked like a dress for Dosya, delicate leaves and flowers embroidered in white against a silken background the color of ripe lemons. I couldn't begin to match her achievements with a needle, but my artistic nature rejoiced at the beauty of her work.

When the children left, the capable Tanya chivvied the lesser servants into setting up a linen-draped table at the far side of the room, topped with covered dishes and brass jugs emitting fragrant steam. Felix and I sat on one side, with Maria and Alexei on the other, and the four of us alternated between conversation and a midday meal that provoked almost as much nostalgia as the house. Stews and fried turnovers, whitefish fillets dipped in batter and sautéed, noodles and pelmeni: although I could see that the cooks had adjusted their offerings for Lent, the differences had more to do with the emphasis on fish than spicing or presentation. Again I felt as if I were back in Crimea.

We had no sooner settled at the table than Maria suggested that for the moment I should stay with her and Alexei while Felix returned to the house where the ambassadors lodged and continued to press them to pursue official inquiries into the fate of his missing cousin.

"There's a danger," Alexei told him, "that Koshkin will order your arrest as well. He's completely unscrupulous when it comes to getting what he wants. If he comes here, I can protect Juliana, but he may seek to force my hand by other means. I've warned my captain to prepare for such a move, so if it happens, shout for my guards. If that fails, don't risk further injury to yourself. Go with his men, and we'll find a way to free you."

"Felix, you can't." I refrained from gesturing at his leg or the cane, a reminder that would convey implicit disrespect. "We still don't know ..."

About to mention our four suspects and the visits of the questionable Lev Glinsky, I stopped. Since my husband's admission that he controlled security, I no longer believed that Alexei had anything to do with the listening devices in the ambassadors' residence, but I as yet had no *proof* that Koshkin bore full responsibility. And even without that, Alexei served the Russians. "Why not stay here as well?" I asked instead.

Belatedly I recalled it was not my house. I raised my hand in apology to my hosts. "If Maria and Alexei permit, that is."

Alexei regarded me through narrowed eyes. It didn't take a genius to guess that he knew why I'd hurtled to a stop mid-sentence. Annoying as he could be on occasion, he was never slow. "You are, of course, welcome to stay," he told Felix. "But I find myself curious as to what you and Juliana don't know that she fears will endanger you."

Faced with two evils, I chose the less problematic admission. He might even confirm it, which would help our investigation. "Someone on your side has been spying on the envoys," I said. "King Sigismund and Queen Bona believed they had a traitor in their ranks, but I found cleverly designed vents in some of the storerooms that allowed people to overhear what was said in the conference rooms above. Including the bedroom where Felix and I sleep, because it's a converted meeting place."

I took a deep breath. Alexei stared at me with a stunned expression on his face, although he hadn't denied the possibility. Felix regarded me more with a look of horror. Maria raised both delicate eyebrows. "Although Koshkin spent most of his time trying to persuade me to withdraw my request for a divorce," I said, "he did mention early on that he was in charge of security. Listening devices seem like the kind of scheme he would develop. But I don't have proof of that, and we don't know how vulnerable we are. That's what I started to say before I realized it might not be wise to share my discovery, even with you."

Alexei still watched me with that steady gaze. "Hmm," he said. "I wonder if that *is* what you started to say. Somehow I think not. But your suppositions about your husband are correct. It was his men who reported the content of your conversation with Lord Felix, although they didn't bother to mention how they obtained that information. I've heard of such devices, but not in connection with the ambassadors' residence."

He didn't say where, and I decided I'd better not ask. He and Maria had gone out of their way to help me, including inviting me to stay in their house. Nor was he pressuring me to admit what I'd really meant, which I appreciated, since I had no intention of confiding that Felix and I thought King Sigismund and Queen Bona might be right about one of their envoys being a traitor, even if it had nothing to do with the listening devices.

Instead, I extended my hand to Felix. "Please, won't you stay here? At least for a few days while we work out how to counteract any attempts by Koshkin to exact revenge for my escape?"

Alas, it didn't surprise me when Felix shook his head. "Better that I return as expected. It makes it less likely that your husband will connect your disappearance with his daughter's visit. Based on what you told me about his regular attempts to persuade you to change your mind, at most we can expect to have a few hours before he discovers you're missing. I'm sure Tsarevich Alexei can protect you as he says"—he sounded not in the least sure—"but any secret is safer if those who want to discover it don't suspect its existence." He hesitated, then added, "The ambassadors would question my absence, too. I still have a mission to perform."

He was right. He did have a mission to perform. As did I. For a moment I fought the sense that I should go with him. But if I did, he would have to defend me as well as himself, and I didn't trust Koshkin not to grab me again. On the contrary, I assumed he would if he saw the slightest chance of success. And I felt certain that in that case he wouldn't confine me anywhere as obvious as his house.

The war of feelings must have shown on my face, because almost as one Maria, Alexei, and Felix said, "You must stay here."

"It's safer for everyone," Maria added.

"Have no fear, Juliana," Felix said. "Despite my injury, I can defend myself if attacked. I don't intend to let your husband get the better of me. And you've already done enough. If necessary, I can complete my tasks without your help."

I wished that I believed him, but I didn't. And if he did complete our mission for Queen Bona on his own, would she still fulfill her promise to me?

I couldn't speak those thoughts in front of Maria and Alexei, however great my gratitude to them. Still less could I express my deepest concern.

Will Felix suffer because I want to divorce my husband? How can I live with myself if I let that happen?

Lyuba returned after Felix left and the servants had cleared the room. She brought with her not only *The Conference of Birds* but *The Tale of Sayf al-Muluk*, an adventure story in which, as in so many Turkic tales, the heroine saves the hero.

"You're quite the scholar," I told her as she settled beside me and handed me *The Conference*. "You read Persian and Tatar?"

"Russian, too," she said. "Don't you?"

"I do." I turned the pages, again admiring the beauty of the painted birds and trees, the horses and flames. "But it's not so common here. Oh, look at this simurgh! Is he not magnificent?" Indeed he was, scarlet feathers and a double tail longer than himself.

I glanced at Maria, chatting in a corner with her husband. "Do you remember the phoenix I drew on your hand before your wedding?" I turned the book so she could see the painting. "Here's my inspiration. I've loved this story since I was Lyuba's age."

A lump formed in my throat as I recalled what else I had experienced at Lyuba's age. I had yet to squash my sadness when the door opened and my husband walked in unannounced.

"Papa!" Lyuba sprang to her feet, but I noticed she didn't approach her father. Instead she regarded him with a wariness I had never seen in her before, not even with me.

"There you are, you troublesome bitch." Koshkin snarled at me, then at Maria. "As for you ..." Alexei rose to his feet, his hands clenched and his pose threatening, and Koshkin cut off whatever insult he'd planned to hurl at his eldest daughter.

"I'll take my wife and go," he said to Alexei. "I've wasted enough time hunting her down. An agent I've been courting is ready to switch sides at last, and instead of coaxing him across the threshold, I'm spending my afternoon chasing a hussy with delusions of persecution."

An agent? As in a Polish agent? Adam Tarlo? "What agent?" I also stood, determined to face him down despite the fear that roiled inside me at the thought of him dragging me back to his estate.

Koshkin paid no attention to me but glared at Maria. "Don't you dare enter my house again without an invitation."

"I'm not going with you," I said.

"Yes, she stays," Alexei announced in the authoritative tone he used with his warriors. "You don't. Leave and don't come back. I'm ordering my men to bar the door at the first glimpse of you."

Koshkin ignored these commands, just as he'd ignored me when I spoke. When he continued to glower at us, his face contorted with rage, I saw Lyuba clutch her skirts with tight fists. She backed away, wide eyes fixed on her father, ducking behind Alexei and stopping next to her sister, who put a protective arm around her waist.

Shocked at the sight, I looked at Lyuba, then at my husband, then at Lyuba once more. Without being completely aware of what I did, I covered my mouth with my hand and stared at the two of them.

The child's head didn't reach her father's shoulders. She was as slender and fine-boned as I had been at her age, beautiful and innocent and, despite her intelligence and her fire, terrified by his anger. And as his daughter, helpless if he chose to hurt her.

She was eleven. He was forty-two, six years younger than the ogre of my dream, who had deflowered me at Lyuba's age, undeterred by my fear and my pain. The master who punished me for screaming and weeping, for daring to resist even inside my own head.

And in that instant, struck by the panic on Lyuba's face, for the first time since that dreadful night I truly *felt* the horror of what my first master had done to me. The first, and those who came after, each more oblivious to my suffering than the one before.

A small sound escaped me, somewhere between a sob and a moan. I collapsed onto the sofa, pulled my feet up, and wrapped both arms around my shins. My forehead touched my knees. Too stunned to cry, I couldn't speak when Maria ran across the room and knelt beside me, pouring concerned questions over me like warm water from a jug. I heard Alexei ordering Koshkin from the room in harsh tones and Lyuba's high-pitched demands to know if I was sick, her pleas that I would get well. I couldn't respond even to the point of raising my head to look at her.

Because in her I had seen Nasrin. *Really* seen her, for the first time in sixteen years. I saw my own vulnerability, my helplessness as a child assaulted by a man more than four times my age who believed, rightly or wrongly, that he had paid for me and therefore had the right to treat me however he liked.

I understood, too, why I thought of my childhood self as dead. Because that night marked the death of hope. Hope that the world would keep me safe. Hope that someone cared for me, cherished me. And hope that my mother, who sang those haunting melodies, would come and rescue me before the ogre struck.

"They're gone." Maria patted my foot. "I told Lyuba I'd find out what upset you and let her know when you feel better."

With a deep sobbing breath, I straightened and glanced around the room. Maria sat next to me, as I'd already deduced from her hand on my foot, but otherwise the room was empty. As I uncurled into a normal sitting position, she went to the door and called for tea, then waited for it to arrive. When it did, she held the brass jug over one porcelain cup, then a second. She placed both on a plate, carried them over to where I sat, and handed one to me. "Do you want to tell me what happened?" she asked. "It looked like more than Papa swearing at you. I'm sure you've encountered that before."

I wasn't sure I did want to tell her, in truth, but I could see from her expression that I'd worried her. I'd heard the anxiety in Lyuba's voice and the anger in Alexei's. Even subjecting them to a visit from my enraged spouse seemed unfair after they'd done so much on my behalf, so

I thought for a moment, then said, "Do you remember that time I told you about my childhood, about being sold into slavery when I was six? About how my master waited five years before claiming me?"

"Of course," she said. I saw a flash of astonishment cross her face, as if it amazed her that anyone could imagine such a story could slip from her mind.

I hesitated, then placed the cup on the floor and let the words flow out in a rush. "I didn't forget that it happened. I've had nightmares about it for years. But it went on and on, master after master, and I could never let myself touch it. Feel it, I mean. I didn't dare. And because I couldn't face it, because I was so sure that if I opened that door and let myself experience the horror of it I would die, I stopped being able to feel anything. That's where I was when you first met me, why I could act the way I did then. It's what pushed your husband away from me, long before he married you."

Maria put down her teacup and took both my hands in hers. She didn't speak, for which I was grateful. I could barely hold myself together as it was, but I returned the grip of her fingers. "When I was held captive in your father's house, I had the dream again. For the first time I managed to get to the end, to the point where I recognized that it wasn't a dream but a memory of that night when my master fell on me and I had no idea what was happening, only that it hurt worse than anything I'd ever experienced. Today when I watched Lyuba back away from her father, I saw how he frightened her, how helpless she would be if she didn't have you and Alexei to protect her. And I realized that's what an eleven-year-old looks like when a full-grown man ..."

I couldn't go on. Tears filled my eyes and flowed down my cheeks.

"Forces himself on her." Maria finished the sentence for me. She released my hands and pulled me into a hug. "Yes, I see," she said after a while. From the sound of her voice, I thought she might have been crying too. "What a terrible thing. I can't find the words to express how angry I am for you. How sad. And Papa, being the self-centered dolt that he is, can't imagine what he's putting you through."

I didn't remember her being so critical of her father when I lived in Russia. She'd grown up. "He sees what he wants," I said. "But to be fair, I never tried to tell him about my past. I did agree to marry him, and I strove without ceasing to fulfill his every desire. It wasn't until I left Russia that I understood I could also please myself." I cringed thinking about my next admission, but after all she'd done for me, I couldn't avoid it. "And I made him jealous," I said. "Flirting with Alexei because I was upset with him—with Alexei, I mean, for rejecting me. I apologize for that. It must have been hard for you to watch. It amused him, you know. He didn't truly care for me, although he wanted me for a time."

"Thank you." Maria straightened her spine and stared at me. "I didn't expect an apology. I suppose you didn't truly care for Papa, either. Why would you, when he's fifteen years older and you'd already been through so much?"

I felt myself blush. "I didn't, no. I wanted safety, but I didn't find it."

"You're in love with Lord Felix," she said. It wasn't a question. "I'm glad, because he loves you too. And I like him. He's sweet, generous, openhearted. A good man for you."

"Did he tell you that?" I stared at her, startled by the certainty in her voice. *Was* I in love with Felix? I must be, mustn't I, to take such pleasure in his kiss? To want more than kisses from him, in fact.

"Not in so many words." Maria's face crinkled into a smile. "But when a man I've never met shows up on my doorstep demanding that my husband help him rescue a woman in trouble, then refuses to leave the premises until he finds out where she is and secures her return, I have to think they're more than friends, whatever he tells me."

"I see your point," I said, and I did. I saw something else as well: that as appealing as it was to stay safe from my husband in Maria's house, I couldn't in good conscience leave Felix to finish our mission alone. We were partners. We'd undertaken this task together, and I owed him my support.

But I could hardly return to the embassy in women's clothes. That would blow my masquerade to kingdom come.

Julian Ossolinski remained in captivity, so far as the ambassadors knew. But I couldn't obtain Polish clothes outside the embassy in any case. "I don't suppose your sister-in-law left her boys' dress here when she went wherever she went, did she?"

Maria's smile vanished. "She went south years ago, to join her brother's horde. She wore her boys' clothes when she left. What are you planning? We agreed your staying here would keep everyone safe."

"I know." I'd shocked her. She'd always been a good Russian girl, even if she had grown up enough to plan and execute my escape from her father's house. "But I can't stand by while Felix puts himself in danger." What more could I safely tell her? I must give her some explanation if I wanted her help. And she'd earned my trust. "Your father mentioned an agent, someone on the brink of switching sides. That's why Felix and I came to Russia, to find out if such a person exists. That's why I was traveling as a boy: so I could act as Felix's translator, and he'd have someone on the staff he could trust besides the ambassadors. I couldn't share that information with Alexei because he serves the Russians. It would put him in a difficult position if he had to juggle his loyalties that way. But I must at least alert Felix to what Koshkin said. It sounds as if the situation is coming to a head."

Maria gazed steadily at me for so long that I became convinced she planned to lock me in the room and run. At last she said, "I have boys' clothes of my own."

She stood and, smiling once more, held out her hand. "We're about the same size. Let's see if they fit."

My goodness, she really had changed.

Chapter Fifteen

MARIA'S CLOTHES REQUIRED ONLY MINOR ALTERATIONS, which she whipped up with her needle before an hour had passed. I waited until twilight before, dressed as a young Russian nobleman, I left the room assigned to me. Alexei intercepted me as I reached the door that led to the outside staircase.

I regarded him, I'll admit, with an expression that must appear more than a little truculent. "You aren't going to stop me, I hope."

"Maria tells me you're in love with him," he said. "I don't suppose it would do much good to try." He handed me a twist of paper. "Show that to Mansur, and he'll let you into the ambassadors' compound."

Surprised, I took the paper and studied the Tatar script, then tucked it in the sash that bound my robes. "Thank you."

Alexei paused, then said, "I was wrong about Lord Felix. He's a good man. I was wrong about you too. I always thought you shallow, but you've changed. Or is it that I didn't see you clearly?"

Quite the admission. "You were wrong about Felix," I agreed. "But only half-wrong about me. Lithuania changed me. Felix changed me. And coming back to Russia changed me in ways I still don't quite understand."

His dark eyes lit in the smile I once loved, and he briefly touched my cheek as he had in Smolensk. "Maria told me some of that. Not the whole, I suspect. Go with God, Juliana. Send for us if you need help. If you can, come back and see us before you leave Russia. I believe Maria has some scheme for persuading your husband to see reason about the divorce. And whatever happens, know that I wish you and Lord Felix a happy life."

"A happy life to you too," I said. "But a scheme? I wonder what she has in mind. Please tell her I'll make every effort to return. You and I can be friends?"

He nodded, and I left, strangely comforted. Friend was not the place I'd once wanted to occupy, but it felt right and left my heart free to follow its own path.

Toward Felix.

I reached the estate housing the ambassadors at about the time the last hint of light shaded into purple. Mansur accepted my note from Alexei without comment and waved me through. I hid in the shadows next to the guardhouse, under the overhang, to take my bearings.

If only I knew exactly what—or whom—I sought! But Koshkin hadn't specified either the name of his agent or his plans for ushering that agent over the threshold, in his words. In retrospect he probably wished he'd withheld even that much, but at the time he must have believed he'd have no difficulty shutting me up in his house for good.

That belief had made him careless, and I had every intention of thwarting him if possible.

I could try to reach Felix, and I would. If nothing else, I had hopes of navigating the storerooms and the inside stairs, at which point I could no doubt wait for Felix in the room we'd shared. But once I did that, I'd be stuck in one place, unable to react to events. And whatever Felix said about defending himself (true, I was sure), his difficulty in navigating stairs remained. So unless I wanted to spend my whole evening in the bedchamber awaiting my chance to warn Felix of potential but vague risks, I'd better take care of the other options first.

That decision made, I walked as quietly as I could away from the guardhouse. Maria's boots were leather, not the silent felt of my artisan's costume, but so long as I controlled my speed and watched where I placed my feet I could avoid tromping soles and clacking heels. I stayed under the overhang, where the shadows were deepest and most impenetrable, for as long as possible. When I reached the point where the wooden walls of the estate met the brick wall that ringed the Kitaigorod, I stopped, still in the shadows, and surveyed the estate.

That was when I glimpsed not one but two shadowy shapes more or less in a direct line between me and the stables. I froze in place, rationing each breath so that I would have enough air to stay upright and move, even run, if needed but would not draw their attention with the sound of inhalation or exhalation.

Like most of the buildings, the stables had lanterns hanging above each door. As the shadows passed down the side toward the main house, I caught a glimpse of light hair and an impression of breadth from the taller figure.

Lev Glinsky? I couldn't be certain. Simon Belsky and Martin Glinsky had light hair as well.

The smaller figure was not distinctive in any way except the smoothness of his walk. A youngish man, I guessed. Not elderly, in any case. He looked about the right height and build for Koshkin, but I couldn't be sure of that identification either.

Once the pair had crossed beyond the light, I slipped along the brick wall, taking care to keep a storeroom or similar building between me and the figures I hunted. As I approached the edge of the kitchen where I had lain hidden from Adam Tarlo, however, I faced a dilemma.

Ahead of me sat the main house. Once I reached it, I could slide along the wall if need be without fear that the men could follow me, as I'd established on the day of our arrival in Moscow, when I explored the compound. But to get there I had to venture out across the courtyard. And before that I must pass one of the hanging lanterns.

A hand clamped around my mouth from behind. Another grabbed me around the waist.

Who? And where had he come from? I'd checked every step I'd taken!

"Don't move," a voice murmured in my ear. "And don't speak, let alone scream. I'd hate to throttle a woman, especially the former mistress of my king, but if you force me to it, I won't hesitate."

My shoulders slumped. My head fell back. I emitted an involuntary "uh," fortunately suppressed by his grip. I did want to scream, but that would be a bad idea for several reasons.

I nodded to indicate acquiescence. The arm around my waist loosened enough that I could twist in my captor's hold, and the man withdrew his hand a short distance from my mouth. He held his palm facing me, as if warning me that he would grab me again at the first sign I planned not to observe his rules. I had no such plans.

From where we stood, the kitchen lantern gave off just enough light for me to recognize the dark eyes and handsome face of Adam Tarlo.

Who had, it seemed, known my true identity all along.

When I put my own hand over my lips to indicate that I wouldn't talk, Adam let his fall. He reached out and did something I couldn't see, and the lantern went out. Then he caught me by the upper arm and pulled me into the doorway the lantern had lit. I deduced that I'd passed him in the dark, although how I'd managed to do that remained a mystery. I must have focused so much on the men in front of me that I'd missed him standing concealed under the overhang.

"Stay here," Adam said quietly in my ear. "You were supposed to keep out of the way and let Felix and me handle things."

I nodded once more so that he'd go away. I had no intention of doing as he asked. I still had no idea whether I could trust him, for starters. Yes, he'd kept my secret, most likely for reasons of his own. And yes, he claimed to be King Sigismund Augustus's agent. But I had only his word for that—and for his assertion that he and Felix were working together. Adam didn't know I'd heard him angling for an offer—from my husband, as it turned out—or that Koshkin had let it slip that one of the Poles had indicated a readiness to switch sides. And if the light-haired man walking with Koshkin was in fact Lev Glinsky, then who more likely for them to be seeking than Adam Tarlo, who had already shown a willingness to discuss such a change of allegiance with Lev?

Adam still had a lot of explaining to do.

I stood in the doorway as instructed long enough for Adam to cross the courtyard, then ran as lightly and swiftly as I could for the passageway behind the main house. By sticking near the wall, I avoided the dim light of the quarter-moon, but I couldn't run and watch for shadowy figures at the same time, making for some anxious moments.

Luck favored me, though. I reached the passageway without encountering Adam, Sandy-Hair, or worst of all Koshkin. I slipped sideways behind the house, then stopped to survey the courtyard.

I saw no one. No large, light-haired body that might belong to Lev Glinsky. No small frame that could be Koshkin. No Adam, and definitely no Felix, who would be unmistakable because of his cane.

Where had they gone?

Although two weeks had passed since our arrival in Moscow, bringing March to its midpoint, the evening air remained cool. After a while, my hands and feet chilled and I shivered. That was when I remembered the small storeroom where I had spent my last night in the compound, after my argument with Felix. It seemed like an eternity had passed since then.

The first day I'd found the outer door locked, but I hadn't barred it when I left, and it had given every evidence of disuse when I slept there. With luck, I'd be able to get into the house that way. I saw little point in lurking in the dark and cold waiting for men who might have left the courtyard altogether, so I decided to revert to my original plan of reaching the bedchamber I'd shared with Felix and warning him. If nothing else, it would be warm there.

With that goal in mind, I repeated my crablike journey along the passageway. Sure enough, the door at the far end remained unbarred. When I entered, I saw that the bedding I'd grabbed that night still lay on the floor. I dropped the bar into place behind me, then gathered up the bedding, intending to restore it to its original location while using it to hide my noble robes. If someone saw me, I hoped he or she would mistake me for one of the servants.

I hadn't reached the stairs when I heard voices speaking in Russian. I looked to my right, where the door to the larger storeroom stood ajar. Of course, the listening vents!

Careful to make no sound, I placed most of the bedding in a pile at the foot of the stairs, keeping one coverlet in case I needed it for warmth or concealment. Then I edged toward the doorway and peeked around the edge.

No one was there. The voices were coming from above, as before, probably from the conference room that had become Felix's chamber and mine. Thank Saint Juliana that

I hadn't stumbled on them unawares. I pushed the door closed, settled in a corner behind the large chest that offered the room's only concealment, wrapped myself in the coverlet, and worked on disentangling the voices.

I identified Koshkin right away; I knew those tones too well, especially after his many visits during my captivity. Adam I'd heard often by now; Lev Glinsky only a few times, but under conditions that burned his distinctive bass into my brain. I didn't hear Felix, which made me wonder if I'd deduced their location correctly. Where was my friend, if not in his room?

At first I thought Adam negotiated alone with Koshkin and Lev Glinsky. That he'd lied to us from the beginning, as Felix and I suspected and the conversation I'd overheard in the kitchen suggested. Then I heard a fourth voice and realized I'd made a mistake. Because while Adam, if a true agent of King Sigismund Augustus, had a reason to wangle his way into a meeting between Russian nobles and the would-be turncoat, I could imagine no reason why Adam would want a witness to his own decision to switch sides.

The fourth voice I recognized as belonging to Martin Glinsky. And as I settled into my hideaway he said, "That offer is acceptable, Fyodor Mikhailovich, so long as you understand that I must work directly with Prince Iosif Shuisky."

The sounds of a crash, followed by raised male voices and the pounding of fists hitting flesh, had me leaping to my feet. I dropped the coverlet and tore up the stairs as fast as my legs could carry me.

By the time I reached the next floor, envoys were pouring into the corridor and racing down the stairs.

Some wore robes hastily pulled over nightshirts; others remained fully dressed. I pushed past them, praying my Russian clothes wouldn't cause the more suspicious types to grab me as I ran toward the bedchamber I had shared with Felix. Although I hadn't heard him speak and didn't know if he was present, the sounds of scuffle came from that direction.

I skidded to a stop before the half-open door and flung it the rest of the way back. The sight within made me gasp. Adam had Martin Glinsky in some kind of chokehold, and Martin writhed in his grip like an eel on a hook. Felix stood over Lev Glinsky, cane raised as if to strike in his right hand while his left clutched the bedpost for balance.

Adam looked up as the door hit the wall. "Didn't I tell you to stay put?" he asked. He sounded distinctly annoyed.

I shrugged and didn't answer. In fact, I couldn't answer, because a man's hand encircled my throat.

"How providential," Koshkin announced in his usual oily tones as he hauled me against his chest. "The very hostage I needed. Back up slowly, my dear, and we'll make our getaway. I'm sure these charming gentlemen want no harm to come to you."

Glancing at Felix, who stared at me in shock, I sighed. This wasn't my night.

"Felix, behind you," Adam yelled. Koshkin had yet to manage more than two steps because of the crowd in the corridor pushing to get into the room and find out what was happening. But Felix's instant of inattention had been sufficient for Lev Glinsky to roll into a squatting position and assume a menacing stance.

Adam's shout did two things simultaneously. First, Felix snapped his head around and whacked Lev's skull with the cane, knocking him down. A couple of junior envoys pounced on Lev. Second, the shout distracted Koshkin, who loosened his grip for a crucial instant. I thrust both hands up under his enclosing arm and kicked him in the shin at the same time. By itself, the effect wasn't enough to free me, although Koshkin did groan and reach for the leg I'd kicked. But as Felix advanced, cane raised once more, I jabbed my elbow into Koshkin's ribs. I heard a satisfying "oof," a swish of the cane, and a sharp cry from Koshkin as Felix struck him across the shoulders. I felt an ignoble wave of satisfaction at the thought of my despicable husband in pain.

The arm around my waist released. I stumbled sideways and clutched at the screen for balance, toppling it. By the time I sorted myself out and had the luxury to survey the room once more, the room was filled wall to wall with Polish envoys and Koshkin was nowhere to be seen.

Chapter Sixteen

FELIX CAME TOWARD ME, CLEARING HIS WAY THROUGH THE throng by tapping ankles with his cane. When he reached me, he held out his arms, then pulled them back. "Julian," he said in a strained voice. "The Russians released you. I'm pleased to see you safe."

Beyond him I could see Adam supervising the tying up of Martin and Lev Glinsky. "Yes," I said to Felix, reminded by his use of my male name that I must resume my masquerade and resist the impulse to throw myself at him. Instead I permitted myself a chaste hug and indicated my Russian clothing. "Tsarevich Alexei heard of my arrest and intervened on my behalf. He seemed to take it as a personal affront that the man who grabbed me just now would accuse one of his charges of spying. I gather they don't get along."

"Fortunate." Felix indicated Martin and Lev Glinsky. "As you see, we uncovered the Russian agents. You're unharmed?"

I nodded. "Congratulations." Most of the crowd, its curiosity satisfied, dispersed. The two who had pounced on Lev remained, as did the ambassadors.

Felix crossed the short distance between us, caught my arm, and led me to a chair at the far side of the room. "Sit, Julian," he said in a more normal voice. "You look ready to fall down. A long day, I think." When I sat as instructed, he engaged in a short but intense conversation with Adam and the ambassadors before returning to my side. At a terse command from Lord Glebow and Lord Tichonowski, the two junior envoys went to summon Alexei's warriors, who soon appeared and hauled Lev and Martin Glinsky off to their guardhouse. After supervising the prisoners' removal, the ambassadors also left, taking the junior envoys with them and promising to send messages of information and complaint to Prince Iosif Shuisky and Prince Dmitry Belsky in the morning. Adam followed them out.

I didn't envy the Glinskys' fate. Tatars favored direct means of persuasion, as a rule—especially with those suspected of betrayal. I'd be lying if I claimed any remorse—our captives' attempts to increase their power and seek revenge would, if successful, have threatened several lives, including Queen Bona's, and risked instability and unrest in both Poland-Lithuania and Russia. But I did recognize that they would pay a steep price.

"What happens next?" I asked Felix.

"We're not sure," he said, standing before me, balancing on the cane that had served him—and me—so well. "The ambassadors will lodge a formal request to try Lev Glinsky before the Sejm for his actions against Poland-Lithuania and its royal family. Most likely, the Russians will refuse. We're on their soil, and Lev is their agent. Nor can we remove him from the Russian lands without permission. But we do know him now, so we can prevent him from doing any more damage. The Russians will no doubt punish him for allowing himself to be caught, and I assume he has the sense to stay out of Poland and Lithuania from now on."

"I see," I said. "Not very satisfying from the king's and queen's perspectives, I suppose, but I hope they'll give us credit for trying. We'll need to warn them to maintain their vigilance against future assassins, though. I doubt Koshkin will stop because one agent fails. What of Martin?"

"Hard to say," Felix said. "The Russians should surrender him, because Martin is a subject of the king of Poland and hasn't yet committed a crime, although his insistence on a close working relationship with Prince Iosif Shuisky, whom he detests, suggests that he planned one. Switching allegiance is not a crime in Poland, only in Russia, whereas attempted murder is a crime anywhere. But Shuisky is one of the most powerful men in the Russian government. If he insists on holding on to Martin, it will be difficult to convince him otherwise."

I considered that. It was complex, but I thought I got the gist of it. Martin hated Shuisky, so he was a Polish subject who had intended to act against Russia, even if he hadn't succeeded. His cousin Lev, in contrast, was a Russian subject acting against Poland. And we were in Moscow, without permission to take either man with us unless the Russians agreed.

"Maybe the ambassadors can persuade Shuisky to release one of them," I said.

"I'm sure they'll propose such a solution," he said. "We'll find out tomorrow."

"We did learn a lot, though," I said, still thinking it through. "Most of what we came for, in fact: the name of the spymaster, the name of the Russian spy, the identity of the man the Russian spy sought to recruit."

"Yes, we did well," Felix agreed. "Enough to satisfy the king and queen, I hope, even if in the end we can't deliver either Glinsky in person. Meanwhile your detestable husband looks fit to escape scot-free."

"He usually does." I sighed. "I don't think the Shuiskys like him much. They may take this opportunity to demote him once more. But I suppose that depends on how the whole matter ends. They might just as easily decide to reward him."

"So it's over," Felix said. "Except for the peace treaty, that is, and the ambassadors' attempt to negotiate the Glinskys' fate."

I looked around. Only the two of us remained in the room. "It is, isn't it?" I stood and wrapped my arms around Felix. I pressed my cheek against his warm shoulder and closed my eyes. A whirlwind of emotions swept me up—relief that we were both safe, that we had succeeded in our task, that we were together; a strange regret that normal life would now resume; residual fear and anger, especially at my husband and his refusal to grant me a divorce. But first and foremost came gratitude for the gift of Felix's presence.

"Yes," he said softly. "It's over. Won't you look up so I can kiss you?"

I tipped back my head. "You kept your promise. To protect me from my villain of a husband. Thank you." I giggled at the memory. "It's terrible of me, I know, but I'm so happy you hit him with your cane."

That made him laugh too. "Does that mean you'll let me kiss you now?"

I tightened my arms around his neck. "Yes, Felix. Please kiss me." And he did.

Some uncountable time later, a knock on the door interrupted us. Probably just as well, although I was irritated when it happened, because Felix and I had again forgotten that the Russians could hear everything we did and said in that room. As Felix had predicted, his reputation would indeed be in tatters by the time we left Moscow, at least among our Muscovite hosts. While I hastily patted my borrowed clothes into place, Felix crossed the room and opened the door enough to stick his head around it.

"Oh, it's you," he said. "You'd better come in."

"Sorry to interrupt," Adam said as he accepted Felix's not-so-gracious invitation. "But tomorrow I'll be caught up in negotiations over the Glinskys. With luck, the ambassadors will succeed in short order, and I can leave with the culprit or culprits while they complete the peace talks. So we need to talk tonight. Unless you two prefer to travel with me."

"Not here." I touched my finger to my lips and walked to the table where Felix and I kept our writing supplies. There I scribbled a note about the listening vents. When I handed it to Adam, his brows rose. I plucked the paper from his fingers, burned it in the candle flame, and pondered our options.

Alexei and Maria were expecting me, but not with two men in tow. I would take Felix there in the morning, but the evening had already advanced too far to impose on them now. None of the conference rooms were secure, and I had no real knowledge of how far the listening network extended. The kitchen might be free, but the ovens had long since cooled by now. It would have to be the small storeroom on the ground floor.

I scribbled another note for Adam and Felix and watched them read and burn it. Then I left the bedchamber once more and descended the inside stairs, collecting the abandoned bedding as I went.

By the time the men joined me, I had constructed a reasonable facsimile of a Tatar sofa from the available covers and pillows. I'd retrieved the coverlet I'd left in the larger storeroom when I heard the scuffle begin and had it wrapped around me. I indicated the two I'd left out of the makeshift sofa for them. "Not the most comfortable arrangement," I said. "And we should keep our voices low. But if we sit close together and talk quietly, I *think* we can speak with some candor."

Felix took that as an invitation to position himself right next to me and wrap his cover around both of us. I pressed against him, relishing the sensation of his arm about my waist.

"You know, then," I asked him, "that Adam identified me in Cracow?" I looked at Adam. "At least, I assume it was in Cracow."

"Of course," Adam said. "The beautiful Lady Juliana Krasilska is hard to miss." He grinned. "Even when she's recovering from the smallpox and facing down a rival with more hair than wit. All I had to do was ask the first courtier I saw. And don't take offense: you make a charming lad, but you don't *quite* have the knack of it."

I closed my mouth, which had dropped open at his last sentence. "Does *everyone* on the mission know, then?"

Laughing, Adam shook his head. "No, no. You're good enough to fool those who take you at face value. Just not enough to allay a suspicious mind. And so you don't have to ask, I wouldn't have dreamed of spilling your secret. Quite unchivalrous, you know." He waved his hand at the ceiling, although this one had no vents that I could see. "But I think you can give up the pretense now. I suspect at least a few of the people in Felix's room tonight heard that man who grabbed you—and who is he to you?—call you 'my dear.' That wasn't a masculine form, you know."

I groaned. Koshkin. Always Koshkin, damn him. "He's my husband," I said. "I had other things on my mind at the time, but of course you're right." I looked over my shoulder at Felix. "Perhaps you should tell the ambassadors? Give them a brief explanation of the masquerade? Even if everyone knows the truth by now, I should probably continue to dress as a man until we reach Vilnius, for safety's sake."

He agreed, and I returned my gaze to Adam, who asked, "Will you both ride with me, then? You can resume your own garb sooner."

Felix tightened his grip around my waist. I couldn't guess what he might prefer, but I hadn't forgotten what Alexei told me as I was leaving. "We can't if it's tomorrow," I said. "I have unfinished business with my husband."

I tipped my head back and twisted my neck to face Felix. "Maria has a plan to persuade her father to agree to a divorce. I can't imagine how she'll convince him, but I'd like to see. And if anyone can, she can. Will you come with me?"

"With pleasure," Felix said. Then he spoke over my head to Adam. "We'll return with the envoys unless our business concludes before you leave. What do you need from us for your journey?"

Adam rose smoothly to his feet and dropped the coverlet on the sofa. "Nothing," he said. "See you in Cracow." Another grin adorned his handsome face. "A pleasure working with you. We made a good team, in the end."

And with that he walked out. I gathered up the bedding, and Felix and I went back upstairs.

Only as we were settling into bed did I recall that I had yet to tell Felix what I'd learned about my past. But right then I was too exhausted to start a long conversation—especially *that* conversation, which inevitably reduced me to a sobbing mess. So I kissed him goodnight and promised myself that I would share the whole thing tomorrow, after the meeting with Koshkin.

We snuggled close, and I slept unmolested by ogres and broken roses. The listening vents prevented any more intimate contact than that.

Lyuba met us the next morning as Felix and I entered the house. "Are you all right?" she asked me, her eyes wide with concern. "I got worried when I saw you so sad."

I bent to kiss her cheeks and led her by the hand as we walked toward the sewing room. "I recalled something very bad that happened to me when I was your age," I told her. "That's why I was sad. I'm sorry I scared you." I reached out with my other hand and pulled Felix toward me. "Do you remember Lord Felix?"

Lyuba freed herself long enough to put both palms together and bow. "Greetings, Lord Felix." Then she tucked her hand back in mine. "Was it Papa who made you sad? He can be scary. And Maria says you don't want to be married to him anymore."

I gulped. What could I tell a child that would explain, even help her, without giving her more information than she could absorb?

"No," I said after a pause. "Your Papa's a good man in his way, and he wasn't the one who hurt me. But he does find it hard to understand that the people he loves don't always want the same things that he does. So Papa is not the right man for me. When it's your turn to marry, remember that. I know you don't get to choose for yourself, but ask your brother-in-law and your sister to pick a man who will love you for the person you are, not the person he wants you to be."

Lyuba stopped then and looked up at me, her eyes solemn as if she were reading one of her books. "Will you marry Lord Felix, then?"

Felix made a choking sound, whether from suppressed laughter or embarrassment I couldn't tell. I frowned at him. "I don't know," I said. "We haven't talked about that yet. And I can't marry anyone so long as I'm married to Papa. But I do like Lord Felix."

He squeezed my hand. "And I like Lady Juliana," he said.

The door to the sewing room opened, and Maria looked out. "I thought I heard voices," she said as she walked toward us. "How lovely to see you both. Do come in and tell us your adventures. Papa will be here soon, I'm sure. Alexei went to fetch him in person."

When I stared at her in disbelief, she giggled. "Yes, I know. Won't Papa be delighted to see him? But Alexei promised to bring him whether he likes it or not, so it made so much more sense than waiting for Papa to dream up an excuse for why he had to go somewhere else today."

"May I come in too?" Lyuba asked. "I want to show Lady Juliana *Sayf al-Muluk*. She didn't have a chance to look at it last time because she remembered the bad thing and felt sad."

"Later, poppet," Maria said. "We're expecting Papa, and he'll be grumpy, because Alexei is forcing him to come here when he doesn't want to. You can show Lady Juliana and Lord Felix your book after Papa leaves. They're going to stay with us for a few days, I think." She raised an interrogative eyebrow at me.

"We'd love to. Thank you." I glanced at Felix, who was gazing at me as if waiting to hear what I would choose. As if my decision would answer an unspoken question about what he meant to me. I turned back to Maria. "We can't say a word at the ambassadorial compound without worrying about it being overheard, so it would be much more pleasant to stay with you."

"So you see, Lyuba, bring your book after dinner, and you'll have plenty of time to show them." When Lyuba agreed and ran off, Maria ushered us in. "Good. Do sit down and tell me what happened last night. I'm dying of curiosity, and I couldn't help worrying that something had gone wrong. You can repeat it to Alexei after Papa leaves. They should be here soon."

In fact, Alexei returned alone, waving a roll of paper tied with a red ribbon and looking extremely pleased with himself. When he finished greeting Felix and me, he bowed and, with a flourish, handed me the scroll.

"Where's Papa?" Maria asked. "Did he beg off after all? I thought you planned to knock him out and carry him here if necessary."

"I did threaten to do just that," Alexei said. He was smiling, and I didn't take him seriously, although with Alexei one could never be certain. He might indeed have threatened to do just that.

"But this is better," he went on. "Juliana gets what she wants, and she doesn't have to face him again. Take a look."

I ripped off the ribbon and unrolled the paper. For a brief moment the heavy black Cyrillic characters swam in front of my eyes. I pulled myself together and read the lines to the end. At the bottom I saw a red seal stamped with my husband's sigil and three signatures: Fyodor Mikhailovich Koshkin, Tsarevich Alexei Bulatovich, and Father Spiridon.

"I don't believe it." I stared at Alexei. "How did you persuade him to agree?"

"What is it?" Felix asked.

I handed him the paper. "A letter of divorce. For desertion, because I've refused to share his bed for five years." I looked at Alexei again. "Is that legal? I thought a bishop had to rule."

Alexei shrugged. "It's customary, from what Father Spiridon said. You can take it to an Orthodox bishop in

Vilnius or Cracow. Show him the letter and tell him you're a Catholic, your husband has agreed to free you, and his chaplain drew up the document and had it signed by a Christian tsarevich as witness. Spiridon thinks the bishop will grant the divorce, although whether the Catholics will permit you two to marry is anyone's guess. But even if he doesn't, Koshkin has surrendered his rights to your person. He won't trouble you again."

"And how *did* you persuade him to do that?" Felix looked as stunned as I felt.

Alexei grinned. "I told him he could sign or I'd knock him out, carry him here, and harangue him until he did, of course. Sometimes it works to be a Tatar sultan, especially one with a father like mine. Koshkin learned the hard way not to cross him. Father Spiridon helped too."

I jumped from the sofa and ran across the room to hug him, then Maria. I heard Felix echo my thanks. I darted back long enough to grab the magic paper and read it again, just to be sure the words were still there, then twirled in joy as the phrases rang in my head.

I, Fyodor Mikhailovich Koshkin, the paper said, *being of sound mind, do repudiate my wife Roxelana, known also as Juliana Krasilska, because she has refused to share my bed for five years and has, moreover, converted to the heretic Catholic faith. To this decision I do plight my word before these two witnesses, who can confirm it to be my true intent to divorce her and to make no further claims upon her, nor she on me.*

They were the sweetest words I had ever read.

"What was Lyuba talking about when we came in?" Felix stood at the door of the richly decorated chamber that Maria had assigned for our use as if he couldn't quite believe his own right to enter, despite the weeks we'd spent together on the road and in the ambassadorial compound in Moscow.

Hours had passed since Alexei returned from Koshkin's house with the precious divorce letter. I'd changed again into women's dress and returned Maria's borrowed clothes. We had eaten dinner and supper, admired Lyuba's books and her learning, shared our stories with Maria and Alexei. Evening had at last fallen, and here Felix and I were alone in this beautiful chamber with no one listening in. I felt blissful and apprehensive at the same time. Blissful because nothing now stood between me and the man I loved, except for the one thing that made me apprehensive: my past.

But I had to tell him. If I didn't, it would always lie there like a fetid pool, poisoning everything it touched.

If only I didn't fear that the reality would cause him to pull away from me, as so many others had done.

"I haven't had a chance to tell you," I said, stalling for time. "When I was locked up in Koshkin's house, I remembered the source of my ogre dream. And when he stormed in the other day—not when he captured me at the ambassadors' residence but after you left me here. He showed up demanding I go with him, and Alexei threw him out."

I stopped, taking gasping breaths, again fighting the raw emotions of that visit. I was becoming incoherent. I tried again. "I saw something, something involving Lyuba, that showed me how wrong it was what happened to me as a child."

Oh dear, not much more coherent, that. "I'm not even making sense, am I?" I asked Felix.

He abandoned the door, crossed the room, put an arm around my waist, and led me to the covered sofa that, here as everywhere else in the house, ringed the walls. There he pulled me down beside him. "Not a great deal," he said. "Start with the dream."

"I'm afraid," I said in a small voice. "Afraid you won't want me anymore when you know the truth."

He hugged me close. "I love you, Juliana. I won't reject you. Tell me about the dream. What you saw in Lyuba. What happened to you as a child. Tell me everything."

I couldn't. He would despise me, and the loss would break me. I'd survived the ogre. I'd survived the opening of the door. But this was too much to ask. "It's poison," I said after a while. "I can't tell you. I'll drive you away, and I couldn't bear that."

He laughed softly. "You won't, Juliana. I gave you my heart that day in the library. With that first line of poetry. Maybe when I saw you beat Samuel at chess. I've been waiting ever since for you to notice."

"That's beautiful. And you said nothing all this time?"

He kissed my forehead. "I didn't want to scare you. So tell me the truth. The whole, if you please. If you had to live it, the least I can do is listen."

I couldn't look at him. I pressed my cheek against his shoulder and closed my eyes. Tell him the whole? Did I dare, even after all we'd been through?

But I owed it to Nasrin, who had suffered so much. Had I not promised myself to nurture her? To find a man who could love her? Or if not, to live my life alone? How could I turn my back on her and walk away when Felix insisted he was that man?

Slowly, in bits and pieces, I told him everything, from the moment my father sold me until the afternoon when I saw Lyuba with her father and finally understood in my heart the price I had paid for my family's well-being. I told him about Nasrin's "death" at the age of eleven, of the second master who provided me with an education and taught me chess but also waited until he got me pregnant to sell me on the grounds that I was no longer of any use to him, of the third who beat me so badly that I lost the second's child and could never bear another, and the fourth who after numerous acts of inspired cruelty at last sold me to Bahadur Bey when I was not yet eighteen. I told him about Bahadur and his son, of Alexei and Fyodor, of Sigismund Augustus—five men who had at least been kind, even if they saw me first and foremost as an instrument for their pleasure. I told him things I had never spoken aloud or even permitted myself to think, because if I stopped long enough to face the truth, I would lose my will to live.

When I at last shuddered to a halt, Felix said nothing for a long time, patting my hair and back while I sobbed against his shoulder. He would reject me now, and I would be alone. Stronger, but bereft.

But when the tears lessened and he did speak, his voice was so gentle I hardly recognized it. "That's the most horrifying story I've ever heard," he said. "How did you survive?"

"I didn't," I said. I felt hollow inside, drained yet comforted by having shared my story with one other person—even if he walked away, knowing that I'd told the truth, that I was poison. "In a sense, yes, I continued to exist. But Nasrin died that first night. She was the part of me who loved and trusted, who believed the world could be a safe place where people valued her as more than a body and a face. Since that night at Koshkin's I've tried to revive her, but I'm not sure I can."

"Nasrin?" he asked, still in that same soft tone.

"My real name." Tears still clogged my throat, but I managed to get the words out. "The name my mother gave me. In Persian it means 'wild rose.'"

"May I use it, then?" His finger brushed my cheek, catching a stray tear. "It suits you even better than Juliana."

When I nodded, he placed the finger under my chin and tipped my head up so that I had no choice but to look at him. "Wild roses are beautiful," he said. "They look fragile, but they're some of the toughest, most resilient plants in creation. Every year they flower anew, clinging to barren hillsides and delighting those lucky enough to encounter them. They perfume the air with their fragrance. Like you, my sweet. I think Nasrin is closer than you imagine. I've sensed her from the beginning, whenever you let your guard down. I'll do whatever I can to help her find her way to the sun. If you permit. Will you? Can you make a place for me in your life?"

Fear tugged at my heart, the pull of the past, the dreadful but familiar. Yet the future beckoned, brimming with hope and trust. With happiness, which in Latin is *felix*.

"Yes," I said. "I couldn't bear to lose you, Felix. Will you make love to me?"

He rubbed my lips with his thumb. "Are you sure that's what you want?"

And to my own amazement, I did. I remembered that moment in the carriage, the nights when we slept in the same bed, the times when we would have made love if not for the listening Russian ears. I thought of the long trip we'd taken together, of the warmth of his arms and the comfort—the *safety*—I felt in his presence.

"Yes," I told him. "It's what I want. I love you, Felix."

"Then I will," he said. "Because I love you too." And he did.

It was magical, a depth of communion greater than I had believed possible. And although I had lost my virginity long ago, that night marked my initiation into passion.

Chapter Seventeen

On the same day that I received my divorce, the government in Moscow—in what I assumed those in power considered a form of compensation for their absolute refusal to turn over Lev Glinsky to face justice in Poland—set Martin Glinsky free on condition that he leave the Russian lands at once and never return. As a result, Adam Tarlo did set off for Smolensk with Martin under guard while Felix and I remained guests of Alexei and Maria.

Less than a week later, on March 23, the envoys received their instructions from the Kremlin. After one final reception in the Faceted Palace, which Felix and I skipped with the ambassadors' permission, Prince Dmitry Belsky, acting in the young grand prince's name, authorized our group to leave Moscow. Negotiations on King Sigismund's proffered truce would continue. Before the month of March ended, Felix and I were on the road toward Poland, sad goodbyes to Maria, Alexei, and Lyuba ringing in our ears.

To no one's great astonishment, Prince Simon Belsky elected to join his kin in service to Moscow. Bogdan Ostrogski, in contrast, couldn't wait to leave Russia and announced to anyone who would listen that Belsky would regret his change of allegiance. Privately I thought Bogdan was right about that last, but I saw no reason to argue with Simon Belsky, whose choices meant nothing to me.

For myself, I was glad to be heading west again, although in retrospect I had to admit that my decision to travel to Russia had worked out much better than I'd feared in my darkest moments. I'd grown accustomed to the changes wrought by smallpox, achieved my divorce, made my peace with Alexei and Maria, atoned for my prior harshness toward Lyuba, taken initial steps toward healing the damage inflicted on me in childhood, and fallen in love with Felix—who, bless him, gave every evidence of supporting and caring for me despite the revelation of the past I'd kept hidden for so many years. Not bad for a journey that had lasted less than three months.

Although some—in truth, more than some—scars remained, the future looked brighter than I could have ever anticipated that day when I heard the doctor pronounce that I would live. With luck, I would attain my promised reward. I had certainly earned it, although I'd be the first to admit that I couldn't have succeeded without Felix.

As before, our party traveled day and night, although by late March the thaw had set in, and with it the *rasputitsa*—the time without roads. Mud slowed our carriages, so that the trip that had taken six days in one direction took almost three times as long in reverse. By the time the massive walls of the Smolensk fortress graced the horizon, our entire party was heartily sick of everything to do with horses and carriages. Felix and I had exhausted our supply of poetry for our contests, the prospect of chess had palled, and I couldn't look at my lute or *The Aeneid* without shuddering.

So it was a welcome relief to cross the brick courtyard and know that, for a day or two at least, we could stretch our legs and sleep in something not lurching from pothole to pothole.

We had yet to find our room when a familiar voice hailed Felix by name. I turned, startled. Sure enough, Adam Tarlo stood not halfway across the room, waving.

I glanced at Felix, who looked as surprised as I was, and without speaking the two of us advanced on Adam. He greeted me with a warm hug. "Still wearing boys' clothes, I see," he said in my ear before he released me to hug Felix.

"As far as Vilnius," I told him. "It seems safer and less likely to raise questions." Adam nodded without comment.

"I thought you were heading to Cracow with Martin Glinsky." Felix put my thoughts into words. "What happened?"

Adam produced a theatrical groan. "You have to ask? The Russians, of course. They refused to let me leave without papers from Moscow, which have just arrived with the ambassadors' escort. So we traveled ahead for no good reason, although at least the military governor hasn't intervened on Glinsky's behalf."

"He's still bound and under guard, then?" I asked.

Frankly, I was somewhat relieved that Adam hadn't managed to reach Cracow before Felix and me. Unfair, perhaps, but if King Sigismund Augustus could send agents of his own without consulting his father, Felix and I didn't need the young king deciding that he and Adam should split the glory for a success that depended in large part on us.

"Yes," Adam said. "At least until we put enough distance between ourselves and the border that we're certain

Martin can't circle back. I'm tempted to keep him under guard until we reach Cracow, even though he never succeeded in actually committing a crime. Of all the mad schemes! What possessed him to imagine that he could attack the head of Russia's most powerful clan?"

"He'll have a fit," Felix noted. "Don't you have to turn him over to the Council of Lords for trial?"

Adam grinned. "No, because he's not charged with anything except drunkenness and stupidity. He's going to travel to Cracow like a good soldier and testify against his cousin. I just want to ensure he remembers that." He flung one arm about Felix's shoulders and the other around mine. "The midday meal's about to start. Come with me, you two, and we'll trade stories over a cup of ale."

Three weeks later, we reached Vilnius, where Julian at last became Juliana once more. I watched with a certain sorrow as Felix's man packed away my boys' clothes. I would miss the freedom of movement and the inattention to my looks, the sense of being taken more seriously because I wore male garb instead of female.

At the same time, I rejoiced at again looking and acting like myself. The pockmarks would never disappear completely, but the rawness had faded, and it took only a small amount of powder to satisfy my vanity. My hair had grown by the breadth of several fingers, and luxuriant brown covered the patchiness of that first day back at court. I still had my figure and my style, and I had learned not to care so much about superficial prettiness.

While in Vilnius, Felix used his connections to secure a meeting with the Orthodox bishop, who accepted my document with suitable gravity, gave it to his staff to copy, then returned it with a promise to consider my request for a formal divorce. His staff would write to me in Cracow, he told me.

"Write to the Ossolinski palace also, if you please," Felix announced. I sent him a startled glance but chose not to argue. The bishop didn't need to know that Felix hadn't confided whatever plan he had in mind to me. When I asked Felix later, he said only that he hoped to see his family and asked me to consider accompanying him. I told him I'd think about it and left the topic there.

With Adam and the guard surrounding Martin Glinsky riding alongside our carriage, we reached Cracow in the last week of May. The sight of Wawel Castle, imposing on its hill, had me wiping away tears. A quick glance at Felix revealed that he too appeared misty-eyed.

When he saw me gazing at him, he clasped my hand. "I'm glad to be home," he said.

"Me too." I smiled and touched his cheek. "But even gladder to return with you at my side."

He pulled me close then and kissed me hard on the mouth. "Agreed, Wild Rose. Are you ready to face the royals?"

"As ready as I can be." I shivered and drew myself up. "I hope they think we did enough to merit our reward."

"You know I'll take care of you if need be," Felix assured me. "You don't need Queen Bona to guarantee you an income."

"I know," I said, because it was true. He'd promised to settle lands on me if necessary. "But if I can, I'd like to bring something to our ... whatever we decide it is rather than be a charge on you."

"What an extraordinary idea," he said, teasing me. "A woman of independent means. And here I thought you loved me for my books by female poets."

I laughed. "Well, you've smoked me out. But don't pretend you're in this for something other than *The Conference of Birds*."

"But I am," he said, so solemn that for a moment I believed him. Then his face crinkled, and he added, "It's Hafiz I have my eye on. And who's the other one? Rumi?"

"You see, a trade!" I held up my hands in mock surrender, and it was his turn to laugh.

"A trade," he said. "Of books. I like that very well."

The throne room hadn't changed since my last visit, except that it again held three thrones. From what I could tell, King Sigismund Augustus had chosen not to summon the lovely Emilia Sobieska to his side.

Perhaps they'd already parted ways. But after a flash of satisfaction at the thought, I decided I no longer cared.

As I walked, Felix's right hand clasping mine and Adam Tarlo to his left, toward the thrones, the ranks of courtiers parted to give us passage. Women pulled their full skirts to one side, but not as they had during that terrible reception when it seemed they would do anything to avoid contact with me. Instead the gentle swish of silk offered a kind of tribute, as did the men bowing over their tight hose. I let myself enjoy the fleeting sense of triumph.

When I reached the dais, I sank into my curtsey, kissed the king's hand, then moved to brush my lips across the queen's, then her son's, while Felix and Adam paid their respects in turn. When ordered to rise, I stood, still at Felix's side. Sigismund Augustus sat directly in front of me, but I gazed at his mother.

The queen's searching glance studied first my face, then Felix's and Adam's, before she smiled. "You've done well, the three of you."

I blushed, and the men bowed. "Thank you, Your Majesty," I said. "It was our pleasure to serve you. I only wish we could have brought the Russian spy as well."

"You've revealed his name," she said. "And according to the report we received from the ambassadors, the three of you can recognize him. Lord Tarlo also had several conversations with him that will, no doubt, prove enlightening. It will do, especially since you've delivered Martin Glinsky into our hands. A foolish man, whose lust for vengeance threatened our desire for peace with the Russians, but he can, we assume, tell us more about what he wanted and what he knew. We're fortunate that he didn't succeed, and the three of you are responsible for that boon too." She nodded at Felix and me. "As well as for Lady Juliana's beautiful prayer page with Lord Felix's hidden message."

"There's also the name of the spymaster," I reminded her. "Who turns out to be my former husband. He's behind the fomenting of unrest and the assassination attempts against you, I'm almost certain, as well as responsible for the listening devices in the ambassadorial residence, which future envoys will know to guard against. I can tell you a good deal about him and what motivates him, as well as what we discovered about the shifting allegiances between the fighting clans."

"And what's that?" Queen Bona asked.

I assumed she didn't want a detailed answer—not right then, in any event. "In brief, the Shuisky clan is again on the ascent, although the Belskys remain strong enough to keep the Shuiskys preoccupied with domestic matters for some time. Their conflict benefits your realm more than victory by either side."

"Indeed," Sigismund Augustus interjected. "You've surprised us, Lady Juliana. Lord Felix's skills at information gathering have long been known to us, but you hid the full extent of your artistry as well as your capacity for ..." He hesitated, looking vaguely uncomfortable, then finished with "creative deception."

Glancing at Queen Bona, who looked as if she wanted to laugh, I suppressed a smile.

When her unhappy son stumbled to a halt, the queen fixed her eyes on me. "It seems, Lady Juliana, that you followed the other advice I gave you as well. Did your husband consent, then, to the divorce?"

"He did, Your Majesty. He gave me a letter abandoning any claim to my person and had it signed by two witnesses, one a priest and the other a Christian tsarevich." Who had wrung the concession out of Fyodor by sheer force of will. I didn't mention that part. "The bishop of Vilnius has promised to consider his request."

I curtseyed again, to thank her for her suggestion. I knew she also referred to her advice that I encourage Felix. She must have seen us holding hands as we came in.

"We will persuade the bishop to issue an annulment," she promised. "And reward the three of you as we agreed. You'll find us generous. The court bailiff has the details." She held out to me a book covered in green leather flecked with gold. "I understand from a prior conversation with Lord Felix that this book has a special meaning for you. Please accept it as a token of our appreciation."

I gasped as she placed Hurrem Sultan's copy of *The Conference of Birds* in my outstretched hands. "Thank you again, Your Majesty!" I curtseyed and once more brushed my lips across her ring. "I will treasure it always."

When the men repeated their homage as well, expressing gratitude for their reward, Bona turned to her husband. "Have you anything to add, my dear?"

A twinkle lit the king's eyes, and I had to fight the urge to hug him. He looked like nothing so much as Saint Nicholas, who enlivened the days surrounding Christmas with his bag of toys—a symbol of Poland to me, since such blessings had never touched my childhood, however well I behaved. "To convey our felicitations for a successful mission," he said. "Otherwise, my dear, I think you've covered the important points."

"Then you may go," Bona said with a graceful wave of her hand. And after one last round of bows and curtseys, go we did.

I walked with Felix in the castle gardens. On this gorgeous first day in June I gloried in the profusion of roses, their scent wafting on the light breeze—not wild flowers these but cultivated in a range of colors from yellow to white, pink to crimson, even the soft peach I recalled from orchards as a child. Again I experienced that deep sense of satisfaction, not only that I'd succeeded in my quest but that it had brought me home—here, to Cracow, with Felix. I turned to face him.

"So are you ready to tackle the Rabbit Warren?" he asked. "I won't blame you if you say no. It's a terrifying place, I'll admit. But it has a wonderful library."

"Thanks to you, no doubt." I held up the copy of *The Conference of Birds* that Queen Bona had given me. "I can't promise to add this yet, because I love it too much, but someday."

"I'm counting on it," he said. "So you'll come with me? We can visit those lands you've just acquired. I know the area: it's not far from Ossolin. Good soil for wheat."

I stared at him, at a loss for words. Despite my yearning for financial independence, I had never once thought of my reward from Queen Bona in terms of land that grew crops, on which people and animals lived. "How do you know that?" I asked as the enormity of the task before me sank in.

Felix laughed. To him, I guessed, the answer was obvious. "I grew up in that region, remember? I rode the fields with my father and brothers from the day I mounted my first pony. No son left my father's house without knowing how to administer his patrimony."

"I'll have to learn these things, won't I?" My face must have revealed how out of my depth I felt, because he stopped laughing and patted my shoulder in a reassuring way.

"We'll find you a competent steward," he promised. "Quite likely you have one already. And I can help you manage the lands, if you like. Teach you how it's done. We can stay at the Rabbit Warren as long as necessary. Or at your estate, if need be. Then, if you're not tired of traveling with me, we could visit Italy. I'd love to show you Florence. Venice, Milan, Padua, Rome? Say the word, and we'll go."

"Italy!" My dream come true. "I would adore seeing Italy with you," I told him. "But are you sure you want to introduce me to your family?" I'd given this some thought on our journey from Vilnius. "We don't know yet if we can marry, and I certainly can't give you children. They may not welcome me."

The mischievous expression I loved crossed his face. "The place is crammed with children already, didn't I tell you? They'll welcome you with open arms for not adding to their number. No doubt you can adopt a couple of them if you like. Besides, the family has already abandoned hope that I will wed; if the women, especially, see even a chance with you, they'll fall over themselves with joy." He put his arm around my waist and pulled me to him. "Won't you come along and protect me from the matchmakers and their wiles, not to mention the dozen cousins named Julian?"

He was absurd. He was my dear companion. I loved him as I had loved no one else—not even Alexei. I understood that now.

"Oh very well," I said, scrunching my nose at him so he wouldn't take my apparent reluctance seriously. "Since you put it that way. But if I'm to sacrifice myself like this, you'd better produce some excellent books as my reward."

"Excellent books and excellent nights," he promised, trailing kisses from my temple to my chin. "Nothing like an Italian poetess to inspire the senses."

"Then I agree," I said. Because really, who can refuse an offer like that from the man she loves?

In the years that followed, I never once regretted my choice. Naturally, I adored Italy, where we spent a good deal of our time, as it turned out—yet I also learned that with Felix, I could be happy anywhere. And although, when Felix and I eventually did marry, I traded in my invented surname for that of Ossolinska, in my heart and his I remained ever after Nasrin, the Wild Rose.

Historical Note

I INTRODUCED NASRIN (PRONOUNCED NAZ-RIN, WITH THE "a" as in "an"), then called by her slave name of Roxelana, in *The Winged Horse* as a foil to Firuza, the heroine of that novel. I realized even then that Roxelana hid her vulnerability behind a façade of sophistication, sexuality, and cunning, but when I brought her back in *The Vermilion Bird*, I still saw her primarily as a fun-to-write character who would give Maria some much-needed trouble. As tends to happen when I write, though, during the creation of *The Vermilion Bird* and its sequel enough of Juliana's past revealed itself to me that I decided she deserved a book of her own. And as you see, she had quite a story to tell. To readers who may recoil from her history, believing it too horrible to be anything but fiction, I wish I could reassure you that were so.

But as today's newspaper articles routinely reveal, the sad truth is that in too many parts of our world—including Chorasan, now part of northwest Afghanistan—parents suffering from poverty still sell their daughters into states indistinguishable from slavery or marry them before they reach puberty to men four or five times their age, who then own and abuse them, beating or killing them if they attempt to fight back. Nor is the problem confined to one country or religion. Even in our supposedly enlightened modern West, each year millions of children suffer physical and sexual abuse from those charged with caring for them, and the effects of such traumas last a lifetime. Nasrin's story may be more extreme than others because of the historical circumstances in which she lives, but alas, it is far from unique.

In terms of the story's historical foundations, most of the details of Felix and Juliana's mission for the Polish king and queen are my invention based on known tensions in and between the Russian and the dynastically aligned Polish-Lithuanian courts. Queen Bona did oppose her son's marriage to Elisabeth of Austria, which she saw as extending the growing power of Poland's Habsburg rivals. There was an unsuccessful assassination attempt against King Sigismund the Old in 1523, although none against Queen Bona in 1541. But the dissatisfaction among certain members of the nobility against the king and queen—based on Sigismund's and Bona's tendency to favor the great magnate families, Sigismund's ongoing attempts to restrain the nobility's demands for increased power and equality, and Bona's land acquisitions—was real.

On the Russian side, the mix is similar. The Belsky princes are not known to have left relatives in Poland-Lithuania, although Semyon Belsky, the youngest of three brothers, did flee there in 1534 and was recorded as visiting Vilnius in 1541 and 1542. There was an ongoing struggle in the 1540s among the noble clans to control the person of the young Grand Prince Ivan, crowned tsar in 1547 and known to history as Ivan IV "the Terrible." Historians disagree over whether the struggle included the entire patronage groups led by the Shuisky and Belsky princes or mostly the leading figures in those clans. The former is more characteristic of what we currently know about how Muscovite society functioned, but some senior members of the clans, including Prince Dmitry Belsky, did manage to stay out of the conflict and as a result survived Ivan's minority unscathed.

I did, however, alter several names. In reality, both of the dominant figures in the 1541–1542 conflict, as well as the grand prince, bore the name Ivan: Prince Ivan Vasilyevich Shuisky and Prince Ivan Fyodorovich Belsky. I changed Shuisky's and Belsky's first names to Iosif and Konstantin, respectively, to save readers from having to navigate conversations involving three princes named Ivan. Note also that the Polish versions of the names Belsky and Glinsky are Belski and Gliński, respectively; I use the Russian forms throughout to make it clear that these are members of the same extended family.

As I noted in *The Shattered Drum*, the portrayal of Poland and Lithuania in this book may surprise my readers. In the contemporary West people do not generally think of Lithuania or Poland as hotbeds of humanist culture or even as politically important states, but in fact they were both. As you can see from the map at the front of the novel, in the 1540s Poland-Lithuania, united under the Jagiellonian dynasty although not yet a single political entity, was huge, encompassing much of modern-day Belarus and Ukraine. It was also culturally and diplomatically tied to many of the other countries that influenced European politics: Hungary, the Holy Roman Empire, the Italian city states, Spain, and France—even the Ottoman Empire, where Queen Bona Sforza, a relative of the Borgia family (and equally suspected of using poisons against her enemies), did indeed maintain a correspondence with the wife of Suleiman the Magnificent. Polish and Lithuanian students attended Italian universities. The Jagiellonian University in Cracow, where Felix completed his education after his accident, was a magnet for foreign scholars and students.

And that was no coincidence. Even before King and Grand Duke Sigismund I "the Old" married Bona, he had embraced what later became known as Renaissance humanism. He imported Italian architects and rebuilt Cracow and Vilnius according to modified Italian styles. By the middle of the sixteenth century Poland-Lithuania could lay claim to a reputation for limited monarchy, gentry rule, religious tolerance—including of its Jewish community—and a level of cultural development that Muscovy could not match, despite Russia's own influx of Italian architects and technicians. The Protestant Reformation also made headway in the Polish and allied lands, especially in Lithuania and Livonia—the former bailiwick of the Order of Teutonic Knights, which fell under Polish control at this time.

In Lithuania, which retained a separate government and nobility until the Union of Lublin merged its state with Poland in 1569, the magnates were a combination of old Lithuanian families, often with Polonized names by the sixteenth century—most notably the Radziwill (Radzivilautas) clan—and Ruthenian (West Russian) princes from the modern states of Belarus and Ukraine such as the Glinsky, Belsky, and Ostrogski families. All noble families, whatever their ethnicity, enjoyed equal rights and status within the dual monarchy. Russian was the state language of Lithuania and Orthodox Christianity traditionally its dominant religion, although by the 1540s Polish had begun to replace Russian at court while Catholicism and Calvinism strengthened their positions relative to Orthodoxy.

After the eighteenth-century partitions of Poland, the palaces of Cracow and Vilnius were neglected. Even before then, a series of fires and renovations modified the buildings' sixteenth-century appearance. Wawel Castle, now a UNESCO World Heritage site, became a museum after the Second World War. Its Renaissance structure, including Queen Bona's garden, has since been restored.

The Grand Ducal Palace in Vilnius fared less well. The shell of the original structure that remained by 1939 was destroyed during the war. But in 2001 the independent Lithuanian state ordered the palace rebuilt in sixteenth-century style based on archeological excavations. As with Wawel, this reconstructed palace is the source of the descriptions in *Song of the Siren*. Photographs of both are readily available through Wikimedia Commons.

On the Russian side, the prior appearance of the Kremlin is even more difficult to determine. Juliana's description of the Faceted Palace interior comes from a 1606 painting, although the ceremonial for diplomats derives from Sigismund von Herberstein's famous account of his journeys to Russia in 1517 and 1526. His *Rerum Moscoviticarum Commentarii* (Notes on Muscovy) first appeared in 1549. Like my characters, he stayed in a house in the Kitaigorod, then called the Great Trading Quarter (I used the modern name here for ease of identification), in the 1520s still without its massive brick wall.

The most remarkable part of the story, the listening devices, is to a large extent true. During excavations conducted in 2017, archeologists in Moscow discovered hidden spy chambers, disguised as rooms for food storage, within the Kitaigorod wall and dating from its initial construction in 1535. The acoustics of these "storerooms" allowed those standing within to hear conversations from outside. But the official explanation—that the chambers were designed to monitor potential attackers—doesn't add up. Who travels hundreds of miles through enemy territory to besiege an impregnable fortress but waits to discuss strategy until he's standing on a rampart trying to scale the walls? And who assigns soldiers to sit around in spy chambers eavesdropping when the enemy is literally at their feet?

The suggestion that instead the chambers were used to monitor diplomats comes from my good friend Ann Kleimola, who has provided so many wonderful suggestions for the Legends novels and now this new series. I thank her profoundly, as always.

Among the many scholarly works I consulted, I benefited particularly from A. V. Beliakov, *Chingisidy v Rossii XV–XVII vekov: Prosopograficheskoe issledovanie* (Chingissids in Russia in the Fifteenth to Seventeenth Centuries: A Prosopographical Study); Elizabeth S. Cohen and Thomas V. Cohen, *Daily Life in Renaissance Italy*; Virginia Cox, *Lyric Poetry by Women of the Italian Renaissance*; Emrah Gürkan, "Espionage in the Sixteenth-Century Mediterranean: Secret Diplomacy, Mediterranean Go-Betweens, and the Ottoman-Habsburg Rivalry"; Helena and Stefan Kozakiewicowie, *The Renaissance in Poland*; M. M. Krom, *"Vdovstvuiushchee tsarstvo": Politicheskii krizis v Rossii 30–40-kh godov XVI veka* ("The Widowed Kingdom": The Political Crisis in Russia in the 1530s and 1540s); Noel Malcolm, *Agents of Empire: Knights, Corsairs, Jesuits, and Spies in the Sixteenth-Century Mediterranean World*; Catherine Merridale, *Red Fortress: History and Illusion in the Kremlin*; and Harold B. Segel, *Renaissance Culture in Poland: The Rise of Humanism, 1470–1543*. Thank you also to Daniel C. Waugh for sharing his articles about Muscovite methods of gathering foreign news and to David Ransel for his work on divorce procedures in sixteenth- and seventeenth-century Russia. As ever, I bear sole responsibility for my fictional use of their research.

My understanding of divorce letters comes from an article by Anna Joukovskaia, although her examples date from the seventeenth century, when literacy was more common in Russia. Still, we have established that Fyodor Koshkin was ahead of his time in that regard, so a written document releasing Juliana from their contract is not beyond his powers.

The poems quoted in chapters 2 and 5 are either my invention or my rather free renderings of versions available online, with the exception of *The Conference of Birds*, taken from the 1889 translation by Edward Fitzgerald—which like the poems themselves, none of which was written later than 1541, is in the public domain.

Acknowledgments

IN ADDITION TO THE SCHOLARS MENTIONED IN THE Historical Note, I tip my hat here to my invaluable writers' group, now in its tenth year, and to the members of Five Directions Press for their encouragement and support. *Song of the Siren* has benefited immeasurably from their comments. Ariadne Apostolou, Courtney J. Hall, Claudia H. Long, Gabrielle Mathieu, Joan Schweighardt, and Denise Allan Steele: I can't imagine writing a novel without you!

To my husband and son—and, of course, the cats, who purred encouragingly at all the right moments—words cannot express my gratitude.

The Author

As a child, C. P. Lesley thought everyone made up stories while falling asleep. It never occurred to her that anyone would pay her for them, and for a long time, she was right—no one would. But after years of producing horrible prose, reading books about novel writing, and pestering hapless fellow-writers and friends to read her drafts, some of the advice stuck, and she finished *The Not Exactly Scarlet Pimpernel*, then *The Golden Lynx* and its sequels: *The Winged Horse*, *The Swan Princess*, *The Vermilion Bird*, and *The Shattered Drum*.

She is currently working on the next book in her Songs of Steppe & Forest series, *Song of the Shaman*, featuring Grusha, another secondary character from Legends of the Five Directions.

When not thinking up new ways to torture her characters, she edits other people's manuscripts, reads voraciously, maintains her website, and practices classical ballet—an interest reflected in *Desert Flower* and *Kingdom of the Shades* (Tarkei Chronicles 1 and 2). She also hosts New Books in Historical Fiction, a channel in the New Books Network. You can find out more about her and her books at www.cplesley.com.

FORTHCOMING IN 2020

Song of the Shaman

SONGS OF STEPPE & FOREST 2

East of the Don, June 1542

SMOKE—STINGING, ACRID, REDOLENT WITH SAGE AND THE heavy odor of dried dung—filled my nostrils. Flakes of ash floated before my eyes, and I coughed as I reached for my drum. All around me, the tent rocked with the pounding rhythm of an instrument not my own, held in hands more experienced than mine, summoning me to the dance. Suzukei—the shaman of this horde, my teacher—whispered to the spirits of the hearth fire, the ancestors of the horde.

Squinting, I settled the plaits over my face to remind those in other worlds that I too was one they had chosen, a journeyer among the realms above and below. When I'd concealed my features, I lifted the rimmed circle, large enough to conceal my torso from waist to shoulder. The familiar heft of the drum, the smooth wood clapper in my other hand, the steady *bam-bam-bam-bam* as I beat the tanned hide—these things drew me out of myself despite the blistering smoke. The beat of the drum, regular as the beat of my own heart, worked its way into my body, resonating in my chest and pulling me away from the present, into the places that lie beyond the middle lands of earth and water.

Against the crackle of the fire, each upward leap of the flames releasing another swarm of ash flakes, I heard the steady croon of Suzukei's voice. Moving to the outer rim of the tent, I joined her song, matching her tone as best I could, adding the percussive rhythm of my own felt-clad feet. Strings of beads and shells, interspersed with metal shapes etched with sacred symbols, hung from the drum's rim, adding sounds soft and sharp. I imagined them whispering my name to the listening spirits—*Gru-sha, Gru-sha, Gru-sha.* I loved the shushing of those beads and shells.

As Suzukei and I danced around each other, I watched her for clues. I couldn't see her face, because like me she had concealed it behind several dozen small plaits—black tinged with gray in her case, light brown in mine. Although half a head shorter than I, she appeared taller, the result of the red felt circle stitched with beaded eyes, nose, and mouth tied around her head and extended by a set of plumes as long as my forearm. Her leather robe, which fell loose from her shoulders, added to the sense of her being bigger than life.

"O ancestors," she called to the spirits of the hearth fire. "O grandmothers, save this child."

"O grandmothers," I echoed. "Return his soul to his body. Make him well." *Bam-bam-bam-bam, bam-bam-bam-bam*—I punctuated each word with a drumbeat. Suzukei nodded her approval.

In response to a second nod, I redirected my dance in an inward spiral, aiming for a spot closer to the fire, beating my drum with every step and adding my prayers to Suzukei's. My job was to assist her in her travels, not to release my own soul in pursuit. She had charged me with monitoring the condition of our patient, the three-year-old Sibai Sultan—second son of Ogodai Khan, ruler of our horde. The child lay sick unto death on a pile of felts next to the rough stones that contained the fire, motionless except for the occasional sobbing breath and croaking cough. As I moved in, she spiraled out, as if we were two puppets pulled by the same set of strings.

"Grandmothers—*bam*—come to us—*bam*—see the child—*bam-bam*—your own descendant—*bam-bam*—save his life—*bam-bam-bam*—so that he can grow strong—*bam-bam*—and one day sire children to continue your line." *Bam-bam-bam-bam*. I spoke to the drum as much as the ancestors, and the drum spoke to me, a wordless conversation.

Suzukei circled the outer trellis, drumming and chanting, as I moved toward Sibai. Her voice rose and fell with the unchanging monotony of waves against a shore, yet beneath it all an otherworldly hum spoke of the realms beyond this one—her destination. I had to take care not to follow her there—to balance my drumming, my chants, and my songs in such a way that I eased her passage without sweeping myself up in the rhythm as well. With the khan's own son at risk, we had agreed that Suzukei's greater experience made her the best person to attempt his healing. My skills at soul retrieval still needed work—my throat singing, too.

As I approached the fire, the inside of my nose itched, portending a sneeze to come, and my throat felt raw. A sharp gasp, a hollow groan, stripped these concerns from my mind, and I whirled to look at my teacher. Her hand pressed her stomach. She winced, staggered my way. I caught her before she could tumble into the fire and lowered her to a pile of felts. She groaned once more, touched her forehead, then lay quiet, her chant stilled.

The trance, so fast? Or has the demon plaguing Sibai attacked her too?

I reached for her, only to stop midway. Her body lay relaxed against the coverings, although she groaned from time to time. Perhaps the mushroom potion she took—and I did not—had worked more swiftly than usual. Or she had ridden her urgent desire to help the khan's son into the worlds beyond. If so, my touch would distract her, robbing our patient of her full attention. I must let her finish, then aid her if need be.

Indeed, I must *help* her finish. If I stopped my singing and drumming, she might fall out of the other world before she could complete her task. I blinked hard and knelt beside the child, softening my chant to a lullaby, like the ones I sang to my six-year-old Stepan each evening. An image of my son's sweet face, his wild blond curls untamable by any comb, his gray eyes and sturdy frame—so like his dead father's—tugged at me.

Why am I here, when I should be caring for my own child?

But Stepan was with my friend Guzel, who would keep him safe. And if I left, who would care for *this* child? Or for Suzukei, using all her strength to aid him?

Sibai's forehead burned under my palm. Three days, and his fever raged as fiercely as ever. His breath became more strained and gasping with each dawn. Neither his aunt Nasan, who derived her medical knowledge from books, nor Suzukei and I with our herbs had succeeded in cooling him or easing his pain. Each time he awoke, his breath rasped as if a man held him by the throat. A spirit had stolen it. That much was clear, the three of us agreed. A wicked spirit, determined to smother a child who should be laughing and playing, not lying as if pierced by an arrow.

Sibai was not rasping now. Lit by flickering flames and the scattered sunbeams filtered by the smoke hole, he lay so still I feared he'd already departed this earth. His soft black fringe pressed damp against my tentative hand. His eyelids, squeezed shut against the smoke, didn't part when I lifted him, intending to slip a few drops of apple juice into his mouth.

The press of the spoon against his lips produced no response. I wouldn't improve his chances by choking him, so I returned him to his pile of felts. I drank the juice myself, then stood and picked up my drum once more, determined to support Suzukei on her journey. *Bam-bam-bam-bam.*

I spiraled outward until I again reached the trellised frame of the tent. My feet danced the helpful spirits into motion. "Look at him, Great Ones. See how he suffers, bereft of his soul! Find it, Great Ones, and persuade it to return."

Sensing no response, I shifted my attention to the spirits painted on my drum—horses and turtles, birds and wolves, tigers and lynxes, strange beasts with long multi-pronged horns—reindeer, Suzukei called them.

Here I enjoyed greater success. As the power filled me, the beasts of the lower world flocked to my call. They swirled around me, sweeping past my face like wisps of the smoke that clogged the fetid atmosphere of the tent. I rejoiced at their embrace. They bore me up, as if I were riding a wind horse through the clouds—I who had never sat unattended on a real one.

Through my inner eye, I searched the other realms for Suzukei, for Sibai. I didn't see them. I begged the animal spirits for aid, but caught up in the drumming, the dancing, the chanting, they answered only with songs of their own. Their unearthly sighs and squawks, whinnies and barks, growls and roars surrounded me like morning fog in the northern woods where I was born.

A chill wind swept over me, as if sent from that wintry land. I saw Sibai, his throat gripped by a demon. And Stepan, gurgling and rasping like the khan's son, clutched in the demon's other hand. As I watched, helpless and horrified, the demon opened his enormous maw, bared his pointed fangs, sank them into Sibai, and devoured him. Then he turned red, glaring eyes toward my son.

I tumbled into darkness.

http://www.fivedirectionspress.com/song-of-the-shaman

Also from Five Directions Press

The Golden Lynx

Legends of the Five Directions 1

Kasimov, Sha'ban 940 A.H. / February 1534

The lynx found Nasan just before the ambush. She glimpsed its tufted ears through the tangled branches of the birch tree, then lost sight of it when her brother launched his attack. Alerted by his joyous shriek, she jumped sideways and stuck out a foot, sending him somersaulting over the blizzard-kissed ground. She pelted him with snowballs, taunting him. "You forgot again, silly. How can you take me by surprise if you yell like that?"

He lurched to his feet, grumbling, and she laughed. Girei tried, but too often he forgot to save his war cries for battle.

He soon recovered. Most of the snowballs bounced off Nasan's quilted overcoat or hit the birch trees that bounded the clearing they had chosen as their private playground. But a few better-aimed missiles sent icy shivers across her cheeks, reddened by the cold. One smacked her on the forehead, knocking her hat to one side.

She pushed the sheepskin cap into place and aimed another snowball at Girei, who yelped when it broke over his neck. While he scooped ice from inside his coat, she leaped in celebration, bending her legs almost double behind her and shouting, "Hurrah!"

Her moment of exultation cost her. Girei darted toward her, grabbed her round the waist, and tossed her into a drift. The impact jarred loose an entire branch's load, covering her in snow. "Yow," she said. "I'm going to get you for that."

Girei grinned. "You didn't hear me coming, though."

She shook her head, giggling. "No, I didn't. Truce?"

He nodded. Nasan kept a wary eye on him as she wriggled free of her drift. A few months ago, he couldn't have picked her up with such ease. But these days he seemed to grow taller with each passing hour; for him manhood lay just around the corner. Sha'ban led into Ramadan, and the ending of the fast marked his fifteenth birthday. Within weeks, he would ride off to join the army with their father and older brother. He couldn't wait to go.

A pair of fingers snapped before her face. "Are you dreaming?" Girei asked. "Wake up."

She rubbed her gloved fist against his forehead, where the unruly hair refused to accept the confinement of his hat. "A nightmare, more like. You off to the army, and I to supervise the kitchens. Is that justice?"

"Oh, sister," he said, "if only you could join me."

"I wish," she told him, not for the first time. "But I can hear *Ana*'s voice now. 'You must marry, Nasan. Bear children for the clan.' She's told me nothing else since the day I turned fourteen. Two years!"

"A hard life you have, sister." Girei scrunched his nose, as if he could imagine no worse fate for himself. "I'll take Father's shouting any day."

"And no doubt I'll be in trouble again when I go home." She stared gloomily at a tree. "Where are those warrior heroines from my book? They must have vanished with our ancestors." Except in her sleep, when the grandmother spirits whispered their promise: life offered so much more than marriage and children.

As if inspired by the thought, she grabbed snow and bombarded her brother. Girei would leave soon, no matter what. Already a faint mustache showed on his upper lip. Each day his resemblance to their father grew—both short and sturdy, with dark hair and black eyes. Genghis Khan might lie buried in the eastern steppe, his grave marked only by the spirit banners where his soul perched between flights, but his illustrious lineage survived in the rulers of Khankirmän, which the Russians called Kasimov.

"Enough of this." Girei ran for his pony, vaulting into the saddle. "Bet you can't catch me."

Traitor! Set on revenge, Nasan leaped for her horse's back. Girei had a good head start, but she rode better than he did. Her sure-footed steppe pony dashed along the flattened snow that formed the road—the frozen Oka River on one side, unbroken forest on the other. The horses galloped nose to tail by the time a dozen men burst from among the trees and grabbed the Tatars' reins.

Russians.

No doubt about that. Many Tatars had European features, but none looked like the leader of this group. A platinum-haired giant, he towered over his men.

Too late, Nasan remembered her mother's warning that more lurked in the woods than screech owls and lynxes.

A man with brown hair and rotting teeth dragged her off her pony as if she weighed no more than the last snowball she'd tossed at Girei. His grip around her waist forced her to gasp for breath.

But Nasan had spent much of her childhood wrestling her way into boys' games. Small as she was, she had learned a few tricks. She drummed her heels against her captor's shins until, swearing, he released her and grabbed his leg.

As she pulled away, hard fingers clamped down on her shoulder. Another soldier materialized in front of her. Although shorter than his comrade, he made up for it in girth, and the slap he dealt her hurt. The man she'd kicked clenched his fists. She cowered, hoping to prevent a beating.

Her plan worked. The man grabbed her above the elbow. With both arms secured, Nasan faked acquiescence. Nothing to do but pray that the grandmothers would show her an exit. Pray and watch: the more she learned about their captors, the better her chances of saving herself and her brother.

Meanwhile, Girei fought the two men who held him, excoriating them as the offspring of rabid dogs and whores. The soldiers stood, stolid as the trees around them, immune to insults delivered in a foreign tongue. After a while, the leader walked over, tipped back Girei's head, and looked at him. "Bulat's son, I vow. Boy looks just like him."

He said the words in Russian. Nasan puzzled them out, one by one, wishing she had paid more attention to the language. She had learned Arabic, Persian, and Chagatai Turkic, but her Russian came from eavesdropping on her brothers' lessons. Custom required her to marry a Muslim; she didn't need Russian. Everyone said so.

Everyone was wrong. Tomorrow she would insist on learning Russian.

The leader examined Nasan as he had her brother. Determined not to show fear, she stared into his frosty eyes and tugged at the unyielding arms that held her. Branches encased in ice refracted the sun's glare in sparkling patterns and cast shadows that shifted with each passing breeze. Bleached by the effect of sunshine on snow, the Russian resembled an ice man. His brows met in the center, like the tufts of a screech owl. A scar, pale with age, bracketed tight, cruel lips.

"Not sure about this one," he said. "Let's not take chances." He tipped his head, considering. Sunshine danced across his face, highlighting an eyebrow, his hooked nose, the whorls of his ear. The hollows of his cheeks remained in shadow, dark as the empty sockets of a skull.

Why had he captured them? He wore the armor of a nobleman, not the rags of a thief. And he couldn't hope to profit from robbery or murder. Even in these troubled times, the khans of Kasimov protected their own.

The man waved his free hand. "We came to avenge my kinsman. No more, no less."

She gasped. Kinsman?

Three months ago, a Russian had killed one of Nasan's cousins in a drunken brawl. The victim's brothers slew the killer and left his companions unscathed—as honor required. Even Russians understood the code of the steppe: a life for a life, and there the matter ended.

Not this Russian, though. The blood drained from her face, leaving her light-headed. This Russian meant death.

http://www.fivedirectionspress.com/the-golden-lynx

PRAISE FOR *SONG OF THE SIREN*

"C. P. Lesley brings sixteenth-century Eastern Europe to life in a vivid and engaging way. Juliana is an inspiring heroine—a woman who overcomes tragedy and heartbreak to reach for that most elusive of prizes, freedom."

—P. K. Adams, author of *The Greenest Branch*

"C. P. Lesley's *Song of the Siren* takes us to multicultural sixteenth-century Poland-Lithuania and Russia in this part adventure, part love story, part narrative of a woman's self-discovery and empowerment. Readers interested in the European Renaissance will enjoy this beautifully detailed historical novel."

—Charlene Ball, author of *Dark Lady*

"C. P. Lesley's *Song of the Siren* whisks us away to Eastern Europe and Russia in this captivating tale of a heroine with a past. This is a wonderful beginning to a new series, and its exotic characters and setting are a welcome addition to historical fiction. Lesley's fans are sure to be delighted, and new readers will quickly become devoted followers."

—Sarah Kennedy, author of *The Altarpiece*

"Across half a millennium comes this tale of a complex and fascinating heroine with threads that will rouse and resonate with women even today. The smart dialogue throughout the book weaves together a cast of characters—of whom we're never quite sure who to trust—through betrayal, hope, fear, conflicting loyalties, determination, and love. Juliana ultimately emerges as a champion for all who think they are broken but instead find undiscovered, unimagined strength."

—Ellen Notbohm, author of *The River by Starlight*

"From a talented author, *Song of the Siren* is well-crafted, nicely paced. An entertaining novel set in the Russian court."

—Weina Dai Randel, author of *The Moon in the Palace*

If you enjoyed this book, please consider leaving a review at your favorite online bookseller and/or on GoodReads.

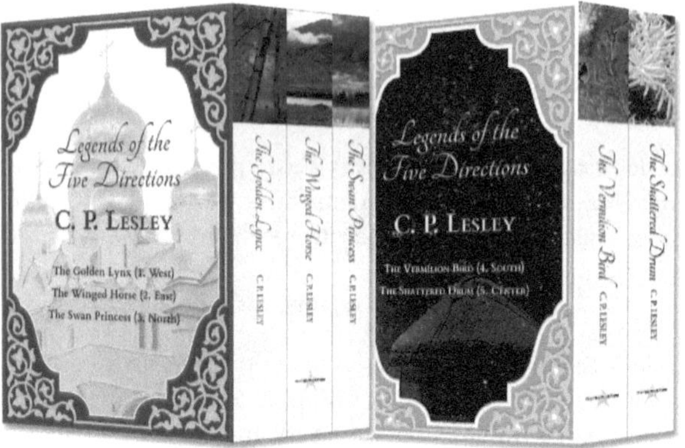

WHO IS THE GOLDEN LYNX?

This question drives the first book in Legends of the Five Directions, a series that will sweep you to the distant world of sixteenth-century Russia, amid the descendants of Genghis Khan and courts that could teach the Borgias a thing or two about political ambition, assassination, and chicanery. Follow Nasan and her kinsfolk as they struggle for power, honor, identity, and love across the steppe and through the vast forests of the Russian North.

"A 'ripping good yarn,' as adventure stories have always been. Enter the exotic, cut-throat world of sixteenth-century Muscovy in the company of a Tatar princess whose skills would have made her equally a heroine on the American frontier. The Kremlin court of the not-yet-Terrible toddler Ivan and his mother-regent Elena Glinskaya, boyar intrigue, arranged political marriages, spirit animals and ancestors pointing the way to restoring balance and order in the universe—what more could a reader want except further adventures, which are heralded by the advent of another animal messenger?"

—Ann M. Kleimola, professor emerita of history

Find out more at http://www.fivedirectionspress.com/boxsets.

www.ingramcontent.com/pod-product-compliance
Lightning Source LLC
Chambersburg PA
CBHW020915200626
46814CB00001BA/349

* 9 7 8 1 9 4 7 0 4 4 1 8 0 *